ONLY THE STRONG

THE DEVIL'S OUTLAWS
BOOK 1

BETHANY DAWN

For my Mom - I'm finally making my dreams come true, but I wish I could share all of this with you.

CONTENTS

Trigger Warnings vii

Playlist 1
Prologue 3
1. Reese 5
2. Callum 10
3. Reese 14
4. Reese 18
5. Callum 24
6. Reese 26
7. Callum 35
8. Callum 44
9. Reese 49
10. Reese 52
11. Callum 56
12. Reese 64
13. Reese 68
14. Reese 71
15. Reese 76
16. Callum 79
17. Reese 86
18. Callum 91
19. Reese 99
20. Reese 105
21. Reese 114
22. Reese 119
23. Callum 125
24. Callum 130
25. Reese 136
26. Callum 144
27. Reese 150
28. Reese 156

29. Reese 160
30. Reese 163
31. Reese 169
32. Callum 175
33. Callum 178
34. Reese 184
35. Callum 185
36. Reese 189
37. Callum 191
38. Reese 196
39. Callum 199
40. Reese 202
41. Reese 208
42. Reese 212
43. Reese 217
44. Callum 221
45. Reese 224
46. Reese 232
47. Callum 235
48. Reese 240
49. Callum 244
50. Reese 246
Epilogue 254

Acknowledgments 269
For Extra Content 271
Also by Bethany Dawn 273

TRIGGER WARNINGS

This is a series about a 1%er motorcycle club, please expect them to act accordingly. Only The Strong depicts torture, gore, blood, extreme acts of violence, stalking, kidnapping, date-rape drugging, mentions of sexual assault of a side character, recreational drug use, and explicit sex scenes. Please be conscious of your triggers, your mental health matters.

Bethany

PLAYLIST

Positions - Ariana Grande
Into It - Chase Atlantic
The Break Up - Machine Gun Kelly
Moonlight - Chase Atlantic
ROXANNE - Arizona Zervas
Train Wreck - James Arthur
If I Would Have Know - Kyle Hume
NUMB - Chri$tian Gate$
Slide - Chase Atlantic
Grind On Me - Pretty Ricky
Please Don't Go - Joel Adams
After Hours - Charlieonafriday
F*CK YOU, GOODBYE - Kid LAROI, Machine Gun Kelly
Slow Down - Chase Atlantic
Party Girl - StaySolidRocky

Playlist available on Spotify @bethanydawnn17

PROLOGUE
REESE

THIS IS MY CHANCE, HE IS HAPPILY DRUNK AND IN A GREAT MOOD, and I've had just enough screwdrivers to give me the courage I so *desperately* need to be this vulnerable.

"Noah, can I ask you something?" I stare at the floor; I can't look him in the eyes.

"Of course, babe." He's holding onto the door frame of the closet while trying to slip off his shoes.

"Why aren't I good enough?" It comes out so softly I'm not sure if he heard me.

"Oh, Reese." He stops with one shoe in his hand and finally looks at me. "Please don't think this has anything to do with you. I just wasn't ready for a relationship when we met. This is all on me, babe." He drops the shoe and steps over to kneel in front of me where I sit on the edge of the bed.

"How can you say that though? You were comparing our sex with your ex. You told her she felt so much better riding your dick. Why would you do this to me?" All of the questions that have been swimming through my head for the last few days come out in a rush. With tears slowly falling down my face I finally look Noah in the eyes, he doesn't have answers there. He looks down to the floor, avoiding my eyes.

"I'm sorry, Reese," he whispers.

1

REESE
NINE MONTHS LATER

GIRL'S NIGHT WAS STARTING TO BECOME MORE ABOUT MY FRIENDS trying to find their next boyfriend and less about actually hanging out with the girls. Except for me, I was still gun-shy. Regardless, the rules were still very strict: dress like you're going to meet the love of your life. Tonight I curled my long natural copper hair and applied my makeup slightly darker than usual, but not too dramatic. Despite the warm March spring weather in Washington, the rain we had this week has cooled the mountains off considerably. I wonder if the girls would approve of me wearing sweats to the bar. Probably not. I choose a black oversized band tee that hits a little below my butt, with a black long-sleeved turtle neck underneath and black thigh-high boots with a chunky heel. No doubt the others would be in skin-tight short dresses or lingerie that they claimed doubled as a top, whereas my curves were hidden under my shirt. Don't get me wrong, I would have been dressed the same a year ago, but ever since Noah, I just haven't had the urge to meet anyone. I'll meet someone when the time is right, it's just not right now.

The drive through The District is short, and I watch the groups of people walking to the restaurants for dinner or the bars for happy hour. Some college students walk into the local bookstore and others are starting games of giant Janga or Cornhole in the outdoor bar, Yardies.

After a short trip in an Uber, we all step into our favorite bar in The District: Mickey's. It is one of the biggest clubs in Merrill Hill's downtown strip of bars and restaurants. The main room is dark, only lit with tv screens showing music videos and dance lights, and neon signs hanging on the walls. There are several tables with chairs around them, a long U-shaped bar, and the dance floor to the left of the bar. A door in the back corner leads outside to a patio with tall lights, a fire pit, and chairs, then a set of outdoor stairs goes up to the rooftop bar. The rooftop is a lot quieter with just a few speakers, a couple of tables and chairs, and a small bar; this is usually where I retreat to once my girls have paired off for the night. There's just something about standing up here, staring off into the night sky and the mountains. Sophie, Emma, and I are sitting around a table while Allie grabs us the first round.

Sophie scans the room, her hazel eyes bouncing between people, guys probably. "How's your first year of law school, Allie?"

"Brutal," Allie sighs, passing around our drinks. "Are you and the doctor still boning?"

Sophie takes a sip of her cocktail. "Dentist." She corrects. "And no, I called it off when he started showing up at the salon and my house unannounced."

"That's fucking creepy! Do you need me to connect you with a judge? I know a great one that can grant you a restraining order." Emma suggests, pushing her dark curls behind her ear.

Allie scrolls through her phone. "I know some guys from The Outlaws that owe me a favor. They could talk to him."

Emma's dark eyes turn to saucers, and she leans forward to speak directly to Allie. "What, like take him out? What the hell,

Allie? You're in law school. What are you doing tangled up with those thugs?"

"I helped out on a case for them. They were really nice and not what you think." Allie shakes her head, her blonde hair fanning over her shoulders, waving her off.

"No, babe. I took care of it. He hasn't bothered me since I broke it off." Sophie squeezes Emma's hand while laughing at Allie.

"Anyways, speaking of judges, what was the verdict yesterday, Em?" I ask, looking at her across the table.

"Custody was given back to the parents. I helped move the kids back home after court." Emma smiles, leaving behind the conversation of gangs and criminals.

I take a drink. "That's great. I know that's what you were hoping for."

"Yeah, the dad got a new job, and they've caught up on all of their bills. These parents deserve their kids, they just fell on hard times and needed some help." Emma loves being a social worker, so much so that sometimes she invests too much into her cases and comes out almost as devastated as the families and kids she's fighting for.

"Celebratory drinks all around then," Allie yells, leaping up to head back to the bar.

After more chit-chat and another round of drinks, Emma and Allie have left us and found the guys they're going home with for the night. Sophie and I relocate to the fire pit outside and continue to talk about our jobs, families, and anything in between.

"Today was pretty draining, I think I'm gonna head out. Wanna share an Uber?" Sophie tosses her plastic cup into the big trash can by our wooden chairs.

I lean my head against the back of the chair to look up at her. "You didn't call Logan?"

Sophie sighs, shaking her head, "No, he's working tonight. Besides, last time he drove me home he ended up staying the night and that's not really helping the whole breakup thing." I nod along to her story even though I don't completely agree with them taking a break when they're both so obviously in love with one another. "Don't give me that, Re. We both need to grow and heal before we can figure our shit out." She sighs, exasperatedly, sitting down on the arm of the chair she just vacated.

I instantly feel bad seeing her tired eyes and hearing the worn out tone of her voice. She's had to defend her decision to break up with Logan to everyone in her life since she did it. She shouldn't have to either; if it wasn't working then it wasn't working, and no one but them know everything that happened in their relationship. When they were together the world just seemed to disappear around them until only they existed; it looked like real love. "I know, I'm sorry."

"You need to stop worrying about my love life and get yourself laid, it's been way too long girl!" Sophie laughs and just like that the somber mood is lifted and I have my carefree best friend back.

I groan, closing my eyes. "Get out of here. I'm gonna finish my drink upstairs and check on the hoe bags one last time." She shrugs as she stands to leave, and I laugh and peer into the main bar for said hoe bags.

Tonight has been pretty quiet. The university's baseball team played and won today, so most of the students are at house parties celebrating. I mean, the college slogan isn't "win or lose, we still booze" for no reason. I make my way up to the rooftop bar and notice that there are more people up here than usual. Avoiding everyone, I walk over to the railing and look out over the mountains, sipping on the remainder of my drink. I love this view. The mountains in the distance are bathed in the beautiful pinks and purples of the setting sun, the breeze is light, barely ruffling my hair. I stare at the view while I bring my drink to my lips, the cranberry juice staying on my lips and the Chase Atlantic song fading into the background. The smell of Axe body spray envelopes me, making me choke, and a man with a square jaw and bald head steps up to the railing, his arm pressed into mine.

Stepping away from him, he laughs and turns to face me. "You looked like you could use a refill, so I got you a drink." His smile doesn't reach his golden eyes.

"Oh. Uh, no thank you." I turn back to the mountains, hoping he'll take the hint and leave.

He takes another step toward me. "It's just a beer."

Another step back. "Sorry, I don't accept drinks from people I don't know." He steps toward me again. This time his chest pressing into my arm.

"Come on, it's rude not to accept." He places a hand on my arm, my eyes widen in alarm, and I snatch it away from him.

"No," I snap, my voice raising.

He grabs my arm again and yanks me into his chest. My mostly empty drink sloshes over onto my hand. Yelling behind me pulls my focus and I watch a tall man stomp toward us. His light eyes are burning and his nostrils flare. He's slightly taller than the prick squeezing my arm, probably 6'2", and his blonde hair blows slightly in the wind, the hair on top of his head longer than on the sides. He stalks closer, and I can feel the anger radiate from him. He's stunning.

2

———

CALLUM

I DON'T USUALLY GO OUT DRINKING IN THE DISTRICT, BUT MY buddy, Finn, is currently crushing on a shot girl at Mickey's, so here we are. At least I was able to talk him into chilling under the outdoor heaters on the rooftop part of the bar. The upstairs is usually less busy and you can have conversations up here without having to yell over the music to be heard. It's getting close to the time that this place picks up speed and turns into a full blown club, and Finn is getting seriously close to getting Hannah or Heather or whatever her name is to agree to go out with him sometime, so my wingman duty is almost over. Finn is drooling over the blonde waitress getting more shots at the small bar while I people watch. A short little redhead saunters over to the railing in front of us. She's wearing a baggy band tee but it's big enough on her to be a dress, despite the loose fit I can still see her supple ass as she sways past us.

"Damn, I've never seen a girl wear a tee shirt and look so damn good," Finn says, looking the redhead over.

"You better look back down at your drink before Hannah catches you and dumps her shots all over you." I nudge my beer bottle with his, not taking my eyes off of the redhead.

10

"You mean Huntley?" Finn laughs and takes a pull of his drink.

Just as I'm about to respond, a guy walks up to Red and starts talking to her. Huntley sits down on Finn's lap and he continues to put his charm on thick, I'm not paying them much attention though because I'm watching this goofy-looking jock keep getting closer and closer to Red as she keeps sliding away from him; every time he takes one step closer to her side, she slides one step away. She's not even facing him and you can tell how uninterested she is, but the big dumbass is either socially inept or he doesn't give a fuck. I should not be watching them like a fucking stalker, but honestly, I don't like the way this douche is looking at her; it's unnerving. He grabs her arm and she pulls it away, but he grabs her again and this time he pulls her into him. Nope, fuck that. I'm going over there. I slam my beer bottle on the small table between us and stalk over to the railing where Red and douchefuck are.

Huntley stops mid-sentence. "Cale, where the fuck are you going?" Finn yells after me.

The bouncer by the stairs sees me get up to charge toward the guy and Red, so he's hot on my heels. What does he think he's going to be able to do? I have no idea. The cops turn a mostly blind eye on the club and our members because we keep our shit out of the city. Murdering this pathetic piece of shit in front of everyone in the bar would definitely land me in jail, but assault? I'd be let go before I even made it to the back of the cop car. It also helps that a lot of the police force is on club payroll.

"I hate to break it to you asshole, but I don't think she's interested," I bark at the jock.

"Fuck off." The dipfuck doesn't even look at me. He lets Red out of his embrace but grabs ahold of her arm again.

"You'd better take your hand off of her arm before I fucking break it." He's a couple of inches shorter than me, and almost just as big. I don't really want to get into a fight in this bar, but I will if I have to.

He turns with his mouth open, ready to tell me to go fuck myself I'm sure. I can see when his eyes fall on my leather cut and things start to click together about who I am and what he's gotten himself into. He's lucky honestly, in most cases I would have already had him laid out, but I didn't want to take the chance of dragging the little redhead into this. Then his eyes shift behind me and fall on Finn. I heard his footsteps following me when he saw I was heading toward the jerk. Most guys tuck tail and run when they're confronted with my brothers and me, but some dumb fucks still try to measure their dicks to ours and come back castrated. Not literally. Well... Okay it's happened once or twice.

"Sorry, man," the asshat mutters as he looks to the floor and rushes away. I guess this guy was smarter than he looked.

"Are you okay?" I ask as our little crowd has wandered away. I lean my head down a little to make better eye contact with her; she's even tinier up close!

"Yeah, thank you for that. He wasn't taking no for an answer." She rubs her arm where red finger marks are starting to appear. Damn her voice is so sweet.

I lean against the railing in front of her. "It's no problem at all, I couldn't stand by while a man was disrespecting a woman."

She smiles a small warm smile, "Well, I really appreciate it." She pauses, waiting for my name.

"Callum." I hold out my hand to shake.

She shakes my hand, firm but light. Her hands are soft enclosed in mine. "Thank you, Callum. I really appreciate it." She smiles and I swear the patio lights strung around the rooftop got a little brighter, must've been a surge in electricity in the bar. "My name is Reese, and I'd offer to buy you a drink, but

I really just want to get out of here." Her eyes drift around the large space before coming back to me.

"I would take thanks in just making sure you got into a cab safely tonight." I scan the rooftop to make sure the jerkoff isn't lingering.

"My friends should still be around, I can Uber home with one of them." She pulls her phone out of a little handbag thing and frowns. "Except they all left." She focuses on her phone, tapping out something.

"I can take you home. I had two beers tonight, I'm only here because my brother wanted some company while he flirts with a shot girl." I quickly spit out without even thinking, she just basically got assaulted. Why would she trust another strange man?

She hesitates while she looks around the rooftop again, probably weighing her options. "Okay sure, it's kind of a long wait for an Uber and I'd rather not wait around alone for one."

"Sure, we can head out then. You ever been on the back of a bike before?" We start walking to the stairs, and I nod toward Finn to let him know I'm leaving; he's standing by the bar while Huntley is counting her tips.

"I have actually, but never in a dress." She laughs.

I look down at her stunned. "I wasn't expecting that."

She laughs as we walk down the stairs. "My dad hit his midlife crisis and bought a Harley. He took me for a ride a couple of times."

I nod, impressed he went with a Harley. "He's got good taste."

3

REESE

CALLUM AND I WALK THROUGH THE BAR AND START DOWN THE street to the big public parking lot at the end of The District. The streetlights start to turn on, lighting the wide sidewalk. I noticed his leather cut on the rooftop and weighed my options when accepting a ride from him, but the wait for an Uber was upwards of twenty minutes and I didn't want to hang around that long. I would also be lying if I said leaving with a stranger who just threatened someone for me wasn't thrilling. I've been so bored of living my normal life. Go to work, go home, cook dinner for one, and go to bed alone. I'm tired of being bored, lonely, and sad. I've heard of the Devil's Outlaws; that they're untouchable, dangerous, but that's it, just heard things about them. No one really knows what they've got going on behind the gates of their compound because they stay to themselves, and whoever is associated with them doesn't kiss and tell. I think that's what adds to the mystery and their allure. When they're in public people almost stop what they're doing to watch, like some sort of celebrity or something. What's worse though? Standing at a bar alone waiting for a ride or going with a supposed criminal stranger? Both are terrible options, to be honest, one's just a

14

little more fun. I texted Allie to let her know he was taking me home since apparently she knows them, so if he kills me then she can send the police to look for my body when she crawls out from whoever's bed in the morning. I haven't ever been around any club members, as I said they usually keep to themselves, but I can't deny that Callum is hot as sin. He has these steel blue eyes that are so piercing and mesmerizing that they seem to stare right into your soul, with a trimmed beard and mustache, it's really just a light layer of scruff laying over a strong jaw. He walks with a sort of confidence that pulls you in and is attractive, but not arrogant. He scans the people around us as we walk down the sidewalk like he's sizing everyone up, but no one rattles him.

I realize that I'm staring at him and decide that I should probably say something before this gets too weird. "So you're a part of the Devil's Outlaws?"

He keeps his head mostly forward, looking down at me from the side. "Yeah, you know anything about us?"

"Only what the rumors say. Crazy parties, scary bikers, illegal activities." I look at him, cocking my eyebrow. I've heard plenty of girls talk about their out of control parties, and the entire city is either terrified or in awe of anyone wearing The Outlaw's leather.

"Hmm. Never heard those rumors I guess," he says with a smirk, looking forward again.

"Yeah, I bet you haven't," I chuckle. "Am I going to be safe with you?" I know it's not smart to leave with a guy you don't know, but my other options weren't a whole lot better.

"I don't need to rape women to get laid, and non-consent ain't my kink." He turns to look at me and I can see the earnestness in his eyes.

At that time we reach a matte black Harley. I start tying my hair into a long braid that hangs down the middle of my back and Callum picks up a helmet off of the handlebars and offers it to me. I thank him and put the helmet on. Callum sits on the bike and stands it upright. I rest my hand on his shoulder, step onto the small footrest, and swing my other leg over the bike. He lays his big hand over mine while I'm stepping up, his head turned and his eyes watching me the entire time. His hand on mine gives me a great view of the tattoos covering his arm, all the way down to his wrist. I look at the other arm resting on the handle bars, just two black bands wrapped around his forearm.

"Good thing I wore spandex under my dress tonight." I laugh, tucking my dress under my butt.

"Damn, here I was thinking I was going to get a show as payment for the ride," Callum says jokingly. "Where am I taking you tonight, Reese?"

I settle in behind him. "You know the Westbrook Apartments by the college?"

"Yeah, are you a student?" He starts the bike. It roars deep under me and now I'm hypersensitive to the warmth of Callum between my thighs. The vibrations of the bike and the presence of this hot as hell man are kind of turning me on. The small amount of vodka I had sure isn't helping the situation at all. I stare at the big patch in the middle of Callum's vest. The cracked skull with devil horns and a snake wrapping around it and through its eye socket. *The Devil's Outlaws* curve above it and *"Washington"* below it. *What the fuck am I doing?* Living on the edge, doing something sweet, innocent, predictable Reese wouldn't normally do.

"No," I stammer, pushing the club insignia out of my head. "I'm the property manager for the complex. Living onsite helps with any tenant issues that may arise."

He nods and grabs the handlebars, I wrap my arms around him placing my hands on his soft black hoodie and hard abs. We slowly drive out of the parking lot and when Callum takes a turn, I lean with him expertly.

"You really can ride, Red." His voice is deep and dark. The lustful tones of his voice have me involuntarily imagining him saying that to me while I'm straddling him instead of his bike. Callum feels good under my hands and the loud sound of the bike seems to turn my brain off. All I can think about are my hormones; Sophie wasn't lying when she said it had been a while. A one night stand isn't something I would normally do, nothing against it, it's just not my thing. So maybe I should do it, a one night stand with a tattooed bad boy isn't going to be boring or lonely, at least not for a while. We slow down to stop at a stop sign and I make my decision before I can second guess myself or think about what if he rejects me.

"Take me to your place." It comes lusty and deep. It sounds weird coming from my mouth and I inwardly cringe.

Callum turns his upper body so he can face me better. "Are you sure?" He sounds shocked and he's looking deep into my green eyes.

"Yes. I'm far from drunk and I'm sure." I'm no longer nervous, and my tone reflects how serious I am. Callum looks around the intersection and turns the opposite way of my apartment and towards the more residential side of town.

4

—

REESE

I LOSE MYSELF IN MY THOUGHTS IN THE SHORT RIDE TO CALLUM'S. I've had casual sex a few times but it's not my thing. I love being in a relationship, at least I used to. Every guy I've ever slept with has been a boy compared to the man sitting between my thighs. The hard muscle of his thighs rest inside of mine, and his arms flex on the handlebars as he slows and shifts gears. He screams masculinity and power and it's an alluring presence. Callum pulls into a nice neighborhood with a freaking cul-de-sac for crying out loud. I feel guilty for judging him and assuming he lived in some run down part of town in a rickety house that has peeling paint and an overgrown lawn. Instead, he pulls into the driveway of an expensive looking brick townhome. He parks next to a big white Ford Raptor and turns the bike off, we walk inside of the townhome and Callum flicks on a light next to the door. A small lamp lights up the living room and I am again impressed with this man's living conditions. The townhome is an open floor design with stairs to my right. The living room has a beautiful bay window overlooking the front lawn, and the long wall that runs the length of the home is black, with every other wall a light gray. On the black wall hangs a giant tv and a tan leather couch sits in front of it with a huge black tufted ottoman, matching leather armchairs flank the couch. The kitchen looks to be all white and very minimal, but with a long island with tall leather barstools on this side of it.

"Are you sure? I can still take you home, Red." Callum hangs his leather cut on a hook behind the door.

"I'm sure." As soon as the words leave my mouth, he's pushing me against the front door and crashing his lips to mine. He's not gentle in the slightest and when he runs his tongue across the seam of my lips I urgently open my mouth. His tongue explores mine and he sucks it hard into his mouth. His mouth leaves mine and starts a burning trail down my neck, licking, kissing, even little nips with his teeth. I grab the bottom of his hoodie and start raising it over his head.

"I can't wait to taste you," he whispers against my neck before sucking more and moving back towards my jaw.

I chuckle and bring the shirt over his head. His chest is a work of art, and I don't mean the curving script and angel on his chest. He is defined, with abs I want to run my tongue down. This man easily has the nicest body that I have ever touched. I can feel his erection growing in his jeans and straining against my stomach. Callum bends and puts his big hands under my butt and lifts me against him, my hands hold onto the back of his neck and my legs wrap around him as our mouths find each other again. He starts to move up the stairs and I won't lie, I am impressed that he is taking the stairs carrying me and without looking, but I'm also nervous he might trip. His confidence doesn't waver and soon I can hear his boot kick a door closed and then I'm being gently laid down on a very plush bed. Callum unbuttons his pants and starts to slide them off while I sit up and throw my dress and boots off. Callum leans down and pulls my spandex shorts off while never taking his eyes off of me. He stands back up to remove his tight black boxers and I can see all of the tattoos on his arm and chest on display. None of my boyfriends have ever had anything close to this many tattoos and it's a huge turn on. I want to lay him down naked and look at every tattoo, tracing them with my tongue. I look down at Callum's cock and gulp, my eyes turn to saucers because holy shit this man is freaking huge! Callum lets out a husky chuckle and starts to walk toward the bed. I slid up to the top and Callum places a big hand on my chest to push me down into the bed.

"I'm gonna make you cum all over my face," he says huskily, pulling my panties down my legs.

"We'll see," I breathe. I'm sopping wet, ready for him to be inside of me. Callum quirks an eyebrow at me in challenge. *Go ahead big guy, anytime a man has bragged about how hard he was going to make me come, I ended up having to finish the job myself at home.* Callum didn't seem the type to ever leave a girl wanting, but did they ever?

He crawls toward me with hunger in his eyes. He pulls my legs apart and dives into my heat. He's slow and tender, unlike his kiss downstairs. He kisses around my pussy until I'm squirming. He places his big hands on my hips to force me to stay still while his tongue starts circling my clit. Callum brings one hand up to my breast to pinch and roll my nipple while he slides two fingers into my soaking pussy. He plays like this until my back is arching, close to coming. I grab ahold of his head with both hands while I start to grind against his tongue and fingers. Before he can stroke me anymore, I'm bursting apart and screaming his name for the whole neighborhood to hear. I really hope he doesn't have a roommate because they are most definitely awake now. As I'm coming down from my high, Callum takes his two fingers out of me and raises them to his lips, and sucks all of my juices off. "So fucking good, baby, but now I need you cumming on my cock," he growls.

Fuck me, I'm going to cum again just listening to him. Callum flips me over and a whimper escapes my mouth, I'm so wet I can feel my release running down my legs. I hear a drawer open, a wrapper ripping, and then Callum is placing a pillow under me and easing his giant dick into me. He's pushing in and I grip the sheets with one hand while placing the other behind me on his thigh, stopping him. The stretch is uncomfortable and something I'm not used to.

Callum leans down next to my ear and whispers. "Relax, Red. Let me in." He kisses the side of my face, since it's buried into the bed, and lightly runs his hand down the side of my body, up and down while I relax around him. "Good girl." He sighs while he sinks further in. He straightens and starts to move inside of me. I moan, the stretch no longer painful, but still so incredibly tight. "Fuck, your pussy is so tight." He hisses, rubbing his hands over my butt.

I'm laying on my stomach and Callum is angled downwards hitting my g spot perfectly, his fingertips digging into my hip and leaving a sweet pressure. He slows his pace to a leisurely roll, and my orgasm starts to build again, but this time much more intense since I'm so full. "I need you to cum for me one more time, baby." Callum leans over my back and breathes in my ear as his hand slides underneath us to rub circles over my throbbing clit.

I cum again, squeezing his cock inside of me. He leans back pulling my hips up with him until I'm on my knees, and then he seems to lose any restraint he may have had and goes insane behind me, pumping into me with such force and speed that he has to hold onto me. My orgasm builds so quickly I wasn't expecting it and I make a slightly embarrassing noise because of how hard it hit me. Callum moans loudly and that just prolongs my orgasm because holy shit that was the hottest sound I have ever heard in my life. His stillness behind me lets me know that he came along with me that time. He eases out of me and I collapse onto the bed, not able to hold myself up on my shaking legs, I turn my head to the side to watch him saunter over to the trash can and toss the condom away.

"My body feels like jelly," I laugh, burying my head into the soft bed.

Callum laughs and walks over to a dresser opposite the big bed, and oh look more tattoos; his back is completely covered, but it's too dark to make out what it is. I get off of the bed and find my shirt and dress while he's pulling on a pair of black sweatpants over his firm bare butt. He turns to see me picking up my boots. "I guess I'm taking you home then."

"I don't really do sleepovers," I say, zipping up my boots. He laughs and pulls a tee shirt and socks out of the dresser.

"Let's get you home then, Red." I follow Callum back down to the living room, he slips on a pair of tennis shoes and grabs a set of keys from a dish on a table by the door. We walk outside, but this time he walks over to the Raptor and opens the passenger door for me. "Your bare legs will be freezing on the bike; the pickup has heated seats." He laughs as he closes my door behind me. Callum made the bike look small beneath him, but in the large cabin of the truck, he looks perfectly proportionate. Watching him handle the steering wheel with one hand while the other rests on the center console has me heating up again and I have to mentally tell myself to calm the hell down. Why is that even hot? Is it just because I can still feel my pussy throbbing?

When we drive into the complex a few minutes later I point to my building. "I'm in building B, the second one up on the left." Callum pulls into a parking spot and surprises me when he opens his door as well.

"I'm not letting you walk to your door alone at one AM, Reese." He laughs as I sit, paused, staring at him with the passenger door open. We walk to my door in more silence and it's only after I've unlocked my door and walked in does he finally break the silence. "See you around, Red." He squeezes my hand before turning and walking back to his pickup. I close the door and head to the bathroom to wash my face and brush my teeth, and when I fall into bed I fall asleep the moment my head hits the pillow.

5

CALLUM

Sundays are always the same old shit. Grocery shopping, hitting the gym and reviewing the jobs I've got set up for the week for CM Roofing. This week we have a few new builds to roof and then a patch job on a house that I'm doing free of charge. The family with the patch job are friends of the club and I always make time for friends. I'm sitting at my kitchen island when Finn calls.

"I thought you went home with that hot redhead last night?" Finn uses in place of a greeting.

"I did," I say distractedly, looking over the dimensions of the new builds.

He pauses. "So that wasn't you last night?"

Now he has my full attention. "What wasn't me?" I look away from my laptop and stare at my phone sitting on the counter.

I hear loud voices trail away in the background. Finn always visits his dad's bar on Sundays and he must be taking our conversation outside. "Huntley said a bartender found that guy you were talking to. He was in the alley behind Mickey's, he was beaten pretty bad and his fucking head was almost smashed in. He's laying in the damn hospital now."

My eyebrows raise. I never pay attention to the news around town like I probably should. If it doesn't involve the club or our associates it's not worth my time. "Oh shit. Can't say he didn't deserve that shit, but it wasn't me."

Finn greets someone walking into the bar and then answers me. "I hear ya."

We hang up and I continue with my day, not giving the miserable fuck in the hospital a second thought. When I lay down later that night, my bed still smells like Reese's deep musky perfume. My dick immediately hardens, Goddamnit that girl is gonna make me throw out my fucking comforter if the smell doesn't fade soon.

6

REESE

ANOTHER MONDAY, ANOTHER COUPLE OF DOZEN EMAILS AND voicemails to wade through. At least this weekend nothing serious occurred, no one was caught skinny dipping in the pool and no one accidentally wrecked their car into the side of one of the buildings; a nice calm weekend for a primarily student apartment complex. Also like any other Monday, it's so busy with phone calls and foot traffic in the leasing building that I end up eating my lunch in my office. Hiding with the lights off, door locked, and pretending I'm not in because if someone sees me they'll knock on the front door until I let them in; my lunch be damned. When I walk up to my front door that evening I'm so irritated to see an envelope pinned to my door. It never fails, some disinclined college kid always leaves a maintenance request or rent on my door because they're too lazy to go into the office. I carefully tear it open before I unlock my door and head inside, just in case I have to take it back to the office. Inside the envelope is a newspaper clipping wrapped inside a piece of paper. The clipping is of an article describing a brutal assault that took place in the alleyway behind Mickey's on Saturday; the man, Lance Wright, is currently recovering in the hospital with extensive injuries, he was beaten so badly he's in a coma. Why would someone leave this on my door? I grab the clipping with my other hand and that's when I see a message on the paper.

"I SHOULD HAVE TAKEN HIS HANDS. I WISH YOU COULD HAVE HEARD HIM SCREAM, REESEY."

I wrap the clipping back into the paper and place it all back into the envelope. With shaking hands, I pull out my cell phone. "Can I come over, I think I might need some legal advice."

"Uh yeah, of course. You okay?" Allie replies.

"I'm not sure, I'll be there in a few." Placing my phone back into my purse I turn around and walk to my Nissan, clutching the envelope to my chest.

The drive to Allie and Sophie's house is brutal. I can't stop staring at the envelope sitting in my passenger seat and my hands haven't stopped shaking since I read the message written in red chicken scratch. When I pull into the driveway, Allie is already sitting on the front porch with two glasses of tea sitting on the table next to her.

"You look like you're going to be sick, Reese. You're as pale as a

ghost!" Allie hurriedly hands me a glass.

"I don't think tea is going to fix this, Al," I say grimly, sitting down in the plush white chair next to her.

"That bad huh?" she asks.

I fill Allie in on the encounter with who I can only assume was Lance on Saturday and then the envelope I found on my door. "I think it was that guy I went home with, Al. The Outlaw that I texted you about." I bury my face in my hands, groaning. "I slept with a criminal and then he went and almost killed someone after he dropped me off at home, or he had his thug friends do it." My stomach rolls, what was I thinking? This is why you don't go home with people you don't know. I look at Allie, her silence sending my fear higher. She's leaning her elbow on the armrest of the chair and scratching her head with one finger, her eyes are roaming the ceiling of the covered porch. "Oh my God, you think he did it too?" I screech. I drop my head back to my hands, her silence says it all.

"It does seem like something they would do." She leans over and pulls my hands away from my face, keeping them in hers. I look into her beautiful blue and mint green eyes, feeling tears starting to well in mine. "But I don't think they are any harm to you, Reese. He was defending you and probably saving future girls that wouldn't have been lucky enough to get away from him."

"What am I going to do, Al?" I groan.

She smiles. "You can't get in trouble for this, you didn't know anything about it until today; but we should call the police and have them take a look at the letter, that way there's no suspicion if more things get discovered. We just won't tell them you suspect it to be The Outlaws."

I shake my head, stunned. "But why not? They're clearly dangerous!"

Allie bites her lip and looks away from me, pausing for a moment before looking into my eyes again. "You've just seen what happens when you get on their bad side, Reese."

"Okay, whatever you think I should do," I reluctantly agree.

"They'll want to see where you found the letter, do you want me to go with you?" Allie hands the letter back to me.

"Yes please." I slip the letter into my purse, my hands finally calming down.

Allie follows me back to my apartment, having called a police officer Allie knows to meet us there. The officer is waiting for us when we arrive and we walk to my apartment together to show him where I found the letter. When we get to the entrance to my apartment the door is slightly ajar.

"Ma'am, did you leave your door open?" the officer asks, placing a hand on his gun hanging on his belt.

"No, I didn't even unlock my door. I grabbed the envelope off of the door and went to meet Allie." I'm shaking again, Allie grabs my hand.

"Let me go in and take a look around, you ladies stay out here." The officer pulls his gun out and slowly enters my apartment. Allie and I stare at the door, silently waiting. He comes back out a few agonizing minutes later. "The place wasn't ransacked, but you'll have to walk through to see if anything is missing. There was forced entry though; looks like they used a screwdriver to break the lock. Do you want me to file a report?" I nod my head, wringing my hands together to hide what must now be permanent shakes. "Okay, go ahead and take a look through and let me know if anything is missing so I can put it in the report." The officer pats my shoulder and gives Allie a half smile before walking to stand beside his police cruiser.

Allie and I walk into my apartment and look through each room together, nothing is missing or out of place, my jewelry is untouched, my electronics, handbags, checkbook. All of the things of value are in their place. I'm checking the laundry room, just in case, while Allie looks in the kitchen.

"Reese. I found something." Allie's voice shakes. I rush into the small dining room attached to the kitchen and see Allie staring down at a piece of paper on my kitchen table. In the same red sloppy handwriting is another message,

"DID YOU GET MY NOTE, REESEY?"

I feel gross, watched, and violated. My skin is crawling and I want to cry, for a long time and in a very hot shower, scrubbing my body of all of the filth I feel. I can't believe I slept with Callum. We walk outside to the officer and hand him the note. His face is stone as he reads it and says he'll add both notes to the report and he leaves.

"This shit is not going to fly." Allie hisses. She pulls her phone out of her back pocket and dials someone, putting the phone to her ear, but when I look at her questioningly, she switches to speaker phone and holds her phone between us. Saint Viotto showing on the screen.

"Miss. Lenkov." A smooth voice answers after a few rings.

"I'm gonna stick your friend with harassment, breaking and entering, stalking, and assault. Maybe I can even convince my firm to try attempted murder. I just thought you should know, our friendship is over and I'm coming for you." I've never seen this side of Allie, she's always been protective over her friends, always sticking up for us, but she's scary right now. Her eyes wide and her voice sharp.

"What are you going on about, Allison?" Allie's eyes darken, she hates being called by her full name, but I don't know if Saint knows that with how casual he threw it out and how calm his voice is.

"One of your club members assaulted a man on Saturday night in retribution for my friend. And now he's broken into her house and is leaving her creepy notes." She brings the phone to her mouth and almost yells into it.

"Who?" Saint snaps.

Allie looks at me, her eyes widening in encouragement. Oh right, she doesn't know his name. "Callum," I say softly to the phone.

There's a long pause on his end before he finally answers. "Give me a moment to check something." There's some moving around and muffled yelling like he placed his phone over the speaker. Allie and I stare at each other and wait. "What time was the break-in and the note left?" He comes back after a few minutes.

"The first note was left while I was at work, sometime between eight and five, and the break-in was between five and six tonight," I answer. Who does this? He seemed so normal, why would he leave these notes and break into my apartment?

"It wasn't Cale," Saint says, back with a calm, almost bored tone.

Allie shakes her head. "Of course, you would say that, Saint."

"No, Allison." *There he goes again.* "I'm looking at time-stamped security cameras right now. He was at his warehouse from seven until five, dealing with inventory and then missing inventory issues. He didn't even leave for lunch. At five he leaves and I can see him getting to one of our cabins at five-thirty, and it's a thirty-minute drive from his warehouse. I'm watching the cameras live right now and he's still there, hasn't left." He covers the speaker again, before coming back. "I can send you copies of the footage if you want, but there's no way he could have broken into your friend's apartment or left the notes."

"What about the assault at the bar?" Allie doesn't give up.

More muffled talking on Saint's end and a long pause. "We tracked his cellphone's movements. He left his house, went to Westbrooke Apartments, and then back home until the next morning when he went to the gym."

"He could have left his phone at home." Allie pushes.

Saint hums. "He could have, but I don't know why he would."

What? "What about the little minions you control?" Allie pushes.

"I've just talked to them, none of them know anything about this, and they wouldn't lie to me." His voice takes on a menacing tone like he's not only talking to us.

"But—" Allie starts.

"Look, I'll call church and ask Cale about the assault, but the break-in wasn't us. I can send some prospects over to watch over your friend and make sure there aren't any more notes."

She sighs and watches me, maybe watching for some direction, but I don't have one. Who broke into my house? Who is leaving creepy messages? My only lead just fell through."It's fine, the police said—"

"You know damn well the police aren't going to do shit. Nobody is going to come near your friend with my guys on her, whoever the creep is will give up after a few weeks." Saint interrupts her... again.

She still watches me, so I shrug. What else am I going to do? The only lead the police could have is if the person left fingerprints on the notes. The odds of stalkers getting arrested though aren't in my favor, and even if they are arrested, they don't stay there for long; only long enough to get more creative and angry. "Okay." She relents.

"Wait for us, I'll send some prospects over soon," he says, hanging up before we can answer back.

Allie leans against her car. "What the fuck, Reese." She sighs.

"I don't know, Al." I shake my head, leaning next to her. "I have no idea who it could be." I start to zone out, racking my brain for any clue.

"I think you should come stay with me and Soph until the Outlaws put someone on this." She turns her head to look at me. Her fear shining in her eyes.

That startles me out of my daze. "No, I'm staying right here until my door is fixed." She nods, I don't take my eyes off of my door until the maintenance guys arrive.

I lean against Allie's Audi next to her as the guys head to repair my door. "So now that Callum is innocent." Allie hedges.

"Not completely." I look at her out of the corner of my eye.

Allie shakes her head, looking at the ground. "I don't think it was him, Reese. The Outlaws." She sighs. "He wouldn't need to cover his tracks if he assaulted that guy."

"Yeah, I guess you're right." I turn my head back to the guys working on my door.

Allie hums as her eyebrows knit together and she cocks her head slightly. "I don't think I've met Callum. Do you have his Insta? Show me what he looks like."

I look at Allie, confused as to why she's choosing now to stalk his socials, but I guess what better time right? "No, I don't. He didn't tell me his last name."

"Scandalous. Isn't that a Carrie Underwood song?" She laughs. Taking my phone out of my hand.

I roll my eyes, leaning into her side to look down at my phone. "Shut up, we're not getting married."

Allie shrugs. "Well lucky for you I'm resourceful. The club has an official Insta, I'm sure he's on there somewhere."

"More like creepy," I mumble but I watch her search the club and locate their page. She starts scrolling and a few rows down I see a picture of him with two guys in black leather cuts. "There." I click on the picture. The caption says *"Hosting our brothers from California. F.A.O."*

"Which one is he?" She asks, bringing the phone closer to get a better look at all of the guys.

"The blonde one with short hair." I point to Callum. "What's 'F.A.O'?" I ask.

"I'm not sure." Allie scrolls through the comments. "Oh. Looks like *Forever An Outlaw*," she says, hovering her finger over a comment saying just that.

Allie scrolls back to the photo and clicks on the tags so they show up over each person. She clicks on Callum's tag and it takes her to his profile. He's following a couple of hundred people and followed by thousands. We scroll through his profile, it's mostly just pictures of him with a dark haired guy covered in tattoos and another guy with longer blonde hair. "That's Saint." Allie points to the guy with long blonde hair in one of the pictures we pulled up. She scrolls back up to the top and clicks follow on his profile before quickly killing the app and locking my phone.

I panic and snatch my phone away from her. "Allie, he's going to think I'm a creep and obsessed with him after one night!"

She crosses her arms and turns to look at me. "Did you like it the other night?"

I sigh, frustrated with her, "Yes, but that—"

"Then stop worrying about what everyone thinks about you and own that shit. You know you wouldn't mind seeing him again and this way you can if you want to."

"Fair enough," I concede. "You might be right sometimes."

She smiles, typical Allie, always glad when she can convince someone to think of things her way. "I'm always right, just be careful they have the reputation they do for a reason."

I shrug. "He seemed nice, even for a criminal."

Allie laughs. "I'm sure he was, they just operate outside of the lines sometimes."

I shake my head, thoroughly confused with Allie's new friendship. "You're a law student, Al, shouldn't you be telling me to stay away from him?"

"Just because I'm going to defend the law doesn't mean I always agree with it. I also can separate a person's character from their lawful, or unlawful, actions." She pulls her hair tie out and runs her fingers through her loose blonde hair.

I stare at her. "You are going to make one interesting lawyer."

She shrugs and laughs. "It's helpful to be able to see beyond the rules sometimes."

7

CALLUM

I WALK DOWN THE CLAUSTROPHOBIC CONCRETE STAIRS INTO THE dimly lit basement. I can hear the smacking of skin beating skin and the groaning of the guy Finn has chained to the chair in the middle of the room.

"Fucking took you long enough." Finn turns around to face me, shaking his hand out.

I step down from the last step and walk over to the tool cart holding the torture tools, or motivational devices, and lean against it crossing my arms. "Sorry, some of us actually have to work at our jobs, not just sit on our asses doing paperwork."

Finn shakes his head, turning around to deliver another brutal punch to the guy's swollen, bloody face. "I fucking hate paperwork!" He roars and something crunches under his fist, probably the guy's eye socket. The guy groans long and low, doubling over as much as he can when his chest is chained to the back of the chair. I shouldn't goad him into beating the shit out of this guy when we need answers, but he left himself wide open for that one. Ever since his garage started picking up business he's had to hand most of the rebuilding over to his employees and he's taken over the books; the stubborn asshole doesn't trust anyone else with the admin shit.

"He give you anything yet?" I turn my head to look down at what tools Finn has pulled out to use on the spy we found staking out our warehouse last night.

Finn shakes his head, stepping over to the tool cart and taking a long drink from a water bottle. Torturing someone for answers is hard work and Finn has been at this for a good fourteen hours, he's got to be exhausted, and the guy in the chair is looking like he has been put through the wringer! His shirt is cut open up the middle, hanging loose on his arms. His jeans are soaked with blood at the knees, evidence that Finn smashed his kneecaps. His torso is bloody with small cuts and stab wounds littering his chest and stomach; each one in the perfect placement to cause maximum pain with minimal damage. The man's face is barely recognizable from the beating and smashing of the brass knuckles looped around Finn's fingers. "He hasn't said a fucking word. Like literally not a goddamn word has left his mouth."

I turn to look at Finn as he leans against the table next to me. "Did you check to see if he had a tongue?" I hide my smirk by rubbing my hand over my jaw. "Maybe he can't physically speak."

The rat in the chair barks a laugh at my joke and Finn picks up the first thing his hand lands on, on the table and throws it at the guy, hitting him in the face and chest. It happened to be the empty five-gallon bucket used for waterboarding purposes, and there was a loud smack and more groaning. Finn glares at me. "I'm not a fucking amateur, Cale. He has a fucking tongue."

"Prove it." I incline my head toward the bloody groaning man in the chair.

Finn shrugs and picks up a scalpel and pliers from the tool cart. He walks over to the man and bends over in front of him.

"Care to share who sent you to spy on the Outlaws?" He places his hands on the armrests, making himself eye level with his prisoner.

The chained up man spits in answer to Finn, his bloody saliva landing on the toe of Finn's boot. Finn stabs him in the stomach with the scalpel, dragging it down a few inches before pulling it out again. The rat screams, doubling over again, his head landing on Finn's shoulder, blood pouring out onto Finn's hand. He stands up, making the man straighten with the movement. "Well, a corpse has no use for a tongue or eyes. Which should I take first then?" The man's eyes widen with fear, the seriousness of this situation finally setting in. "Give me some answers and you can keep them," Finn says, his head cocked to the side.

"I don't know! I don't know," The man screams.

"Mmm. Not good enough." Finn shakes his head.

"The Coalition. I work for The Brothers Coalition, but I don't know who hired me. Please." He begs.

Finn turns to look at me, but I shake my head, not knowing what he's talking about. "Okay. Thank you." Finn says, turning back to our prisoner. He lets out a big sigh, relaxing a bit. In a flash Finn stabs the man in the eye and grabs ahold of his tongue with the pliers during one of his wails and pulls it out of his mouth, slicing it off with the scalpel. Finn drops the bloody tongue on the floor and walks around to stand behind the guy, grabbing his hair in his fist and yanking his head back, gliding the scalpel across his throat in one fluid movement. Blood spurts out in front of him, covering the floor at his feet, the man coughing and choking, making more blood release with his jerking movements. Finn and I lock eyes and he smirks, still standing behind the man bleeding out. "I didn't specify what he got to keep." I bark a laugh while he drops the man's head, letting it hang over in front of him, and leans down to pick up his tongue. He walks over to me smiling, and I grab a bloody rag off of the cart already anticipating his next movement; he drops the tongue into the rag in my hand smiling like a fucking maniac. "Told ya he had a tongue." I continue laughing and drop the tongue and rag onto the workbench I'm leaning against. Finn strides over to the utility skin against the wall and starts to clean his hands and arms of the blood. "What the fuck is The Brothers Coalition?" He asks without looking at me.

I stare at the man hanging limp in the chair. "I have no fucking clue."

"Shit." Finn hisses, turning around and wiping his hands with a paper towel. "Someone big is watching us. Someone who can train minions to withstand torture."

Before I can add anything else to this brewing shitstorm my phone dings with a text.

SAINT:

Chapel ASAP. Shits gone down.

Well fuck, I grab Finn's cut from the table next to the tool cart and toss it to him, he's reading the message as well. I flick through my notifications, noticing one saying a Reese Thomas followed me on Instagram. Is that Reese from last weekend? I wouldn't mind seeing her again if it were. Finn pats my shoulder as he walks over, breaking my train of thought from the redhead I should have made more of an effort to get to stay over. We both look over to the dead guy and shrug. Putting in a call to the prospects for a clean up as we head up the stairs and into the small cabin that the club uses to hide out at. Emergency church is only called when things have really hit the fan so we break a few speed limits to get to the clubhouse fast.

———

"DID Saint tell you what's going on?" Finn asks when we take our seats at the long rectangular table in the chapel. Everyone except our VP and President is here. There are six of us, everyone sitting around the table smoking, talking to the person next to them, or staring down at their phones. I nod to all of my brothers in a greeting.

"Nah, only that shit went down and to get our asses here." I switch my phone to silent while I answer him. Don't want my phone going off and interrupting church, instead of God smiting me, fucking Saint would do it instead; I don't know who's more fucking powerful.

Saint and Ronan walk in talking to each other in hushed tones, Saint rakes his hands through his long blonde hair when he takes a seat next to our President, Ronan. Fuck. Saint, our VP, looks stressed, this meeting should be fucking good.

"Now that we're all here, I'll let Saint go ahead and tell you all why we called you in tonight." Prez rubs his temple as he talks, looking to his left at Saint.

"A friend of a friend needs some protection. The law school student that helped me out a few weeks ago has a friend that recently found herself a stalker. Dude seems fucking weird and a little dangerous. We're gonna put prospects on it to watch her apartment, but of course, we have to vote on it. The girl's a sweet one and she and our friend are pretty spooked over this. Allie called in a favor with us and I want to honor it."

"Can we get the full story before we vote?" Tobias booms from the end of the table. "Not trying to undermine your friends, I just want the full story out there before we put our guys on it." Tobias is never one to rush anything, being the oldest here he's always the most level headed of all of us young guys. Ha "young guys", we're all in our mid to late twenties but Tobi says he feels fucking ancient compared to us at thirty-five. It's not about age, he says he's just in a different place in his life than the rest of us. He's got kids, a wife, and an ex-wife to care for and stress over. He's been in this life the longest and has seen a few things in his time on a bike. Ronan's a few years younger than Tobi both in age and in years in the club, despite Tobi being here longer we all still chose Ronan when our last Prez retired out. Nate is Ro's age, and Saint, Finn, and I are all twenty-five. Our prospects are a mix, Mason is a few years younger, Wyatt is closer to Tobi, and Leo and Jack can barely drink legally.

"Of course." Saint rubs his sharp scruffy jaw. "Reese Thomas was at Mickey's on Saturday night and some guy was..." Saint continues recapping the entire story, but my heart dropped into my fucking stomach at the mention of Reese, I know I stopped fucking breathing because by the time he's done talking I gulp in a breath, and Finn side eyes me; seeing the worry all over my face. He leans over and whispers, "That was your girl wasn't it?" I can't speak over the lump in my throat so I just nod.

"There's a police report," Saint continues, "but since he broke into an apartment building and no one saw a thing, they're pretty freaked. I'm sure it's nothing, just a little college fuck with a crush that lives at the complex, but they want a tail just in case." Saint leans back in his chair, looking at each of us sitting around the table. "Ready to vote?"

I lean forward in my chair and raise my hand to catch Saint's attention. "Saint, I have something to add before we take a vote." He motions for me to continue. "I know Reese, I met her Saturday and saw that guy grabbing on her. I want to be a part of her tail." I look Saint in the eyes so he knows although this sounds like a request, it's not.

"Were you the one who beat his ass and put him in the hospital?" He asks.

I shake my head. "No," I answer honestly. "Reese and I hung

out that night and after I took her home, I went home and passed out."

Saint nods slowly. "That's what I thought, but I had to ask." I nod along with him, not upset for him asking. It's not like it would be that out of character for one of us to do something like that.

"You can manage the prospects and keep us updated." Prez is leaned back in his chair with his hands clasped together in front of him. I nod, leaning back in mine again, trying to suppress my nerves but it's fucking hard. Someone broke into her damn apartment and is leaving creepy ass notes.

We go around the table all voting yes to helping Reese; we always honor friends if we're able to, and none of us like creepy stalker fuckers. Ronan raises the gavel, ready to smack down on the table and end the meeting when Finn clears his throat.

"Actually, Prez, we got one more thing." This brings my head back into the game, focusing on Ronan's face instead of the knots in my damn stomach. Finn spins his lighter between his fingers, his nervous tick. We all have great respect for our president, of course, and Ronan has never run this club like a dictator; we really do feel like brothers and like we're more equal than the ranking hierarchy implies. Regardless of how comfortable we are within our friendships, this topic is incredibly sensitive and I wouldn't want to have to be the one to present it to the club.

Ronan shifts his heavy gaze to my best friend, setting the gavel back down on the table in front of him. "Is it about the mole from last night?"

Finn nods. "He wouldn't give anything up for a long fucking time, but he finally said he doesn't know who hired him, but he worked for The Brothers Coalition." The room goes silent, and that's probably the most telling and terrifying thing yet.

Ronan stares down at the table in front of him, nodding his

head slowly. "So this was professional," Ronan surmises. He looks at Finn again. "Did he have any ink?"

Finn shakes his head, keeping eye contact with Ronan. "None." Everyone exchanges confused looks around the table. Tattoos are like organization name tags; if the spy was a part of anything then he should have had a tattoo linking him to someone.

"What the fuck is The Brothers Coalition?" Nate barks from between Saint and Tobi.

Ronan shakes his head. "No fucking clue. Have Mason look into it."

"What about who hired him in the first place?" Tobi asks.

"The Kings of Mayhem?" Finn suggests.

Ro shakes his head, dismissing Finn's idea. "We've had the peace pact going with them for over a decade."

"But they were forced into that, and they have that new president." Finn continues, but Ronan shakes his head again, not convinced.

Tobi leans his elbows onto the table. "What about Los Lobos?"

Nate scoffs. "In the words of our young prospect, 'they're more useless than stoplights in *Grand Theft Auto.*'"

Ronan chuckles. "He's right, their numbers are too low to be of any concern to us. One on one maybe, but they know a war would bring in our other charters and they don't have enough bodies to try to compete with that."

"You get a name at all?" Saint changes the subject, slipping his phone into his jeans pocket.

All of our eyes bounce between Ronan, Saint, and Finn. "He didn't have any I.D. on him."

Ronan rubs his bottom lip with his finger. "Call the prospects and tell them to get his prints before dropping him off at Doc's." He looks at Saint. "Get Richards to run his prints through the police database and see if he pops anything." Saint nods, pulling his phone out of his jeans pocket again. "Anything else?" Ronan looks around the table. With no one saying anything more, he slams the gavel down on the table and we all start to rise from our seats, checking our phones and casting concerned glances at one another. Ever since leaving the cabin, I've had a bad feeling about the rat. We still have more questions than answers, and all signs are pointing to a major shit storm in our future.

8

CALLUM

Leaving one giant clusterfuck to attend to another, I turn the corner from the chapel and see the prospects sitting at the bar; they're not allowed into church since they're not patched members yet. I walk straight toward them, not wasting any time, and fill them in on Reese's story and what we're gonna be doing. We have four prospects, so I figure shifts with me checking in is the best way to handle this, according to Saint, we're not worried about safety, mostly just want to catch the sick fuck. We're not concerned about the beating that Lance took, fights are always happening between drunk students in The District, and the chances of Reese's stalker actually doing anything are slim; he probably just read the news and is taking credit to spook Red. I pull my phone out while walking to my bike, clicking on the follower notification from Instagram earlier. Sure enough, it was my newest little responsibility. Ignoring the followers because I don't care, I scroll through her pictures quickly. Taking a seat on my bike and pulling my helmet on. They're all of her and a group of girls, lots of pictures of desserts, and a few pictures of the mountains with hashtags like #hiking, #nature, and #Washington. I follow her back before sliding my phone into my pocket and starting my bike.

Wyatt, the oldest prospect, follows me to Reese's apartment, and when we enter the parking lot it sounds like an entire charter is coming with the echoes bouncing back and forth between the buildings. Reese and a short blonde are leaning against a car, the woman's arm draped over Reese, so she must be Saint's friend Allie. Wyatt and I park our bikes a space away from them and when Reese sees me she says something to Allie and then walks toward us. She looks so sexy in her black dress pants with a bow in the front, a tan tank top, and tan heels. Her heels click against the pavement as she moves toward me and I can't help but stare at her legs. Not the time to be remembering how they felt wrapped around you just a few days ago, dickhead. My thoughts sober when I see her grimace and can see just how freaked out she is, shit I kind of feel bad now.

"You're a prospect?" Reese crosses her arms and rubs at the backs of her arms like it's freezing outside, despite the warm weather.

"What? No. What?" I scratch my head, looking over her shoulder to see Allie opening her car door.

"Saint said prospects would be coming to help." She looks at my cut and then her eyes shift back to Wyatt behind me.

"No, I'm the Sergeant at Arms." I crook my thumb behind me to Wyatt. "Wyatt is one of our prospects, I'm going to be monitoring them and helping out. I wanted to check in and make sure you're okay." I place my hands over hers to stop her frantic rubbing.

She looks into my eyes. "Did you assault that guy after dropping me off on Saturday?"

I should have expected that, but I answer anyway. "No, Red. I didn't spare that dick a second thought after you got on the back of my bike." She searches my eyes, I hope she sees the truth. "I went home and went to bed."

She lets out a breath, eyes still holding mine. "Okay, I believe you."

Allie clears her throat while taking a few steps over to meet us. "So how's this going to work?" Damn this one is all business, but I guess I can't blame her; Saint sent me pictures of the notes Reese had been sent and they did look a little creepy.

"I have four prospects who are going to take shifts watching Reese, and I'll check in when I can and whenever I'm needed. I run a roofing business so I can leave when needed, but I can't abandon it completely. I've also got a tech buddy that's going to come out in the morning and wire the whole place with cameras and a security alarm." I cross my arms, I feel like Allie is sizing me up, wondering if I'm fit for the job, or maybe for her friend. I'm sure as fuck qualified to watch after someone and scare off creeps, not so much for relationships. Those are a waste of my damn time, energy, and money. Reese was a great lay and her safety will be a top priority, but it ends there.

"You're going to be following me everywhere and putting cameras in my apartment?" Reese's eyes are huge and she rubs between her eyebrows with one delicate finger.

"Yes, someone will be watching you from a distance, but we won't be putting cameras in the apartment, just on the exterior doors. The security system will have an alarm if the doors or windows are forced open or the code isn't entered after opening the door." I shift my weight from side to side while I keep an eye on the maintenance guys finishing up fixing Reese's door. That answer seems to calm her down a bit and she nods while she looks down at her shoes. "Wyatt is going to go home and grab his cage so he can sit out here and watch the apartment tonight. Can I come in and look around? I need to send the specs of your apartment to my guy so he can get what he'll need to fit the place." Reese just nods again, not saying anything more.

Allie's phone pings and we all pause while she brings it to her face. She scrunches her little nose. "I have to go to the office, will you be okay here with him?" Her gaze swings to me quickly before focusing back on Red.

Reese nods and we say goodbye to Allie and the two maintenance guys, we finally walk into her apartment. The guys eye me when they see me behind Reese, but once they pass and see my cut they quickly look away, not wanting to get on my bad side. Reese's apartment is comfy looking, but everything is white, like everything. The white puffy couch, white carpet, white stone coffee table, and even the pictures on the wall are of white flowers. A complete opposite of my place.

"I feel like I'm in an asylum," I say looking around at everything, it looks like a showroom; I feel like I should take off my shoes before I accidentally track anything in.

"I think it's calming. The white is easy and bright." She watches me look around the living room.

"At least your couch looks comfortable." She kicks off her heels by the front door and walks into the small kitchen.

"Oh it is, I wanted the place to be as comfortable as possible. I love watching movies and shows, so I invested in my couch, TVs, and bed," she says, grabbing a spoon from a drawer.

My phone vibrates in my pocket, Wyatt telling me he's in the parking lot outside. "I'm gonna go ahead and look around and then I'll head out. Wyatt's watching from his car outside."

Reese grabs a pint of ice cream from the freezer. Typing something on her phone the entire time. She turns around to face me. "Um, would you be willing to stay with me tonight? I keep picturing someone coming through my bedroom window while I sleep, and all of my friends are working late into the night or out of town." Her eyes are on the floor and when she looks up at me she looks so scared.

I shrug out of my cut and lay it on the arm of the couch. "Of course, Red. Whatever you need. I can sleep on the couch, see how comfy it really is." I pat the back of the couch.

Reese puts the spoon straight into the tub of ice cream and pegs me with an unamused look. "Your tongue was on my clit, I think we can share a bed." I put my thumb in the corner of my mouth to hide my smirk and shake my head. Scared as shit and still making crude jokes, what a girl!

9

REESE

Even waking up at every little sound, I still slept a lot better than I'd expected; having Callum next to me helped tremendously. We kept to our own sides of my bed, the no cuddling rule I implemented last night standing strong. My alarm wakes us, beeping loudly and causing Callum to curse under his breath.

"Red, why is your alarm so fucking loud?" He rubs at his eyes, his voice is deep and gruff with sleep.

"I'm a heavy sleeper usually." I laugh. "Sorry, I haven't shared a bed with anyone in a while." I turn my head to look at him and bite my lip. How can he make bed head and half closed eyes look sexy?

"Yeah me either. What was it you said? *I don't do sleepovers.*" He pushes the covers down his torso and stands. He only slept in his tight boxers last night so his back tat and tight butt are on full display as he walks to the bathroom. It's only now that I'm noticing his back is a giant colorful mural of an old ship with a sea serpent and the word 'Outlaw' across his lower back.

I roll to my side to watch him walk away. "I'm so glad my

stalker could make you break your rules for me!" I laugh and throw a pillow at his retreating back.

"I think you could make me break a lot of my rules, Red!" He yells from the bathroom and I roll my eyes.

I'm about to get up when Callum's phone starts vibrating on the bedside table. "Hey, Callum, your phone is ringing!" I yell towards the bathroom again. He saunters into the bedroom, muscles and tattoos flexing and relaxing as he walks and dries his hands on my hand towel, and I can't help but stare at him, his blonde hair is messy and falling into his eyes.

Callum runs his fingers through his hair, pushing the strands off of his face. His lips form into a cocky grin and he bites his lip. "If you keep looking at me like that, Red, I'm going to decline this call, spread you out over this bed, and fuck you until you forget your own name."

"Uh," I stammer, stunned silent while my brain short circuits from how hot his dirty talking is. He chuckles and answers the phone, walking out of my bedroom, and closing the door behind him.

I get up, shaking my head to clear the lusty fog, and walk into my bathroom to wash my face. As I'm applying my skincare, Callum walks in and leans his butt against the double vanity. He crosses his arms and his muscles flex, my eyes tracing the designs on his skin.

"I gotta head outta town for a day or two. The prospects will be around, but I just wanted to let you know that I won't be here." He looks down at me.

Panic sets in, but I try to ignore it. "You're leaving?" It sounds desperate even to my ears and I inwardly smack myself; I shouldn't be leaning on this guy to protect me, he doesn't owe me anything just because we hooked up once.

"Yeah, I have to meet with a lighting consultant for my warehouse. Everywhere is backed up right now and this is the only supplier that doesn't have a six month wait." I nod, not able to say anything else. As much as I don't want to rely on him, I don't feel safe with anyone else. "Red, I don't want you freaking out while I'm gone; you should come."

"No. It's a work trip, I'll be fine here." I shake my head and start to run a brush through my long hair.

He puts his hand around my free arm and I stop to look at him. "It's gonna be boring, you'd make it a whole lot more enjoyable." He looks into my eyes. "Besides, it'd probably be a good idea to get you out of town for a few days. I just wasn't sure you'd be able to leave work with such short notice."

I put the brush down and turn towards him, resting my hip against the counter. "My regional manager told me to take a few days for myself after what happened yesterday."

Callum smiles. "Good. Start packing, we can stop by my place for my stuff after." He walks past me and into the bedroom.

10

REESE

WE SWITCHED THE BIKE OUT FOR CALLUM'S RAPTOR FOR THE hour ride to Seattle. We made it a little before lunch, so Callum dropped me off at a hotel he booked for the night so I could freshen up and relax while he went to the warehouse to pick out the lighting fixtures for his business. After showering, changing, and nailing down a place to grab lunch, I decide to call my friends and fill them in on everything that happened with my new creepy stalker.

"This is so messed up, Reese," Emma says down the line.

"I know." I fall back against the bed.

"And you associating with the Devil's Outlaws? They're criminals Reese, I see them down at the courthouse all of the time." She harrumphs.

"I know, Em, but Allie thinks this is the best idea right now, and Callum isn't what you think." She grunts like she wants to argue with me. Changing the subject because I am so tired of talking about this stupid situation. "Hey, could you go over to my apartment and take a package inside? It was delivered after we left and there's some students that keep stealing people's packages off of their porches. There's a key tucked inside of the wreath hanging on my door." I stare at the ceiling, kicking my legs over the edge of the bed.

"Of course, Re." I know she's coming around because her voice is soft again. That's one thing that makes her so great with the kids she works with; her sweet voice could end wars.

"Take someone with you just in case." I hate that I have to ask my best friend to ask someone to go along with her to my apartment because she might be in danger if she goes alone. Frustrated and bitter, I end the call shortly after and wait for Callum to get back from his meeting.

A while later, on our way to lunch Callum's phone dings in the cupholder between us.

"Would you mind checking that, Red?" He keeps his eyes on the road.

I pick up his phone and he tells me his passcode to open the message. "It's from Ronan and he said to call him."

Callum curses under his breath. "Hit call." I press dial on Ronan's contact and the phone starts ringing through the vehicle's speakers.

"Cale." Ronan's voice is deep through the phone.

"I'm with Reese, I brought her with me to Seattle." Callum quickly interrupts.

Ronan hums on the line. "That's fine. I need to meet with Alessandro, so I told him you're in Seattle and he's flying down to meet with you tonight over a deal. Finn is on his way to... oversee that everyone is cordial."

Callum tenses and his grip on the steering wheel tightens. "Why am I meeting with him?"

"Because Saint and I are meeting with a supplier." The grumbling of bikes comes through the line. "I'll let him know you have company so Reese can go as well."

Callum glances at me quickly. "Yes, sir," he says before hanging up.

We pull into the parking lot for the sports bar and I turn in my seat to face Callum. "Who is Alessandro?"

Callum rubs his hand over his sharp jaw and groans. "Look I don't want to lie to you, Red, but I can't tell you who he is or what we're meeting him for." He meets my eyes and I can see the honesty there.

"Criminal things?" I ask, lifting my brow, but Callum just stares at me, giving nothing away. I can tell he doesn't want to lie, but he can't divulge the truth. I stay in my seat, holding his gaze. "What can you tell me?"

He pushes out a breath, pausing. "All I can tell you is that Alessandro is a club associate and we're meeting with him for club business."

"Will this be dangerous?" I stare into his eyes.

He shakes his head. "No. Ronan wouldn't let you go if he thought it would be."

We get out of Callum's Raptor and walk into the restaurant. After ordering our drinks, a news segment flashes across the big screens in the sports bar. "Oh my gosh, Callum look!" I watch the TV screen horrified.

His head snaps up from his menu. "What?" He follows my gaze to the screen behind the bar.

"Michelle Davis, the wife of Senator Buxley Davis, was found murdered in their Washington home last night."

The news reporter continues the story and Callum lets out a giant breath. "Oh shit."

———

DURING LUNCH, Callum had gotten a text about where we were meeting his 'club associate' and told me we needed to buy me something nice to wear tonight. Apparently, this Alessandro guy has expensive tastes because Callum even stops in and buys a nice button-up for the dinner meeting. When I walk out of the bathroom wearing a white cropped tank, high-waisted gold glitter mini skirt, and nude platform stilettos, Callum's gaze slowly slides down my body; lingering on my tan legs that look longer due to the short skirt and tall heels. He's standing in front of the window with his leather over a deep blue button-up shirt rolled up and tucked into black jeans with his motorcycle boots. The shirt shows off his muscled arms and tattooed forearm. The moment seems to stretch on forever, with us both staring at each other and I move my hands up to fluff my red curls to break the tension.

Callum clears his throat and turns around to grab his phone and wallet off of the desk next to him. "Finn's waiting for us at the bar downstairs." I turn around and walk to the door, swinging my hips a little more in the heels. I hear quiet mumbles behind me and turn my head to look at Callum, his eyes quickly meet mine from where they were watching my ass in my skirt. I've never had this effect on a guy, they've never watched me walk away, or told me all of the dirty things they wanted to do to me. My life has always been boring, and I've always felt like I blended into the background. The grin doesn't leave my face the entire way down to the bar.

11

CALLUM

We meet Finn in the hotel bar. The big fucker is scowling over his beer watching a game on the TV in front of him. He always has a resting bitch face, but when he sees us his entire face lights up. I chuckle under my breath and Reese turns to look at me with her head cocked, I just shake my head to say that it was nothing. Finn is the biggest sap in the world when it comes to his family, everyone else gets the big scary biker with the scarred knuckles and glares. He tosses cash onto the bar and the bartender grabs the money without making eye contact. He pushes the sleeves of his shirt up to his elbows and walks over to us. I told him the restaurant had a dress code tonight, not that he's in some fucking suit, he's wearing his cut and a black long sleeve tee shirt with black jeans and a less scuffed up pair of biker boots. Finn is a good few inches taller than me and almost double my size, putting him around 6 and a half feet. The dude is a hulking mass of muscles and tattoos. His black hair is slicked back on top and shaved on the sides, tattoos cover his neck and the shaved sides of his head and they continue all the way down to his fingers; basically, the only thing he doesn't have tattooed is his clean shaven face. Reese tenses next to me and takes a slight step closer to my side, watching Finn stalk over to us, even smiling like a goon he still intimidates her.

Finn pulls me into his chest and thumps my back with his big hand, when he releases me he looks down at Reese, his cool eyes run over her in a calculating way. "I'm Finn, you ready for tonight?" He holds out his hand to shake hers. Finn doesn't trust people easily; he's always cold to people he doesn't know, but props to Reese for not running the other way from his judging stare, a lot of people don't have the backbone to withstand Finn's glare.

Reese shakes his hand, keeping eye contact even though she's still tense. "I'm Reese, and I'm not sure. I don't know what I'm supposed to do." She looks between us.

Before I can answer, Finn cuts in. "Just sit there and look pretty darling." She scoffs and Finn waves his hand laughing. "Not in a sexist way, we're just gonna be talking business and there really isn't anything else for you to do."

I shake my head laughing. Attempting to pull my brother's foot out of his mouth, I cover for him. "Just enjoy your drink, Red."

Outside we each get into our vehicles, my Raptor and Finn's Hellcat, and head to the upscale restaurant in the Bay Area of Seattle. The cars are a lot safer and easier in the city traffic compared to the bikes. Finn is a gearhead, if his owning a body shop and garage wasn't evident enough; He's a fan of muscle cars, old and new.

We walk along the water to the restaurant, on the other side of the bay the Space Needle shines like a beacon. When we walk into the restaurant it's empty, with only minimal staff walking around.

A hostess steps forward. "Mr. Moran, Mr. Evans. Mr. Valenti

and Mr. Segreto are waiting for you. Follow me please." She gestures us forward and Finn and I exchange a confused glance, who the fuck is Mr. Segreto? We follow her along the empty water-front restaurant, past vacant tables with white table cloths and low lighting, to a big round table in the back sitting in front of a large floor-to-ceiling window. Alessandro is sitting on the back side of the large table with two other Italian guys seated next to him and four large goons standing behind them. Alessandro stands to shake our hands, an expensive suit tailored to fit his frame perfectly. He gestures to his guests as they stand. "Gentlemen, I'd like to introduce you to Sebastian and Nico Segreto of Sicily. *Oh shit. Sebastian Segreto is the Don for the Cosa Nostra with Nico being his second in charge. What the fuck!* I'm pretty sure Finn's head explodes at the same time that mine does. Although we've never done business with Alessandro Valenti, we've met the head of the Valenti mafia in New York a few times.

Sebastian eyes us all closely, his dark hair styled and his deep brown eyes focused, bending forward to shake our hands. "Callum Moran, Finn Evans. Thank you for meeting with me tonight, I was hoping that we could discuss some business." He extends his hand to Reese. "Miss. Thomas, It's very lovely to meet you, as Alessandro said, my name is Sebastian Segreto." Her eyes go wide at him using her name.

She shakes his hand and stutters out. "It's nice to meet you as well." After shaking both Sebastian's and Nico's hands, I pull her into my side and sit her in between Finn and me.

I rest my hand on her leg to hopefully give her some reassurance because although she shouldn't know the head of the Sicilian Mafia, it's still weird for someone you don't know to know your name. "We're not really operational in Sicily," I say, not sure what we could do for him in Italy. Sebastian orders some expensive ass wine for the table, but Finn, Nico, and I order whiskey instead and leave the wine for Reese, Sebastian, and Alessandro. None of us wanted to sit around and wait for food so we decided tonight's meeting would just be over drinks.

Sebastian leans back in his chair, sizing me up. "I would be hiring you for a job in the states." My eyebrows raise, but he looks away from me and tilts his head, and focuses on Reese. "Are you enjoying Seattle, Miss. Thomas?"

Reese takes a sip of her wine. "It's nice, though we haven't seen much of the city to be honest, and please call me Reese."

Sebastian nods, his stare turning into a smile; but it looks evil on him, not welcoming. "Reese." He pauses. "The name means fiery."

Reese laughs, looking at a section of her red hair in her slender fingers. "I guess it fits me then." Finn tries to cover his laughter on the other side of her and I glare at him.

Fire seems to dance in Sebastian's eyes as he watches her. "Yes, I suppose it does. Anyway, I much prefer Sicily."

Reese groans. "I've always wanted to go!" It's kind of funny, her unknowingly making light conversation with a mafia boss.

Sebastian's dark brown eyes bore into Reese's green ones. "If you ever find yourself in Sicily, I'd be delighted to show you the island." I'm starting to get irritated with the attention he's paying to Reese, but this is also a fucking mafia Don and I can't throw my weight around like back in Merill Hill; so I have to let this play out for a little longer. We came here for business, not so he could try to get his dick wet. "Reese, how did you find yourself in the company of The Devil's Outlaws?" He looks down her body and back up to her face, well as much of her body that he can see while she's sitting.

"Uh..." Reese pulls at the bottom of her skirt, obviously nervous.

Not liking the way Sebastian is looking at Reese and making her uncomfortable, I interrupt her. "She's friends with the club." My tone is harsh and Finn looks over to me, his eyes telling me to calm my shit, but I've had enough of his bullshit. "Is there a reason for this meeting?"

Sebastian finally stops staring at Reese and looks over at me. "Of course." He adjusts the cufflinks on his dark suit. "The reason I asked to meet with you tonight is that I had a roofing job for the club." Sebastian raises his wine glass and takes a drink. He's talking in a code so that Reese doesn't know he's asking us to make him illegal bullets.

I lean onto the table, keeping one hand on Reese's thigh. "We're currently overbooked," I say, thinking about how we've already started making bullets for the O'Connell Irish mob.

Nico looks over to his boss. "We're aware of your job for the O'Connells."

Sebastian interrupts him. "We'll double their offer."

My eyebrows raise to my hairline and Finn leans back in his chair, spreading his thighs wide and resting his arm across the back of Reese's chair. He isn't touching her, he's just trying to make it very obvious that Reese is protected by the club. "How big is the job? We'll be redoing Killian's entire compound, so the project would have to be equal in size for us to take your offer instead." O'Connell said he was gearing up for something big and asked for regular shipments, normally we deliver to him on an as needed basis so his need this time is huge.

Sebastian clasps his hands together on the table. "What a coincidence, Alessandro's family is also in need of all new roofs. I assure you the jobs would be equal in size, and as I said, I will pay double what Killian O'Connell is currently offering."

Finn and I look at each other over Reese's head. Silently communicating that we're on the same page; Finn and I can't make this decision on behalf of our club, especially since we've already taken Killian's job on. "We have to take your proposal back to Ronan, and he'll be in touch with his decision," I say, taking a drink of my whiskey. Finn and I have barely taken a drink since we're both driving.

Sebastian nods, although his Cheshire cat smile is gone now; I don't think he gets told 'no' very often. "How is the wine, Reese?"

Reese swallows the drink she just took, wiping the red liquid from her plump lips with the white cloth napkin. I need to stop fucking watching this girl so closely, but everything she does is just so feminine and addictive. "Divine. Thank you." She smiles all warm and sweet and I want to taste the wine on her tongue.

Sebastian smiles a flirty smile and motions for a waiter to bring something over. "I'm glad. In my opinion, Massetos is the best wine in Italy. I've arranged for you to take a bottle of the 2004 Tenuta dell'Ornellaia home with you."

His flirting with Reese starts to make my stomach knot a little, but I chalk it up to not having eaten yet. "That is so kind of you, but I couldn't." Reese looks at the waiter with wide eyes and her eyebrows raised.

Sebastian waves his hand. "Please, I've greatly enjoyed your company this evening."

The waiter hands the unopened bottle to Reese. "Thank you so much." Her voice is so innocent, too sweet for someone talking to the Don of the Cosa Nostra.

Another waiter comes out from the back. "Gentlemen, I've also ordered you each a bottle of a limited edition whiskey that I recently came across on my last trip to Japan. Please, take it as a thank you for meeting with me tonight." The waiter hands Finn and me each a bottle and my eyebrows raise as I read the label, stating it as Hibiki 21 Year Old Mount Fuji Whiskey. I've never had Japanese whiskey, but I suppose if this snobby guy drinks it and it's limited edition and 21 years old then it's gotta be pretty good right? One of the goons discreetly slips a phone into his pants pocket and steps forward to whisper into Sebastian's ear. Sebastian's jaw clenches and he lets out a deep breath before quickly returning to the easy smile he just wore, he turns to Nico and gives him a pointed look, then Sebastian, Nico, and Alessandro stand from the table, buttoning the button on his suit jacket he says, "It was a pleasure meeting with you all, and I hope you'll consider our proposal. If you'll excuse us, we have some business to attend to in New York."

I nod, standing as well and helping Reese to her feet. When Sebastian and his men are walking beside us he reaches out to shake my hand again. Shaking his hand I say, "Ronan will be in touch." Sebastian nods and walks to the front doors of the restaurant.

Alessandro stops to shake my hand. "Thank you for meeting with us." I nod, now wondering why the Segretos are doing business in America personally, normally they let the Valenti's take care of any issues on their behalf. Taking Reese's hand, the three of us leave the restaurant; Finn walks behind us to add an extra layer of protection for Reese. "Come on, Red, let's go drink that fancy ass wine on the rooftop of the hotel." Her laugh echoes through the restaurant and her smile brightens her face, she squeezes my hand as we walk out into the warm night air.

When we get into my pickup and pull out onto the road Finn revs his engine before going in the opposite direction.

Reese looks into the side mirror, watching his taillights. "Where's he going?"

I look at her out of the side of my eye. "Home. He wanted to see Huntley."

She nods. "Is that his girlfriend?"

I laugh, shaking my head. "No, but that's not from lack of

trying." Finns been on this girl's case for a little while trying to get her to let him take her on a date. He doesn't ever spend any more time on a girl than it takes to fuck her. He says he'll settle down when he finds a woman like his mom, but I don't think he really thinks he'll ever find a love like his parents had. So for him to be trying so hard says something about her.

12

REESE

WHEN WE GET TO THE HOTEL WE STOP IN THE BAR TO GRAB TWO empty wine glasses and some dinner to take up to the outdoor rooftop lounge, "Positions" by Ariana Grande playing softly through the outdoor speakers. I lounge back in the wide plush chair, my heels resting on the low table between us. "Why'd you join the club?"

Callum takes a drink of the wine, his throat working to swallow it. He cocks his head, looking down at the glass in his hand. "Not bad by the way." He looks up at me. Since we turned the lights out here off the only light is from the sitting room inside. Callum is a work of art in the daylight, with his sharp jaw and scruff on his cheeks, but in the low light he looks like a fallen angel, his features shadowed and making everything look like he was cut from marble. "I always liked bikes and I heard about a club function, so I went and some guys convinced me to prospect. I liked the idea of brotherhood and the guys were all really cool and like me."

I nod along with his answer. "And tonight's meeting was about a roofing job for your company? I thought your president set up the meeting."

He pauses, leaning back into his chair, and looks into my eyes despite the lack of light. "Something like that." I watch him, staying quiet to see if he's going to say anything more. "I'm not going to lie to you, it wasn't for CMR but something that the club does. That's all I can say, Red."

I know he's keeping secrets about the club and what they do because I'm sure it's illegal; I mean I've heard the rumors about them, but I do appreciate him not completely lying to me, or at least not wanting to. Not wanting to push him anymore I drop the subject. "What is something you can tell me about you then?"

He smirks and slides his eyes down my body. "That all night I've been picturing bending you over, sliding that little skirt over your ass, and eating that sweet pussy."

My heart stops in my chest, but I try to play it cool. "Oh have you?"

Callum nods and points to his right. "Over there."

I follow his finger to the stone wall overlooking the city. Downing the rest of my wine I stand and slowly walk over to the wall that stands to my chest. With us having had dinner up here as well as finishing the entire bottle of wine from Sebastian it has gotten pretty late, and with the lights off up here you can't see anything other than our silhouettes; no one has come up here since we got here so what are the chances anyone would come up now? I lean against the stone and look over my shoulder at him. Callum places his glass on the low table and makes his way over to me, his tongue coming out to wet his lips. I jolt with excitement when his lips land on my shoulder, his hands slowly gliding up my thighs to the hem of my mini skirt, kicking my legs apart with his boots. He places a hand on my lower back to lean me against the wall and kneels behind me, sliding my lace panties down to my knees.

I look over my shoulder at him. "You look good down on your knees."

He laughs and slides a finger inside of me and I jolt with excitement. "Don't get used to it, Red."

He pumps his finger inside of me a few more times before replacing it with his tongue and moving his finger to circle over my clit. I suck in a breath at the new sensation mixed with the warm night air flowing over my exposed ass. He laps at my pussy, his tongue flexing and flicking. This man's tongue is like nothing I have ever experienced; oral before this used to be boring and make me self conscience, but Callum eats me like a freaking dessert and he doesn't rush through it, he treats fore-play like it's just as important as the actual sex. I'm climbing towards my orgasm, my moans turning into begging until he pushes harder against my clit and I explode, my orgasm rolling through me like waves; my moans filtering into the city night.

He rubs his hands up and down my thighs while I run through the aftershocks of my orgasm. When I'm finally back he places a kiss on my bare ass cheek and pulls my panties up. "As beautiful as you are bent over like this, I want to watch your tits bouncing on my dick." I stand up straight and fix my skirt, with my legs still shaking in my tall heels, I take his arm and we walk into the sitting room. Passing a beautiful sleek piano Callum stops. "You wanted to know something about me right?" I nod my head and he walks over to the piano and sits down, leaving enough space next to him on the bench for me. He takes a deep breath, staring down at the keys. "I haven't played since high school." He places his fingers on the keys and plays a couple of notes. After testing out the piano he starts playing; the song is slow and sad, almost haunting. I watch his face as he focuses on his playing, he seems relaxed and like he's starting to lose himself in the song. The song crescendos and his playing becomes quicker until it slows and quietly ends, the last note hanging in the air like a dark cloud.

He slowly closes the key lid and I take this time to collect myself. There is so much I didn't expect about Callum, and every day he does something else to surprise me. "That was beautiful."

He lets out a soft laugh, flashing a smirk. "Thanks. I wrote it."

"What?" I stare at him shocked. "When did you learn to play?"

He leans his elbows on the key lid and looks at me over his shoulder. "I started taking lessons when I was a kid, every week until I graduated high school. My parents wanted me to go to college and do something with it, but I chose to work and prospect for the club instead. I wrote that song for my final recital."

I lean against the piano, resting my head in my hand facing him. "Is that why you haven't played since high school?"

He keeps staring ahead at the blank wall at the end of the piano. "Yeah. My parents said I was wasting my talents to become a criminal; that I was disgracing the Moran name. We don't really talk anymore." My heart breaks for Callum, how could parents abandon their child? You spend nine months, ten really, preparing for a child, eighteen years preparing them for the life that they choose, and are supposed to spend the rest of your life loving them; how could you just give up on them? Callum isn't a bad guy, he saved me from a handsy guy at the bar, and volunteered to watch out for me from my creepy stalker, he may be a criminal, the jury is still out on that one, but he isn't a bad guy. I've met bad people and Callum isn't one of them, and as far as I'm concerned, The Devil's Outlaws aren't either.

13

REESE

The next day we came back to Merrill Hill and I decided to get some work done from my laptop. The day goes by quickly, with me sitting on the couch and binging Netflix while I work. I periodically look out of the window but every time I see a guy about my age, twenty-three, sitting in his dark gray Chevy pickup watching my apartment and looking down at his lap; every time he catches me looking he smiles and waves and every time I feel embarrassed to be caught looking. By the time dinner rolls around and I start to pile my meatball sliders onto my plate I realize that I haven't seen the guy eat the entire day. I start to load up a plate for him as well and then decide to invite him in to eat since he's been stuck in his pickup all day. I slide my slippers on at my front door and walk out to his car in the parking lot. He watches me walk to his driver's side window in confusion and rolls it down when I get close enough.

"Is everything okay, Reese?" He's cute with dark brown hair hanging into his sea green eyes. His tan skin and sunken cheek-bones make me instantly envious. With his black hoodie up over his head and his tablet in his hand, he looks like a hot techie guy.

I shake my head, tearing my eyes away from his odd-colored eyes; they're gorgeous, but they haven't got anything on Callum's slate blue eyes. "Yeah everything is fine, I was just wondering if you wanted to come in and have dinner?" He looks at me skeptically, with one eyebrow raised. "It's just dinner, I haven't seen you eat anything all day." He pauses, biting his lip. Then he places his tablet in the passenger seat and turns the ignition of the pickup off, rolling up his window before opening the door. We walk back to my apartment in silence and he quietly shuts the door behind him, following me into the kitchen. I pick up my plate and hand him an empty one. "Help yourself, although I slightly burned the rolls. I forgot to set a timer."

He laughs while loading his plate. "Anything is better than that shit Wyatt was going to bring me." He comes to sit next to me at the table and pulls his hood down to sit around his neck. "My name is Mason by the way." He holds out his hand to me and I shake it.

We start to eat, but the silence is starting to get awkward. "Thank you for watching over me."

Mason shovels food into his mouth, talking between bites. "Yeah, no problem, Princess." I roll my eyes at his nickname and take a bite out of my slider. He laughs and takes a drink from the energy drink he brought in. "Sorry, we all just started calling you the Princess of the Devil's Outlaws since we were guarding you like knights."

Overcome with guilt, I look down at my food. "I'm sorry you all are going to these extremes for me."

Mason places his hand over mine on the table. "I didn't mean to make you feel bad, we all want to help. You're not an inconvenience to us."

I look into his eyes. "Why? You don't even know me."

He rubs his hand over his shadow of stubble. "I guess because we didn't like that someone was terrorizing an innocent woman." I focus on my food again, not able to continue to stare into his earnest gaze. "I mean I always begged my mom for a little sister that I could protect, I guess I saw this as my opportunity to finally do that." I look up at him again and his grin is goofy. I laugh and shake my head and his grin gets wider.

After we've finished dinner Mason helps me load the dishwasher and clean up the table. I walk him to the door, and after he walks out I stand in the doorway and lean against the frame. "Dinner is usually done around seven and I always make enough for leftovers, so if you don't mind my subpar cooking you're welcome to join me again."

He turns around, pulling his hood over his head. "Are you sure?"

I grin and nod my head. "Yeah, I enjoyed tonight."

Mason grins his goofy grin. "Well in that case I have to be honest with you." He starts walking backward, his face still towards me. I stare at him and wait for him to continue. "Subpar is a compliment to your cooking." He laughs so loud it echoes through the common area.

I glare at him though he can't see it in the dim light of my porch light. "You're uninvited!" I shout at him.

He rights his body but turns his head so he can look at me over his shoulder. "I'll see you Tuesday, Princess! I'll bring the beer!" he yells back.

14

REESE

A WEEK HAS GONE BY SMOOTHLY, BEING WATCHED BY PROSPECTS outside of my office and Callum and I spending the weekend days together. April is almost here and we've started preparing for most of the students to sublease their apartments for the summer. I've started looking forward to the weekends and thinking of Callum as a friend. The conversations are easy and I feel more at ease with him around. On Friday I'm finishing up a move-out inspection form when the bell over the office door dings.

"Hello!" I greet the customer, finishing up the last few check-boxes. I look up from my desk just in time to see a tenant step up to my open door.

"Hi, Miss. Reese." The young man shuffles from side to side in my doorway.

I smile, he's always so nervous when he comes in here to talk to me. "Hi, Tyler. What can I do for you?"

He stares down at a small stack of papers in his hands. "A girl from my psych class has been missing for a week, and I was wondering if I could put a missing flier on some of the community boards around the complex?"

My heart drops, poor girl. "Of course!" I answer immediately. "Actually, if you let me have one, I can scan it and send it as an email to all tenants, some don't pay attention to the community boards."

Tyler nods and steps into my office, passing me a flier. Bailey Darren, nineteen, missing. My eyes scan her photo. She looks sweet and young. Red hair, big blue eyes, and freckles. I hope she's just off ignoring the world, perfectly safe and happy. I scan the flier and hand it back to Tyler. Then I write up an email about Bailey and send it out to all residents, hopefully, someone can help find her.

That night I'm so ready to hang out on my couch and fall into a sugar coma with a good movie or two. The prospects have been keeping an eye on me from their vehicles outside and every night after I make dinner, I bring them out a plate. They're all really sweet and two of them are way too close to my age to be calling me 'ma'am'. On my way out of the door to take some enchiladas to whichever guy is here tonight, I stop in the doorway to see Callum walking up the sidewalk towards me.

"I sent Jack home, I thought I could hang out with you tonight." His eyes rake over my oversized tee and booty shorts, lingering over my legs before coming back to my eyes. If anyone else were to attempt this it would be so sleazy, but everything he does is so hot to me.

"Yeah that's fine, I made dinner if you're hungry." I raise the plate in my hands.

He takes the plate from me and follows me inside the apartment. "This doesn't smell half bad."

I spin around, my mouth open in surprise. "Did your friends say I'm a bad cook?" Callum scratches the back of his neck as he walks past me over to the dining table. "They can eat shitty takeout from now on." I grab a beer from the refrigerator for him and scoff.

Callum laughs loudly, taking a seat at the table. "They'll eat anything you place in front of them, and they're very thankful for you feeding them."

"Well, I'm better at desserts." I hand him his beer, our fingers pause over one another's and Callum pulls away smoothly, clearing his throat.

"So I think we're gonna pull the guys off of watchdog duty. There haven't be

en any issues since the break in, so I think we either scared him away or he moved on," he says between bites.

I nod my head. "Yeah, I think you're right," I agree. It's been quiet around here. No creepy notes, no heads in boxes, joking, I've been watching too many horror movies. My life is back to normal, with the exception of Callum.

After dinner, I was able to talk Callum into watching a movie. Callum takes off his leather cut and lays it over the back of the couch. "Alright, Red, now's your time to redeem yourself from those enchiladas." Callum laughs and slumps into the couch. "Damn this thing really is nice." He burrows into it further.

"And redeem myself I will." I carry a bowl into the living room and sit down next to him.

He looks into the bowl. "Popcorn and Reese's Pieces?" His unamused gaze switches to me. "Is this some sort of namesake thing?"

I bark out a laugh. "No, that was unintentional. Just trust me." I tip the bowl towards him.

He holds my eyes as he pops the popcorn/candy mixture into his mouth. "Much better than the enchiladas." He nods his head.

"Shut up!" I push at his arm gently. Callum is quick and he grabs the hand that was on his shoulder and pulls me into his lips. Although I'm caught off guard, I melt into his kiss immediately. His tongue glides over my lips and I open my mouth to let him in; our tongues dance together while he grabs the bowl in one hand and places his other on my hip. He guides me into his lap and places the bowl on the floor next to us. Again, I'm impressed with how smooth this man is with his eyes closed. His mouth moves down to my neck and I grind down onto his dick. He slips his hands under my shirt and starts to raise it.

"Wait. I don't want a relationship." I stop moving my hips and place my hands on his shoulders.

He stops kissing my neck and looks into my eyes. "I'm not asking for your heart, Red, just your tight cunt." *Well, that I can do*. I smash my lips into his, our kiss becoming fervent and urgent. He slides my shirt over my head, cupping my breast, and my hands slide up his sides to cradle his face. I break the kiss by biting his bottom lip and standing to slide my shorts and panties down my legs. Callum pulls his shirt over his head in an unreasonably sexy move with one hand, his muscles flexing deliciously. He undoes his belt buckle and button and raises his hips, pushing his jeans down as well. He pulls a condom from his wallet that was in his back pocket and tears it open, sliding it down his long length, and my mouth waters at the sight of his monster cock. Callum smirks at my staring and grabs my hand to pull me down on top of him. "Ride me like you own me, Red." I slide down his dick, filling me completely and he hisses. Determined to give this man the best damn ride of his life, I circle my hips, holding him deep inside of me while I relax around him. When the slight pain from the stretch has subsided and all I'm left feeling is absolutely full I rise onto my feet and start bouncing on top of him. One hand is behind me on his thigh and the other is holding onto the back of his neck for balance. Callum's honest to God moans are the sexiest noise I've ever heard and are what I'm living off of at this point. Callum leans his head on the back of the sofa and watches me through a heavy-lidded gaze. One hand cups my breast, flicking his thumb over my nipple and the other pinches my clit and I explode, my pulsing pussy tightening on his cock. Callum grunts and I stop with him fully seated inside of me, riding out my orgasm. I moan low, my head falling backward. When I finally come down, Callum raises his hips and holds under my thighs to keep me in place, pumping into me with quick deep thrusts. He's pumping into me so quickly that I feel myself riding the edge of another orgasm. When I feel his dick swell inside of me I reach down between us and vigorously rub my clit, pushing me over the edge. "Fuck!" Callum grunts as we both watch my fingers work my clit. With a roar, he thrusts deep inside of me one last time and comes. He drops back down onto the couch, "Holy shit." he breathes, dropping his forehead to my shoulder. My laugh comes out raspy and after a moment sitting in his lap, his dick still inside of me and his head on my shoulder it starts to feel a little too much like cuddling so I roll off of him and my back hits the couch next to him. Callum laughs and drags his hand down his face, "Sorry, Red. I had to catch my breath there." He pulls the condom off and drags his pants back up, walking into the kitchen to throw the condom away.

"You can stay the night again if you want." I offer, grabbing my shirt off of the floor and sliding it on.

"I think that's called a sleepover, babe." He leans his forearms against the counter and eyes me over the bar.

"It's allowed when you stay on your own side of the bed." I slouch into the couch.

"Tonight I won't be." Callum stalks over to me, his slate blue eyes turning a stormy gray. He lifts me from the couch like I weigh nothing and my arms and legs wrap around him automatically, my hands resting on the back of his neck. He walks me to the bedroom, promising more orgasms and working his mouth down my neck.

15

REESE

I WAKE THE NEXT MORNING WITH MY FOREHEAD PRESSED INTO A surface that is a lot harder than my pillow, pulling away and opening my eyes, I see Callum's arm. During my sleep, I moved to his side and wrapped myself around his arm. I stiffen and jerk my arms away, *what the fuck?*

"Morning, Red. I didn't take you for a cuddler." Callum rumbles next to me.

I slide my eyes up from his arm to find him already watching me. "I'm sorry, I didn't mean to."

He shrugs. "Mmm. I didn't mind it." I slide out of my bed and make my way into my bathroom. I lean over the sink and splash cool water on my overheated face. No cuddling with the hot biker that's only supposed to be a one time fling. Or four times. Five? Six? I've honestly lost count. "I'll start breakfast, come join me when you're ready!" He calls as I hear my bedroom door open.

After taking my time washing my face and brushing my hair and teeth, I walk into the kitchen and boost myself up onto the kitchen counter to watch Callum make breakfast burritos; he's a much better cook by the way and he knows it. We laugh the entire time, poking fun at each other and talking about some of his upcoming projects.

We inhale our breakfasts silently, too starved after last night to make conversation, but after we've replenished ourselves I ask what I've been thinking since meeting him. "This is going to sound really cliche, but why are you single?" He laughs a deep laugh. "Shut up. I mean you run your own company, you're hot, you have great taste in interior design, and you're clean. Do you know how rare it is to find a man that cleans? What is it?" I pick up our plates and take them to the dishwasher.

Callum stretches back into the dining room chair, putting his arms behind his head. "The townhouse wasn't all me. When I moved in and the landlord gave me free rein of the place, a couple of the girls who work for the club came over and told me they were decorating with or without me; apparently my room at the clubhouse looked like a watered down version of a frat boy's room and they weren't going to let me ruin this place." He laughs. "They picked everything out, but I vetoed some things and showed them pictures of things I liked." He picks up his glass and finishes his orange juice, grabbing both of our glasses, and joins me at the dishwasher. He turns around and leans against the counter, crossing his arms. "As far as a relationship, I haven't had one since after high school, about seven years ago. I dated one girl all through high school and then she came to college up here and I stayed home and started my first carpentry job. I'd make the thirty-minute drive from Oak Creek to come see her every couple of days and we'd spend the weekends together. She started wanting to spend the weekends with her friends, which was fine 'cause I started prospecting for the club and I was getting busier. I decided to propose." He sighs and shakes his head. "So I planned everything out, I came up to surprise her. Her roommate let me into their dorm while she was supposed to be at the gym. She didn't even see me sitting on her bed at first, she was too busy making out with the guy." Callum rubs his index finger across his bottom lip. "I didn't even say anything, I just walked out. She tried to call me for weeks after, I guess her roommate told her I was waiting for her with the fucking ring, but I never talked to her again." He pushes himself off of the counter, picking up the skillet and utensils and setting them in the dishwasher. "Well shit, that killed the fucking mood." He laughs, but it's not his gleeful laugh, it's laced with sadness. This is the first time I've ever seen Callum anything but happy and joking since he played the piano for me in Seattle.

"My ex cheated on me too," I say quietly, adopting the same stance he'd held a moment earlier. Hoping to maybe distract him from his memories.

"Wanna talk about it?" He leans against the counter in front of me, crossing his arms. I really don't want to talk about Noah, but how can I not when Callum bared his heart to me like he just did? I take a deep breath and get mentally ready to spill that still healing part of me when I'm interrupted by Callum's phone dinging in his jeans pocket. He pulls it out and starts tapping away on the screen. Saved by the freaking bell, or the text. Callum grimaces and slips his phone back into his pocket. "I need you to go to a party with me tonight, Red."

I frown and cock my head to the side. "Why?"

He uncrosses his arms and places them on the counter behind him. "The prospects are doing something for the club and I have to be at this party tonight."

I laugh. "Well I guess I don't have much of a choice then, do I? What do I wear?"

Callum smiles a genuine smile finally. "It's real casual."

16

———

CALLUM

Reese walks out of her room wearing an orange short sleeve tee that she tied in a knot just under her big tits and some high-waisted jeans, there's holes in the jeans and she's got a little bit of toned stomach showing. She looks hot as hell. I mean this girl can rock a tee shirt, and when she asks if her 'mules' will be okay for the bike I just stare at her like she just spoke another language, because for all I know she did; she laughs and walks ahead of me towards the door. After laying in bed for the rest of the morning, Reese and I went back to my townhouse to get some clean clothes for me so we didn't have to stop on our way to the party. I took a shower and got ready in her guest bathroom, then I watched a few episodes of a Swat show while she got ready. I don't ever take girls to the clubhouse parties, one of those 'why bring sand to the beach' types of things, but also these parties are when I get to let all the way loose with my brothers, and I don't want to be worrying about some chick. Tonight's different though; for one, Reese is a friend, definitely not sand, and two, tonight's party is mostly business. When we pull up to the clubhouse, the party is in full swing, music bleeds from the building, and I back my bike up into the line with the

79

others, Reese watching me the entire time with her arms crossed under her perky tits, turning her head to look in every direction. I turn off the bike and walk over to her, placing my hands on her arms and leaning in to speak over the booming music leaking from the clubhouse. "Relax, you're with me tonight, no one will bother you." She looks into my eyes and nods. I grab her hand and walk in front of her into the clubhouse, pulling her along with me. The clubhouse smells like it always does during a party: a shit ton of perfume, smoke, and leather. Classy, I know. People part and stare at us as we pass; both wanting to stay out of my way, and shocked to see me with a girl. I lead us straight to the bar, spinning a barstool around for Reese.

Peyton smiles at me from the other side of the bar, with the dark purple lipstick she always wears and the small black crop top barely holding in her tits. "What'll it be, handsome?"

I lean my forearms against the bar next to Reese. "Just water for now, I'm driving tonight."

Peyton looks at Reese, smiling like a damn fool. I told you I never bring chicks here. "And for you sweetie?"

Reese looks behind Peyton's bright pink head to scan the liquor shelves and restaurant-grade coolers lining the wall. "A vodka-cran, please." Peyton walks away to grab our drinks for us and Reese takes the moment to scan the clubhouse, in her defense it is an odd place if you've never been in one. The place is packed with our guys, our guests of honor, some friends, and of course strippers and cut sluts in all stages of undress.

This room is the main room of the building; there are tables and chairs spread around the room, with a pool table to our left; behind the bar leads to a professional kitchen. Down the hallway at the back of the building are two rooms, one being the chapel, where church is held, and the other is the little strip club we have here; it's got a couple of poles and lots of mirrors, we call it Purgatory. Upstairs are several bedrooms that prospects live in with attached bathrooms. The rooms are available to patched members as well, but we usually have a place of our own or share with another member.

Peyton sets our drinks in front of us and moves on to get drinks for others stepping up to the bar. Reese pegs me with a knowing look, one eyebrow raised. "What?" I ask, taking a drink of my water.

Reese talks over the rim of her cup, a smile in her voice. "You've slept with her haven't you?"

I choke on my water, not expecting her to be so direct. "No." I laugh when I recover. "What gave you that idea?"

She can barely get her words out, she's laughing too hard at my choking fit. "You guys were flirting."

I shake my head, setting the water bottle down. "I never claimed to be a choir boy, but I was just being nice. Peyton flirts with everyone, if you'd give her a chance she'd flirt with you too."

Reese barks a laugh and takes a sip of her drink. "She makes good drinks." She shrugs.

Now I'm laughing. "And that's why I'm nice to her."

Finn saunters over and stands on the other side of Reese, he bends over and leans against the bar on his forearms, looking at Reese over his shoulder. "We really need to work out a schedule for our man here." He points his index finger at me with his free hand. Reese cackles and leans back in her chair, looking between me and Finn.

I cup Finn's shoulder behind Reese and shake him a little. "Oh, Finny, are you jealous?"

"Just miss ya is all." He leans behind Reese's chair and slaps my ass. Shaking my head, I change the subject.

"Where's Huntley?" I try to look behind his hulking frame but it's useless, the fucker is huge.

He holds up a finger to get Peyton's attention. "Finishing up a paper for one of her classes, she said she'd swing by after." He gives Peyton his drink order, then he leans down so he's face to face with Reese. "How are you doing? Heard anymore from that creepy fucker?" His voice is gruff, but you can see the sincerity in his eyes. That's why he's my best friend, his heart is just as big as he is, he just only shows it to people who mean something to him.

Reese's spin stiffens. "No, I haven't gotten any other notes and your guys haven't reported seeing anything unusual." She takes another sip of her drink.

Finn hums and nods his head, his brain clearly at work. "Well, I don't trust it." He looks up at me and meets my eyes. "Keep an eye on your girl, Cale. I don't think this guy is done yet." Finn checks the time on his phone and then motions with his head toward the chapel. "It's time we head in there man, don't wanna keep Ronan waiting."

I nod my head and motion for Peyton. "Can you take a break and hang with Reese?" Peyton nods and hops onto the bar, swinging her bare legs over to drop into the seat I was standing next to, Reese laughs with her brows knit together, she'll get used to Peyton's antics soon.

Finn picks up his drink from the bar top and we make our way to the back of the clubhouse and to the chapel. "You into the bombshell, or is it just protection?" Finn's question is directed towards me, but he's looking behind us at Reese. I can't help but look back as well, and when I see Reese over the crowd, our eyes meet and we stay like that for what feels like an eternity until she looks down at her drink and pushes her straight hair behind her ear. "Guess that answers my question." Finn laughs, now looking directly at me, rubbing his chin and smirking.

"No. I'm not into Reese, we're just friends and I want her safe. I don't like the idea of some asshole getting off on scaring her." I push past him and towards the chapel doors.

"Uh huh." Finn follows me inside, sounding less than convinced.

"Yeah okay, we sleep together, but honestly she's just really fun to hang out with. We're just friends, you know I don't do anything more," I say, taking my usual seat at the table.

Finn sits down next to me, in his usual spot, and pulls out a joint. Rolling it between his fingers, he looks at it thoughtfully. "You can let more people in, Cale. Not every woman is gonna do what Kaity did."

"You're right because I'm not gonna let them." I take the joint from him and light it with a lighter that's sitting on the table. I take a hit and let it seep into my lungs, I'm not gonna talk about my cheating ex and all the damage she caused while being sober if I don't have to. Not with Finn, he can see through any lie I try to throw at him; it's why he won't let it go with Reese. He knows damn well she's quickly becoming anything but "just a friend", but like I said, I don't do relationships. Not anymore.

This meeting with the O'Connell crime family is to broker a new deal. There's been word of a war brewing between the O'Connells and the Segretos, which explains why Sebastian wanted to meet with us, and they both need ammo. Our less-than-legal ammo distribution is the club's main income source, and it's highly sought after here on the West Coast. We don't deal guns; we choose not to have those wars hanging over our heads, but if the fight has already started and they're gonna need bullets anyway might as well make our buck off of it. We like to flirt with the line between moral and morally corrupt.

Killian and Conor O'Connell and a few beefy Irishmen stroll into the chapel. Killian and Conor take a seat at the opposite end of the table from Ronan, their muscled cousins standing like a wall behind them. Killian and Conor took the reins of their family at a young age, with Killian being our age and Conor being a few years younger, and although they're cousins they look more like brothers. Both with floppy brown hair and strong jawlines. The only difference between the two is their eyes; Killian has vibrant green eyes while Conor's are light blue. They're both closer to my build, still tall but shorter than say Finn and Sebastian, and just as muscled as me.

Without wasting any time, Ronan gets straight into business. "Look, I'll be straight with you, Killian. Sebastian Segreto made us an offer, but because of our friendship I wanted to offer you a chance to outbid him." Ronan says, leaning back in his chair, looking like a goddamn cucumber he's so chill. The meeting shouldn't turn violent, the O'Connells are long time buyers and friends of ours, but there aren't many sellers with as much stock as us, and desperation can make a man do some stupid shit.

Conor, Killian's second, curses when hearing Sebastian's name. "Of course the Italian prick would try to get his bullets through our fucking connection, it's just like that slimy fuck!"

Killian raises his hand to calm Conor. "How much?" He looks at Ronan.

"Double." Ronan crosses his arms, deliberately placing his hand over the butt of his gun holstered under his arm.

Killian drags a hand down his face. "We'll triple it." Conor shakes his head in frustration, his cool stare glaring at his cousin, but Killian shoots him a stern look that causes Conor to look away. Holy shit, that's a fuck ton of money. We're gonna be goddamn rich after this shit starts up, well more than we already are. Between our own businesses and our underground ammo distribution, the biker lifestyle has been quite lucrative. It's been a while since a good Italian mafia/Irish mob war went down, and now I can't fucking wait.

Ronan leans forward, resting his forearms on the table. He's smiling and his friendly demeanor is back now that business is taken care of. "Great, I'll pass my regards to Sebastian." He stands and walks to the middle of the table, right behind Saint and Nathan, Killian joins him and they shake hands. No true business deal is sealed without a proper handshake, because that's exactly what this is, business. "Enjoy the party, brother, we threw it for you," Ronan smirks, the smug bastard.

"As ya fucking should have, asshole. Seeing as I'm paying for it with the amount of money ya just scammed me out of." His Irish accent peeking through now that he's relaxed and laughing. Ronan just shrugs and opens the door, clearly ending the meeting.

17

REESE

THE MOMENT CALLUM WALKS AWAY I FEEL A WEIGHT ON MY CHEST. I feel so stupid admitting this, but it's easier to breathe when he's around. I can't help but watch him walk away, the crowd is different here, they don't part when he walks by, scared of who he is and the patch on his back. They still move away from him but here he has the respect of everyone in the room. He's different here too, his shoulders are more relaxed and he isn't constantly scanning the room; he's at peace here with his club brothers.

"So you're Callum's girlfriend?" Peyton pops a cherry into her mouth and smiles.

I tuck my hair behind my ear, turning my attention from Callum to my drink. "No, we're just friends; he's helping with a problem of mine."

"Callum doesn't bring girls here." She slides her gaze up and down a passing guy, thoroughly undressing him with her eyes. When she catches my eyes again she shrugs and smirks, grabbing another cherry from the small bowl in front of her.

I ignore her comment, Callum only brought me here

because nobody else was available to babysit me. "So you're a bartender here?"

She turns her chair so she's facing the rest of the club and leans her arms behind her onto the bar, pushing her small chest out. "I bartend at The Second Circle, but when the club has parties, some of the bartenders and strippers get our shifts switched to here."

I choke on the sip I just took. "Strippers?" I manage to cough out.

Peyton cackles so loud the guys playing pool look over. "Yeah, the doors the guys just walked into," she points across the clubhouse to two sets of double doors, "the ones next to it are used as a club. The best strippers always work the club parties." My eyes are bugging out of my head, but Peyton hasn't noticed, she just keeps talking. "It's called Purgatory. Since the club owns the strip club, The Second Circle, most of the strippers are sweet butts just trying to get some Outlaw dick, but you know, whatever floats their fake tits."

Now I'm giggling, partly out of being uncomfortable and partly because this girl is just hilarious! "Did you just call them 'sweet butts'?"

"Yeah, sweet butts, cut sluts, it's like a groupie but for bikers. Nothing like you, you're Old Lady material." I roll my eyes and take another drink, I'm not going to spend my night trying to convince her Callum and I are just friends; even if he does make my body do irrational things. Mason slides onto the barstool on my other side, combing his brown hair out of his eyes. Peyton eyes him, laughing. "Speaking of sweet butts, how's Jessica, Mase?"

Mason chuckles, turning in his seat to face us. "Same as ever. Sucks like a vacuum and fucks like a rabbit."

I gag and Peyton cackles again. "I did not need to know that." Mason shrugs off my comment. "Is it serious with Jessica?"

Another scantily dressed girl brings Mason a beer and he takes a drink. "Well, she walked directly from my room into Leo's so no I'd say it's not serious."

"Sounds like you didn't please her well enough." Peyton pops another cherry into her mouth.

Mason takes another drink while scanning the room. "I didn't hear her complaining when her legs were spasming around my head."

As I start to throw up in my mouth, Peyton inclines her head toward the stairs she said led up to the bedrooms. "I guess she finally had enough." A short blonde with huge, presumably fake, boobs walks into the party tucked under the arm of one of the younger prospects, Leo.

I turn my gaze to Mason with a bored expression. "She looks nice."

Mason chuckles again, flashing his goofy smile that's become a comfort over the past few weeks. "What can I say? I like blondes."

I roll my eyes because of course he likes the pretty blonde with the huge boobs. "I thought you wanted to find something serious?"

Mason sighs, turning to face me. "I do, I'm just really busy with the club and I haven't found anyone worth making time for."

"You'll meet her when you least expect it." I smile at him, already excited for his future. Mason is so different from the rest of the guys in the club, they're all serious and slightly cold, but Mase is bright and warm. He's always smiling and making jokes. I know he would bring that same kind of playful energy into his relationship; she's going to be a lucky girl, whoever she ends up being.

Mason playfully rolls his eyes. "I didn't know when I asked

for a little sister I'd get all of this sappy girl talk." I push Mason's shoulder while we both laugh.

Out of the corner of my eye, I see the doors open to the room that Callum had gone through a little while ago. A couple of guys shuffle out and then I see Callum and Finn walk through, his eyes scan the room until they meet mine, his gaze is so intense and my stomach erupts in butterflies. This drink must be stronger than I thought and it's just making me queasy and hot. That's why my heartbeat is quickening as he gets closer and I'm starting to get warm. *Just keep telling yourself that, Reese.* Finn looks up from his phone and looks my way as well, he raises his giant arm and starts waving it dramatically at me, a huge grin on his face. Next to him, Callum's shoulders start shaking with laughter and he shakes his head. I subtly wave back to Finn, not able to hold back my laughter.

"Dumbass," Mason whispers. I elbow him in the side and he laughs, picking up his beer bottle.

That distraction was enough to cool me down a little, but the butterflies are still going strong. I need a minute to get a hold of myself, I turn to Peyton. "Is there a bathroom I can use?" She looks over to the door on the other side of the pool table and grimaces.

Peyton tilts her head towards the boys still walking toward us. "Ask Callum to take you to a bathroom upstairs, they don't get used during parties and I wouldn't let you use this one, someone's probably already came or puked in there." *Well, that's a hard no.*

I laugh, although it was more of a nervous laugh than a real one because *ew*, and slide off of the barstool and walk towards Callum. When I'm a few steps away from him I feel a sharp sting on my butt and a loud smack, I suck in a surprised breath, but before I can turn around to see who just slapped my ass, a huge blur passes by me. It all happens so quickly I can't get my bearings, I'm quickly spun around and I feel strong hands grasp my arms and a very solid presence behind me. Before my eyes focus, I hear the thundering sound of flesh hitting flesh. When I realize what's going on Finn is behind me holding my arms, and Callum is straddling a guy on the floor. His hand is around his throat and he's bleeding profusely from his nose, and his eye is already starting to swell. Mason is standing above Callum looking ready to jump in if needed and there's a wide circle around us with Callum and the guy on the floor in the middle of it.

The guy on the ground holds up his hands in surrender. "I didn't know she belonged to ya, I thought she was one of ours!" His Irish accent wheezing and strained under Callum's hand.

"You okay, Red?" Callum squeezes harder, his eyes boring into the man's skull.

"Yes. Come here." My voice is breathy and just as lustful as I feel. What is wrong with me, isn't violence a red flag? This just seems to be turning me on.

"If I see you around here again I'll break your fucking arms." He pushes away from the guy and stands, wiping his jeans off. He turns and walks to where I stand, Finn dropping his hands from my arms. Callum cradles my face in his hands, looking deep into my eyes. "I'm here babe." It's a whisper, meant only for me, and I can tell he means a lot more than he's just here physically. I know I can trust Callum, not just with my safety but maybe my heart as well. He grabs my hand and cocks his head to the door. "Let's get out of here."

18

CALLUM

We pull out of the clubhouse gates and start towards a little surprise I have in mind. If Reese ever thought the security at her apartment was intense, her mind would be fucking blown at the shit we have at the clubhouse. Giant privacy gates with security code access and electric volts running through them, motion detecting alarms, security cameras over every inch of the property, and alarms on every door and window; this place is a goddamn fortress.

"You hungry, Red?" I yell over the sexy rumble of my bike when we stop at a red light.

"Starving." She leans in close to my ear, pushing her tits into my back and making me rethink the food plan altogether.

We make our way to the closed bar and grill that is Big Dawg's, it's Finn's dad's place, but he lets Finn and I have keys so we can stop in whenever we want, or to open and lock up the place for him if he can't. Finn's dad became like my second father whenever Finn and I started prospecting for the club and became friends. The lights are all off and the parking lot is empty, as I expected. I pull up right by the door and stop the bike, turning the engine off and waiting for Reese to hop off.

Reese puts her hands on my shoulders and presses into my back, tempting me again. "I think this place is closed, Cale."

I hold up my keys and dangle them in front of us. "Not for us." Laughing, Reese steps off of the bike and waits for me.

Once we're inside with the security alarm turned off and the door locked behind us, I walk through the small bar and turn on only the bar lights. I don't want all of the lights on and people to think the place is open again. I walk to the back storage room to get all of the ingredients and leave Reese to look around the place. There isn't a whole lot to look at, but one long wall is filled with pictures, basically just a fucking shrine to Finn and his mom. Randy, Finn's dad, has pictures of everything Finn has ever participated in or accomplished, with Finn's mom always at his side, both always smiling like it was the best day of their life. Finn's high school graduation was the last picture of the two of them together, then I came along; now Randy captures every club moment with the two of us.

I walk back into the bar with my arms full of food and find Reese exactly where I thought she'd be, making her way down the wall. "Is this Finn as a kid? Is this the both of you when you got patched?" She walks to sit at the bar in front of the grill.

"Yeah, Finn's dad owns this place. He says he takes pictures of everything he's proud of so he can show off his family to the customers of the bar." I start to reheat the pulled pork on the grill and drop the fries into the fryer.

Reese steps up to sit on a barstool in front of the grill, resting her chin on her hands as she watches me. "Need any help?"

I laugh and start to warm the barbecue sauce and melt some cheese in pots. "Absolutely not. That would be an insult to *the* Randy Evans' famous barbecue."

Reese laughs and tosses a cardboard coaster at my back. "So you and Finn are related?"

I stir my sauces and mix around the pork. "No, even though Randy calls me his son and drunkenly said he was leaving this place to me and Finn when he dies. I met Finn when we started prospecting for the club together; we hit it off really quickly and he started bringing me around here. Randy taught me how to cook at this grill." I motion to the grill with the spatula.

I pull the fries out and dump them into two to-go containers, topping them with the pork, barbecue sauce, and cheese.

Placing the container in front of Reese, she takes a bite and then looks at me with wide eyes. "This is delicious!"

I laugh, taking a bite of my own. "Did you doubt me, Red?"

She shakes her head, laughing. "No, it just doesn't look that appetizing."

Between bites, I answer her, because this is fucking delicious. "Finn and I came up with it one night after drinking. Showed it to Randy the next day and he added it to the menu." I shake my head. "Named it 'Fallum Fries'."

Reese's laugh could damn near be heard in fucking Antarctica. "He shipped you guys together?"

I groan into my fries, "Don't say it like that." Reese keeps laughing, tears forming in her eyes, smug little thing. We eat the rest in comfortable silence, and when we're both finished I pick up the plastic container. "If you're done mocking me and the great food I slaved over for you, do you want to play some pool or head home?" I jokingly toss at her while I throw our containers into the trash at the end of the bar.

"Pool, I don't want this night to end yet." She makes her way over to the pool table at the back of the bar, swinging her hips way too fucking perfectly.

I follow behind her, rubbing my hand down my face, no girl has kept my attention for this long and it's fucking with my head. I switch on the light above the table and set the balls while

Reese starts a playlist on the modern jukebox. A soft bass and heavily autotuned voice fill the bar. "I like this." I hand her a stick so she can break.

"It's 'Into It' by Chase Atlantic. I thought it fit the vibe." She leans over the table, lines up her stick with the cue ball, and smacks the ball into the middle of the triangle, two make it in; it was a decent shot. Reese is still bent over the table and smiles up at me, and goddamn I've never seen a girl look like the most beautiful angel dropped from heaven and the most seductive vixen all at the same time. My stomach does a flip and I scratch the back of my neck and focus on the table instead of what the fuck my heart just did in my chest. "I guess I'm stripes." She smiles and walks around the table to find another shot. Lining up another shot, this one she misses. She chuckles. "I"m not that good, but I enjoy playing. I'm also enjoying the company this time around a lot more." She stares down at the table. "I used to go to a pool hall with my ex a lot, but that usually just ended with us arguing because he was flirting with the waitress or checking out other girls in front of me." Reese tries to smile, but I can tell it still hurts her, that type of shit hits your ego hard and it's not easy to let go of.

My blood boils at the pain and insecurity she must have felt, probably still feels. I brush past her, laying a hand on her waist as I pass because I just can't fucking resist touching her. I line up my shot, sinking it because I'm a damn pool shark. "Your ex was a fucking idiot." I sink another shot. Reese leans against the table, resting her hip right in my line. Of course the next shot I miss because I'm too busy watching the curve of her hip.

Reese laughs and looks for a shot.

I figure throwing questions back at her is a good distraction. "What about your family?"

Reese finds a shot and starts to line it up. "We're pretty close.

I'm an only child and my mom stayed home most of the time, so she and I are best friends."

I rub chalk on my stick, watching her. "Have you told them about your stalker?"

She's bent over the table, about to take her shot, and she quickly glances up at me and then back down to her cue. "No, it would scare them too much and one of them would come down here. I don't want to bring either of them into this."

She misses again by the way, and the mood needs to be lifted after that last question. "You're not very good, babe." This gets me a shocked face. "I'll let you have a free shot to catch up." Now she's glaring at me, but her glare just makes me laugh because she still looks too sweet to be angry. Reese swishes over, swinging her hips and keeping eye contact the whole time, she steps in between me and the table and bends over the table just inches in front of my dick. The cue ball isn't even on this side of the table so I know she's doing this deliberately. I decide to test how far she's willing to take her taunt. I take a step forward, our bodies molding together and my cock hardening. I place one hand beside her on the table and I glide the other up the side of her leg and then set it on the table too, caging her in. I lean forward to whisper in her ear, "Are you trying to distract me, Red?" She shudders and goosebumps rise on her arms. Smirking, I move above her and lick up the column of her neck to her ear.

Reese pushes her ass farther back into my dick and moves her hips side to side. "Is it working?" Her voice is breathy, and there goes any restraint I might have had.

I stand up and turn her around all in one movement. Our mouths crash together and we kiss like we're fucking starving for each other because honestly, that's how it feels right now. She finally parts her lips for me and my tongue dives in, claiming her. I unbutton her jeans and start to slide them down her sexy legs. She gasps and pulls away, looking around the bar. "There aren't any cameras," I assure her and she looks back at me and nods, giving me consent to continue. I move my mouth to her neck, biting and sucking while my hand slides under her shirt and into her bra. I roll her nipple between my fingers and she throws her head back moaning.

Her head comes back to look at me, her eyelids half closed. "We're friends right?"

I bring my fingers to my mouth and suck on them. "Of course, Red." I put my wet fingers back into her bra and roll her nipples again.

Another moan leaves her mouth before she whispers, "And this is just sex?"

I pause as I'm leaning into her neck. Of course this is just sex, I've been trying to convince everyone of that all night. *Then why does hearing her say that make my stomach turn into knots?* Probably because the thought of her being 'friendly' like this with anyone else makes me fucking homicidal, but I can't do relationships, I can't go there again. "Yeah, babe, just sex." *It has to be.*

She pulls my face into hers and I lift her to sit on the pool table, pulling her jeans the rest of the way off. She lays down and I kiss up the inside of her thighs until I get to her sweet hot center. I push her lacy panties to the side and start worshiping her pussy. My tongue rubs circles over her clit and I slip two fingers inside of her to stroke her perfect spot. Her fists fly into my hair to control my movements, she's moaning and letting out breathy curses and before I know it, she's grinding into my face and pushing herself into my fingers. I add another finger and replace my tongue with my other hand to pinch her clit. She fucking bursts, her pussy squeezing my fingers and her thighs shaking. I slow my movements to let her ride it out, her eyes roll back into her head and she lets out a long groan. I could spend fucking forever watching her lose control like that because of me, it's the most beautiful fucking sight. When she comes back down, I start to lean back down to start that all over again because once was not enough for me, but she sits up and moves off of the table. I'm confused as hell because I know I just rocked her world, but she smirks and pushes me back a step, then she sinks to her knees to undo my belt and jeans, and pull them down to free my fully fucking ready cock. She pushes me as far into her throat as she can and uses her hand for the rest. "Yeah, babe. Just like that," I rasp, my voice dark with need. I fist my hand into her hair to control her pace and her manicured nails dig into my ass, adding a burning sting to the pure fucking ecstasy that is her mouth. She works me over, hollowing out her cheeks and twisting her hand up on the upstroke. She moves her hand down to roll my balls while she pushes me deep into her throat and my balls start to tighten with the fucking glorious sensation of my impending release. I warn her that I'm about to come, because I'm a fucking gentleman. She pushes me further into her throat, choking on my cock but swallowing despite the tears forming in her eyes. I explode and Reese eagerly swallows every drop, her throat eagerly milking out every last drop. "You're fucking addictive." I run my fingers through her hair. When I've emptied all I had into her throat, she licks up the bottom of my shaft and swirls her tongue around the tip, making me fucking shiver and goosebumps rise on my thighs. I pull her up to her feet so I can kiss her and show her just how much I appreciate her. When I look into her light green eyes, there's something more there, more than the jokes and the sex, she looks vulnerable and like she's letting me in. Overcome with the feeling of coming harder than I ever have in my life, and the emotion in her eyes, I say the one thing that's been stuck in my mind since I first saw her at Mickey's. "I'm never going to let you down, Reese." I promise her. Her eyes flash to mine, and we stay locked like that for a few minutes. Just staring into each other's eyes. I hope she sees the truth in mine. I finally look away, my orgasmic haze subsiding and I remember the small amount of anger I was holding onto the entire game. An idea comes to me, and I think it's one of the best ones I've had in a while. This will be fun, I just have to get Red to agree to it.

19

REESE

Callum leads us outside and I watch him lock up the little bar. "I have one more stop for us if you're not too tired?" Cale says, handing me the helmet.

"Okay. Where?" I ask, wondering what more we could possibly get into tonight.

His easy smile turns mischievous and his eyes sparkle under the streetlamp. "Can you find out where your ex is right now?"

"What?" I balk. My ex? Why?

"Can you?" He ignores my question.

I shake my head, confused as to where he's going with this. "Yeah, but—"

Callum nods and licks his bottom lip. My attention immediately falls to his lips and I forget what I was saying. "Great. Figure out where he is, I have to make a call."

Callum leans against his bike to make his call and I sit down at a nearby wooden picnic table and pull out my phone. I click on Instagram and look up Noah. It's a Saturday night, which is when he usually did something with his friends and he more often than not documented it on his story. Pulling up his profile I roll my eyes at the initials in his bio. If he had a penny for every time he put a girl's initials in his bio he would never have to work another day in his life. But sure enough, the multicolored ring spins around his profile picture. I click on it and flick through a multi-slide story of him drinking with his friends at a bar. From the logo on the cups and the small glimpses at the background in the story, I can tell exactly where he is.

I quietly approach Callum, his eyes following me the whole way, and show him the slide from Noah's story with a clear shot of the logo on the cup, which was taken about five minutes ago. His grin turns victorious. "He's at McCann's," He says into the phone. "Meet us in the District parking lot." Then he hangs up and moves to straddle his bike.

———

WE PULL into the parking lot and stop at the entrance. "What does he drive?" Callum yells over the sound of the bike.

I lean forward so I can talk into his ear instead of yelling. "A white Toyota Camry."

He turns his head to look at me, his eyes squinting, but without saying anything he shakes his head and turns back around so we can cruise through the lot looking for Noah's car. There are several street lamps around the lot so when I see it a few cars down in the corner of the lot, I point to it. We park in front of it and step off, pulling our helmets off.

Callum eyes the compact car with disdain. "You know, you can tell a lot about a man by what he drives."

"Are you saying I was supposed to know he was a cheating asshole by his choice in transportation?" I ask with a laugh in my voice.

"I mean does this scream trustworthy to you?" He gestures to the car with a very serious face, not breaking at all.

I shake my head, willing to play along. "Okay, so what do your vehicles say about you then?"

Callum smirks. "Well the Raptor says I'm confident, clean, maybe even accomplished. The bike says, trustworthy, fun, and responsible." He looks back at the Camry. "A Camry isn't manly."

I cross my arms over my stomach, genuinely interested in his argument now. "And how did you get these qualities from a car?

Callum sits, full on sits, on Noah's hood. No regard for the paint or respect for someone else's property. "As I'm sure you've noticed, A Raptor is loud and big and when you drive by people notice, that's not for an insecure person. It says I'm a clean and professional person because of how well I take care of it but also because of the architecture of the car, beautiful lines, and flares. It's a beauty of a truck, and I don't know if you've checked the prices on those things, but they are not cheap so you have to have some cash to afford one."

He tries to continue but I can't help but interrupt him and burst his bubble. "One could say you are overcompensating with your big loud truck, and that you're financially irresponsible for purchasing such an expensive vehicle."

His smirk drops, which makes mine only grow. He stands and strides towards me, his eyes drawing me in and not letting me look away. He stops inches from me, my nose almost brushing his chest. Callum gently takes my hand and runs it down his hard pecs and abs, and down over his jeans. He palms his growing erection, my hand in between his and his jeans. "Am I overcompensating, Red?" He cocks his head and raises an eyebrow.

I clear my throat, trying to give myself a chance to remember what words are and clear the fog in my head. I'm spared from having to answer when a pickup pulls up behind us and Callum smiles at whoever is there. I pull my hand out of his while he's distracted. I turn around to face the pickup and see Ronan, Saint, and Jack getting out of the cab and walking around to the bed of the truck. They lower the tailgate and sit down, Ronan smiling from ear to ear, Saint swaying a lot, and Jack looking like he always does, lost.

"Did you bring what I asked for?" Callum asks, standing in front of the guys.

"Sure did!" Ronan says, dragging a sledgehammer from behind him and sliding it into Cale's hands and then slinging his arm over Saint's shoulders. Jack grabs a tire iron from behind him and hands that to Callum too. "Prospect, put on some mood music and grab my bottle of Crown."

Jack hops off of the tailgate and disappears around the side of the pickup. Callum turns towards me, his grin splitting his face and I stare at him questioningly.

"What are we doing?" I ask slowly.

"I think you can put two and two together, Red. Heavy tools, a cheating ex's car." He laughs and holds the tools out to me. "Which one you want?"

I take the tire iron hesitantly as Machine Gun Kelly's "The Break Up" starts playing out of the pickup speakers. Not loud enough to draw attention, just enough for us to hear it. "This is insane." I stare at the tire iron in my hand. "We can't do this."

"Why not?" Callum asks, already beside Noah's Camry.

My brows pull together. "Um, it's illegal."

Cale shakes his head. "You won't get in any trouble. I promise." He crosses over to me and angles my face to his with his hand on my chin. "Do you trust me?"

I hesitate. Yes, no. "Kind of." I finally answer.

Callum chuckles. "Close enough." He switches the tire iron out for the sledgehammer and moves to stand behind me, wrapping around me and placing his hands on my arms. He raises our arms and smashes the hammer down onto the windshield.

The screen smashes and Ronan's laughter can be heard over the car alarm. I glance back to see Ronan and Saint passing the bottle between them with lazy, drunk smiles. "Hurry. Smash whatever you want!" Callum yells to be heard and hands me the tire iron again.

The music and laughter set me off, the adrenaline pumping and I no longer care about the law. Callum and I set to work smashing all of the windows and lights, and putting dents into several places on the car. The smashing and smacking, remembering the messages and pictures I found on Noah's phone, spurs me on and every hit gets harder and harder. I finally stop when the one place I was hitting over and over is too dented to do anything more. Callum is standing off to the side and Ronan, Saint, and Jack are still on the tailgate. They all watch me.

"That's the fucking spirit, Princess!" Ronan hands the bottle to Saint and hops off of the truck. Saint downs the rest of the liquor in one long gulp. "But one last thing." He pulls a butterfly knife out of his back pocket and flicks it open.

"Hey!" A man yells as he runs over to us. I drop the tire iron, my eyes going wide, It's practically daylight out here with how many streetlights are around the parking lot, there's no way he doesn't know what we were doing. Jack slides off of the tailgate and steps into the path and the man abruptly stops. "Oh shit. Sorry, man," He stutters out and turns to walk away quickly.

Jack turns to face us. "We'd probably better wrap this up, the woman he was with was on the phone." Just as he's finishing his sentence, police sirens sound in the distance.

"Not the best place to trash someone's car, Cale," Ronan says as he bends down to stab a hole into both tires on our side and walk around to the other side.

"You getting too old for a little chase?" Callum counters, ever the presence of calm, despite the sirens getting closer.

Ronan barks a deep laugh. "Yeah right, just worried about

the Prospect's ability to get us away." He stabs one tire on the passenger side and then motions to Jack. "Get us back to the clubhouse without getting us pulled over alright?"

Callum grabs my hand and pulls me towards his bike, tossing the tools back into the bed of the pickup before Ronan, Saint, and Jack speed away. We quickly fasten our helmets, the sirens only a few blocks away now. "Hold on tight, Red," Callum says with an unmistakable grin in his voice.

20

REESE

I'm woken up by Callum lightly brushing my hair out of my face, with my eyes still closed I start to place my hand over his. We made it back to my apartment last night without being stopped and I immediately crashed from my adrenaline high. I vaguely remember scooting close to Callum and when I felt his heavy breaths on the top of my head, I didn't jump to get away. I just enjoyed his presence and the warmth of his embrace. Before I can reach his hand, I hear the bathroom toilet flush, and the featherlight touch on my face is immediately gone. My eyes snap open and I scan the room, my heart beating out of my chest, but I don't see anything. The bathroom door is mostly closed, only a sliver of light leaking through the small opening. The barely rising sun doesn't let a lot of light into the room, so I sit up and turn on the bedside light, there's no one here. The bathroom light turns off and Callum shuffles back into the bedroom.

"I'm sorry, babe, did I wake you?" His voice is rough with sleep, his eyes are still half closed.

Shaking my head I turn the light off and lay back on my bed. "Come back to bed." He hums his agreement and falls back into

105

the bed. He pulls me to his side and I rest my head on his big chest. Callum getting out of bed must have shifted the bed and my hair fell over my face. I fall asleep knowing I'm safe and feeling adored. I should move, I know I should, but it feels too good to be in his arms right now. I'll worry about why that feeling doesn't scare me when I wake up, right now I'm not going to let it ruin the night we had together.

THIS TIME when I'm woken up it's by the sunlight streaming right into my eyes. Groaning, I roll over and check the time on my phone, it's late morning. Callum's voice startles me in the doorway.

"Good morning, sleepyhead, I was just about to come wake you." He sits on the bed and holds out a glass of orange juice for me. I accept it and take a big drink. Callum stares at my lips as I lick the juice off of my bottom lip. "I was going to wake you with my face buried between your thighs, but I guess we'll have to take a rain check until tonight. Our presence is requested for a day of drinking with Finn and his girl."

My cheeks flame red at the thought, I've never had someone be so blunt with their attraction to me, or so damn smooth. "I don't know if I could have taken that, I'm pretty sore after all of our activities last night." Callum smirks over the lid of a Starbucks coffee. "Did you go out to get that?" I smile, imagining this tattooed bad boy pulling through a Starbucks drive-thru and ordering a Pumpkin Spice Latte and the cute barista almost fainting when he pulls up to the window.

He shakes his head, swallowing his drink. "I had Mason bring it. You don't have a coffee machine." He smiles at me.

"I don't like coffee," I say sweetly. Callum looks at me with his eyebrows pulled tightly together, but before he can say anything about my dislike of coffee, I remember the rest of his previous statement that was clouded in my sex hazed brain. "Why are we going day drinking with Finn?"

Callum lets his argument go and shrugs. "He said he wants you to meet Huntley. I'm sure he just wants to fulfill some girly teenage dream of going on a double date." Callum takes another drink and leans against my headboard, stretching his long legs out in front of him. "We're meeting them in a few hours, but I wanted to take you somewhere first." I stare at him wide-eyed and scramble to get out of bed quickly to get a shower in before we have to leave. Callum smacks my butt as I hurry past him to the bathroom. "Hurry that sexy ass up, babe."

A while later, I'm ready with my makeup done, hair pulled into a ponytail, and dressed in white jean shorts, a thin tan belt, and a jean-looking-button-up. I tucked part of it into my shorts and it's hanging off of one shoulder. I grab a small shoulder bag to slip my phone and wallet in and slip on some nude sandals. Callum is still sitting on the edge of my bed, but now he's showered and dressed in jeans, a charcoal tee shirt, leather cut, and boots. When I walk out of the bathroom he looks up from his phone and shakes his head while smiling. "What?" I lean back into the bathroom and check my reflection.

He stands up from the bed and strides over to me. "You look damn good, Red." He reaches out for my hand. "Let's go." I place my hand in his and he guides me in front of him to walk out of the bedroom.

It turns out Callum's surprise stop was a shooting range. I let him take my hand and lead me into the storefront because I'm truthfully scared. I've never shot a gun before, never even held one. I've never felt the inclination, but I guess with everything going on it wouldn't be a bad idea to have an understanding of how to handle one. When I tell him of my weapons skills, or lack thereof, he shakes his head and asks for a few handguns. I miss the names because I tuned into "Moonlight" by Chase Atlantic playing through the speakers in the ceiling of the store. The girl lounging behind the counter on her phone must be the one controlling the playlist. Callum leads me through a set of double doors into the shooting range. Several long lanes are set up with targets at the end, and a few are occupied by older gentlemen. We walk all the way across and to another door. In the room are another two lanes with an employee setting up the guns Callum asked for. "I reserved the private lanes since you've never shot before." He walks to the back of the room and starts grabbing clear eyeglasses and headphones for us. "I wanted to be able to teach you without the distractions of the other people."

"Oh, okay." I nervously walk over to the lane where three small black guns are laying on the table. "Are you qualified to be teaching me?"

Callum shrugs. "It's one of my job skills."

I turn around, with my back against the table holding the guns. "You need to know how to shoot guns to run a roofing business?" I snark at him.

"I wasn't talking about CM Roofing." He hands me the eyeglasses, putting his on as well. "I would have brought my personal ones for you to try out, but there's too many to travel with." *Too many to travel with? Are you a small army?*

I cross my arms and stare up at Callum. "I guess the rumors are true then, huh?"

Callum shakes his head and chuckles deeply. "You and those damn rumors, why are you so obsessed with them?"

"Because they're all I know about the club since everyone side-steps around it." I snap, starting to get a little irritated at his constant diversions of the topic.

He leans against the wall of the small cubicle with his arms crossed. "I can't tell you about the club babe, and I told you I won't lie to you." I turn around, frustrated with him for not sharing things with me, but also appreciating that he's not lying to me when it would be the easier option. Callum's hands come to rest on the table on either side of me, his lips grazing my ear. "The truth is far worse than the rumors," he whispers. "But I will always keep you safe." His mouth moves from my ear to kiss down my neck. I tilt my head to give him better access and feel the vibration of his deep chuckle. "You want me to bend you over right here? I gotta admit, you next to these guns is doing something to me." His chest shakes behind me and I realize he's laughing. His laughter is infectious, it always has been, and it makes me laugh along with him. "Are you scared?" His laughter dies out and his voice turns serious.

Am I scared? Of Callum? Maybe. No. Should I be scared? Probably, yeah. Am I scared of the club? Again, I know I should be. All I know is the rumors and they paint them as dangerous people. Cold, scary, and unpredictable. I know Callum is into illegal things, he'd be more open with me if he wasn't, but he hasn't ever put me in danger. The guys in the club are some of the nicest and most selfless people I've ever met. So can whatever they be doing be that bad? What makes a person a bad person? That they do illegal things? Is a criminal a bad person? Where do we draw the line? At hurting others right? But what about if they're doing it to protect people who can't protect themselves? My lines on these kinds of things used to be so clear-cut. Everything was black and white, but Cale has come to mean a lot to me, and that's where Callum and the club reside: in the gray area of life.

"No." I finally answer.

"Why?" His hand snakes up my front, stopping at the base of my neck and rubbing back and forth softly.

My mouth goes dry at the contact and I swallow to bring some moisture back. "Because I know you'll always protect me."

Callum's hand starts to move again. Running up my throat to clasp around my chin. He gently turns my face to the side and he leans over my lips, inches away. My breath catches when I look into his slate blue eyes. "Always, Red." When I think he's going to kiss me he pulls away and I can feel the air rush back into my lungs with the distance. I take a deep breath and clear the fog from my brain. "Alright, let's do this," he says from beside me again.

After giving me the rundown speech on safety and what each part of the gun is meant for we finally move on to the actual shooting. Callum positions me in front of the target, with the gun aimed and my arms locked straight, my legs parted slightly. He stands behind me and lightly holds my arms up, his big body enveloping me with his pine scent. He smells like a forest and I lose my focus for a second, his body emitting heat down the length of me.

"Whenever you're ready, Red." He snaps me back to reality and the weight of the gun sits in my hands. I pull the trigger. *Pop!* I stare wide-eyed at the target. I didn't hit anywhere near the bullseye, but I hit the target at least, more importantly, I just fired a gun. "You're a natural, Red. You didn't even flinch."

I lower the gun to look at the target, smiling. "I kind of liked it."

Callum chuckles behind me, his chest shaking against me. "That's my girl. Pop off a couple more and then you can try the other ones."

I raise the gun and fire, checking to see where I hit. Still not close, but at least I'm hitting the target. I fire again, *pop, pop, pop.* Callum laughs his intoxicating deep laugh and lets go of my arms and steps to stand beside me. He loads the next two guns and hands me one. I set the previous one down and try out the next one. After trying both of the other guns, my aim getting slightly better, I grab the first one again. Callum pulls the target in and replaces the sheet with a clean one. This time I focus more on my aiming and I get dangerously close to the bullseye. I let out an embarrassing squeal and turn to look at Callum. His grin is huge and he looks as proud as I feel. I'm no stranger to Callum, we've been hanging out for a few weeks now, but this time together feels different; I feel more of a connection to him like I actually care if he's proud of me or not.

We stare at each other, I bite my lip and his gaze lowers to my mouth before he pulls his attention away from me with a sigh. Callum pulls his phone out of his pocket and checks the screen, pulling his earphones off and placing them on the table; I follow him in doing the same. "Which one did you like, Red?"

I set the gun I was holding back into its case. "This one."

Callum nods and starts to close the case. "I thought so. You looked most confident with it." He sets his glasses on the table as well and picks up the case. "Come on, babe, we have a double date to get to."

He holds the door open for me and I walk through and back into the public lanes. The lanes are about as busy as they were when we arrived, not much, and I turn to read a poster on the wall about a women's shooting night when I slam into a person. Rushing out an apology, I look up to the stranger that I just assaulted. "Eli?"

Eli's chocolate brown eyes widen. "Reese! Wow, I haven't seen you since..." He trails off looking over my shoulder to Callum.

"Since Noah and I broke up, yeah. How are you?" I feel Callum move a little closer to me, but I ignore how badly I want to lean back into him.

Eli smiles, his smile was always the most handsome thing about him. "I'm good. You look great though. I mean Noah hasn't taken the whole thing that well but..." He shrugs.

I roll my eyes. "Yeah, I'm sure." I highly doubt my cheating ex was all that heartbroken when we broke up, yeah I'm sure he cared about me, but I know he didn't have any trouble filling his bed after I left.

Eli leans in like he's going to tell me some secret and looks into my eyes. "Really, I mean he's acting super weird and running off without telling anyone. He never wants to hang out with any of us anymore. I think he's hiding something; all of us guys are worried about him."

I nod, trying to hold my tongue. I'm sure the only thing he's hiding is an STD. I notice the earplugs in his ear and the handgun case on the table next to him. "I didn't know you liked shooting." I gesture to the small black case on the tabletop.

He flashes that charming smile again and his eyes hold a mischievous glint in them. "Oh yeah, I've always loved to hunt."

I nod again, not knowing what else to say and Callum lightly taps my waist, getting my attention. "Well hey, we have to meet up with some friends so I'll see you around okay?"

Eli looks between Callum and I, smiling. "Yeah. Definitely. See you around, Reese."

The boys do that guy nod thing and Callum places his hand on my lower back to lead me to the door that opens into the store part of the shooting range. He leads me straight to the front door and out to his bike. "That was Eli, he's best friends with my ex. They work together in the IT department for the college." I fumble with my hands, standing on the opposite side of the bike looking up at Callum as he watches me.

Callum smiles and shakes his head. "You don't owe me an explanation, babe."

I let out a sigh. He's right, I don't owe him anything, but I still didn't want him to get the wrong impression of Eli. Although he's always been charming and he is handsome, it was never like that between us and it never would be; he's Noah's best friend and I never saw him as anything other than that. "I know. I just..." I stop flustered. "Whatever. Are you stealing that?" I point to the gun case still in his hand.

Callum laughs and unlocks the box on the side of his bike. "No. I bought it for you. I told the guy working to charge my card for whichever one you picked." He puts the case into the box and closes the lid. "You don't have to carry it until you're ready and have more practice, but I want you to start getting comfortable with it."

I stand there stunned. "You didn't have to do that. " I start.

"I know, but you looked sexy as hell shooting it." Callum smirks and swings his leg over the bike.

21

REESE

A few minutes later we're cruising down the streets on Callum's bike. The wind breezing past us and the sun warming our bodies. The air is fresh and I love the feeling of the wind on my face. I feel so safe on the back of the bike with Callum's big frame breaking all of the wind in front of me. He looks like he belongs on the bike, he handles it with such confidence and power. It's strange how close we've grown in the few weeks we've known each other, sitting here with his hand resting on my knee and my hand resting on his side feels so normal. I can feel myself slipping into normalcy with him. I know my feelings for him are growing deeper than just friendship, I'm still fighting it, but with every joke and promise, he's making his way further and further into my heart. I need some time to myself to get a grip on this and some time away from him to get these feelings under control. We stop at a red light and I hear the roar of another motorcycle behind us, turning around I see another bike barreling towards us. They stop next to us and I recognize Finn's huge grin under his dark sunglasses, a beautiful blonde is behind him. I couldn't see her when they were behind us because Finn is so huge he completely eclipses her. She smiles while Finn reaches over and pokes Callum's butt between my legs. "What is up with him and your ass?" I lean forward and say into Callum's ear.

He leans back and turns his head to speak into my ear. "He wasn't joking about sharing me." I look at him with wide eyes, completely stunned, and he laughs so hard he doubles over, clearly joking. I glare at him from behind my giant sunglasses and he and Finn fist bump before taking off once the light turns green. The rest of the ride is Finn trying to get Callum to race with him, and Callum thankfully declines every time. We're heading out of town, and I can admit I have no idea where we're going. The Douglas-fir trees are getting thicker the further we travel away from town, but briefly, there is a clearing in the trees with a beautiful view of the mountains. I stare at it as we pass and try to commit it to memory, no matter how many times I see the mountains I never get tired of them.

We pull into a small parking lot in front of a small wooden building with a giant deck wrapping around the place. We get off of the bikes and Finn and Callum do the manly bro hug thing and Callum hugs the blonde briefly, much more gentle than he is with Finn. As we're walking up the steps of the deck and heading straight to the back Finn turns around "You ever been to Whiskey Springs, Reese?"

"I can't say I have." I look around, taking in the small bar. There are wooden high-top tables all over the deck, most are empty. It's right up against a mountain so the back has stairs leading to grass and about 100 feet away is a small stream and then the steep climb of the mountain. There are massive Evergreens and Douglas firs surrounding the small building, blocking out the sun. This place is beautiful, I can't believe I never knew it existed.

"You're in for a real treat then." Finn smiles devilishly, pulling out a seat for the blonde.

She smirks. "It's not that great, but they do have good margaritas. I'm Huntley, Finn obviously forgot his damn manners." Huntley holds out her hand to me with a huge smile.

We shake hands. "I'm Reese." Huntley is stunning; tall, thin, waist length light blonde hair. Her legs look endless in her little jean shorts, her white racerback tank is knotted a little above her belly button, showing off a toned stomach. She tied a flannel around her waist and topped it all off with white converse. She's not a sweet type of beauty, hers is dangerous and has venom; she's so beautiful it makes her intimidating. Callum pushes my barstool in for me after I take a seat across from Huntley.

"Hey better not let Nathan hear you rag on his place." Finn leans back in his seat, manspreading to the extreme, although I guess when you're that big it's not really all that extreme.

"And what's he gonna do?" Huntley cocks her perfectly arched brow.

"Not a goddamn thing to my girl." Finn leans in and kisses Huntley hard, when they part her laugh is just as beautiful as she is. I glance at Callum and he's watching the exchange, smiling like the cat that got the canary.

Finn notices too. "Shut up, brother." He rests his arm behind Huntley and stares at Callum.

"I'm just happy for you, brother." Callum places his hand on my bare thigh under the table. Finn waves him off and our waitress comes over at that time and ends all conversation.

After a few drinks and lots of laughs, Callum finally asks the question I've had since this morning. "So why did Reese need to meet Huntley? So they could hang out at club functions?" Callum takes a drink of his beer and I rub my cheeks because they're sore from laughing and smiling.

Finn rakes his fingers through his hair and Huntley shifts in her seat uncomfortably. "I thought she could help Reese with her stalker problem."

"How?" Callum's hand flinches on my thigh, then starts to rub reassuring circles.

Finn blows out a breath and looks down at Huntley. She lays her hand over his on the table, her hand so delicate next to his big tattooed one, and squeezes it. "I can do it, babe. It's okay." He nods and leans over to kiss her on the cheek.

"You can stay and hear this, brother, but I'm gonna go wait at the bar, or else I'm gonna slit the motherfuckers throat." Finn stands, but before he can walk away Huntley grabs his hand.

"In due time." I think she whispers, but it was so low that I'm not sure. He grabs the back of her neck and cradles her head while he kisses her one more time before stalking away. Both Callum and I watch him go. Huntley clears her throat and we both focus our attention back on her. She squares her shoulders and she looks like the badass beauty she did before we mentioned the reason for the meeting. "Finn told me about your stalker, Reese, and I offered to teach you some self defense. I don't like it when men terrify women for amusement." She rests her arms on the table. "I was assaulted at a frat party almost a year ago, drugged so I couldn't defend myself."

"Holy shit." Callum breathes, looking down at his beer and shaking his head.

Huntley folds her hands together on the table and shakes her head. "The details don't matter, what matters is that I learned how to fight back and I want to teach you. I'm trained in Mixed Martial Arts, and I teach a self defense class at the university gym once a semester. I don't want you to be afraid anymore, not of that sad piece of shit."

I grab her hand on the table, this girl doesn't even know me and she wants to help me; she understands what it's like to be afraid of shadows and not know how to protect yourself. "Thank you. I would really love that." She smiles and nods, squeezing my hand.

"I would really love that too." Callum's hand leaves my thigh and rests on the middle of my back. "I'm gonna go check on the big fucker, make sure he's taking his anger out on a drink and not a person." He stands and pats Huntley on the shoulder. Huntley laughs and sits back in her chair.

Huntley and I talk more, I learn about what she's going to school for, and more about her training. "I'm gonna call Finn and see where the hell they went, there's a slut here that's always trying to get him to take body shots off of her." Huntley pulls out her phone. "Damn my phone died." She rolls her eyes.

"You can use mine." I slide my phone across the table.

"Thanks. I'd really hate to beat some bitches ass the first time I meet you." Her smile is pure evil and it only makes me adore her more. She taps on the phone and holds it up to her ear. Her smile turns into a grimace, her eyebrows knitting together. She pulls the phone away from her ear and ends the call, only to type the number in again and place the phone to her ear, she repeats this one more time while the guys walk up to the table laughing.

"Angel, you didn't even give me enough time to answer." Finn laughs, sliding into the chair next to Huntley.

"Shhh!" She hisses as she ends the call again and looks at me, panic barely peeking through her hard exterior. "Reese, your phone has been cloned."

22

REESE

"How do you know?" Callum demands, still standing next to the table.

Huntley sets my phone in the middle of the table and dials Finn's number again, quickly switching it to speaker phone. "Did you hear that?" We all shake our heads, just hearing normal ringing. She growls under her breath and redials the number "Listen for a clicking right before the ringing starts." She hits 'call' again and turns it to speaker, and just as she said there's a faint *click* right before the ringing begins.

Finn curses under his breath, Callum looks like he wants to murder someone, and Huntley slides my phone across the table back to me, but I just feel cold.

"What does this mean?" I ask, afraid of the answer. a cloned phone doesn't sound positive.

"It means that someone copied your sim card onto another phone and they can see everything that you do on your phone." Huntley's calm voice is the only sound I hear despite the light wind blowing through the deck and the steady flow of water in the stream. "They can see every text you send and receive, listen to every call, basically use your phone as their own." She looks between Callum and I, biting the side of her lip.

I feel the chilling fingers of fear that hadn't been around in weeks, crawl its way up my spine again. We've talked about my stalker, but with no signs of him I was beginning to think he'd been scared off by the constant protection of bikers or had become disinterested, but it turns out this whole time he'd been reading my text messages and listening to my calls. The cold in my spine turns to my stomach turning into painful knots and I feel like I'm going to vomit.

Callum grabs my hand and breaks me out of my panic. I swing my head to the side to look up at him. "Come on, Red, we're leaving." He pulls me to my feet.

"Where are we going?" I follow his quick steps, not letting go of his hand.

"To get you a clean fucking phone." He gets on his bike and I climb on behind him.

Finn and Huntley climb onto his bike next to us. "We'll follow, brother, just in case." Callum nods and we speed out of the dirt parking lot, the wheels kicking up dirt as we speed out.

———

WE ARRIVE AT MY APARTMENT, Finn deciding we were fine to be alone after leaving the phone store with my new phone and new number. "I'm staying with you tonight, and the Prospects are back on watch duty." Callum holds my hand as I step off of the bike.

I nod my head and pull my hair tie out and ruffle my loose hair. We had one week of peace, but I guess that was just in our heads. "I would like that, but I think you should go home and grab your stuff and let me shower and get my thoughts in order."

He looks at me with his brows knit together. "I'm not leaving you alone, Red."

I set my jaw, ready to fight. "I haven't had a moment alone since this creep put that envelope on my door. I'll be fine in my apartment with the security alarm on; you'll only be gone for a half hour tops!" He shakes his head. "While I appreciate you protecting me, this is my life and my choice. Please don't fight me on this." Callum and I have spent any spare moment together in the last few weeks, and if I'm going to be able to keep my feelings for him at bay I need some time to get my heart and mind on the same page.

Callum sighs. "I'll be thirty minutes, that's it. Lock the door and set the alarm." I nod and lean in to kiss his cheek. "Don't answer the door for anybody. I'll call when I'm here and you can let me in."

After my shower I'm no closer to burying my feelings for Callum, all I did was reflect on how much fun we have together and how he's always been so reliable. He's never lied or hid anything from me, other than club stuff. As much as I don't want to get hurt again, he hasn't given me any reason to believe he's anything like Noah; he's more like me than anything, with his ex cheating on him too. He's been single for so long though, would he consider going monogamous just for me? Why would a guy want one girl when he could have as many as he pleased? Great, now my head is more of a mess!

Turning off the shower, I open the shower door and wrap myself in a fluffy pale pink towel. Stepping out of the stall I look up at the foggy mirror, in the corner, there's a small smiley face drawn in the condensation. My stomach falls to the floor and I can hear my heart beating wildly in my ears. This was done while I was in the shower, the end of the mouth is still dripping down my mirror. I walk to the closed door as quietly as I can and I lean my ear against it and listen, I don't hear anything, no security alarm, no voices, no movement. I want to stay in the bathroom, but my phone is laying on my bed and the ensuite door doesn't lock, just the door to my bedroom. I have to get to my phone and then I can lock my bedroom door and hide in my bathroom and call Callum. I grip my towel tightly; one breath, two, three. I open the door just a crack to be able to listen better, there's no sound at all; I open it more and see my phone still on my bed. Another deep breath and I swing the door open wide and run to my bed and grab my phone, as I pick my head up to run to the bedroom door I see my once bare white wall covered in big red block letters. *Mine* is written on my wall, still dripping from whatever he used to paint it. I freeze, my knuckles turning white around my phone. I want to scream, but my throat feels like it's closing up. After what feels like a century, the red liquid drips getting closer to the floor, something in me finally snaps and I remember to breathe. One, two, three. I quickly reach the door, close and lock it, and run back to the bathroom. I shut the bathroom door and sit on the opposite side of the room, against the closet door. Dialing Callum, I start to cry and realize I'm shaking again.

Callum answers, the roar of his bike in the background. "What's wrong, Red?" concern evident in his voice.

I let out a shaking sob. "He was here while I was in the shower," I scream. "He was in my bathroom while I was showering!" I take shuddering breaths between sobs.

Callum yells, "I'm a few blocks away. I'll be there in two minutes. Fuck!" He roars and then hangs up and I curl into the wall and stare at the door.

A few minutes later I hear the front door slam into the entryway wall, loud footsteps stomp until they are outside of my bedroom door. I can hear the handle moving and then fists bang on the bedroom door. "Reese, it's me. If you don't open this door in five seconds I'm breaking it down to get to you."

"Coming," I croak, running to the door. I tear the door open and stare into the eyes of the most handsome man I've ever met, my friend, my protector, the only person I want to chase away my fear. I crash into him, burying my face into his chest. He strokes my wet hair, whispering apologies into the top of my head.

"Fuck babe, you're naked. Can you go get dressed while I look at what this sick fuck did this time?" He rubs his hands down my arms and pulls me back so he can look into my eyes.

I nod. "He wrote on the wall and drew a face on my bathroom mirror, but I'm sure without the steam it's gone."

Callum looks over at the writing on the wall. "Pack a bag, you're staying with me for a while." His tone leaves no room for arguing, and if I hadn't come so close to meeting my stalker today, I might have; but despite the emotions warring inside of me, fear is still coursing through my veins and I think staying with Callum is the best thing for me right now.

While I'm packing my bags, I hear Callum making a few calls. One to a prospect to come get my bags and take them to his townhouse, another to an Officer Richards who apparently does favors for the club, and the last to the guy who installed my alarms. I walk into my bedroom with my bags, Callum is sitting on the edge of my bed watching me. "The police have added this break in to your file and a friend on the force is coming to test the stuff on the wall."

I nod and step in between his legs, his hands run up my thighs and stop just under my butt. "Why didn't my alarm go off?" I rest my hands on his shoulders.

He signs and inclines his head to look at me. "Miles said the door was unlocked with a key and the code was entered." He shakes his head. "There's no video, it was hacked and erased for the time he was in here. He was in and out in less than ten minutes." He turns his head and kisses my arm. "He didn't have time to linger, just leave his creepy messages and get out."

I nod, relieved that he didn't watch me shower, and freaked out that we severely underestimated my stalker. "How'd you get in?"

He rubs his hands up and down my thighs, marginally calming my nerves. "He left the door unlocked and the alarm unarmed, he probably left in a hurry and didn't want to take the time to close up on his way out. It's not like we were going to question if he was here or not."

I let out a breath, my voice shaking. "What's on the wall?"

He looks into my eyes, pausing. "Blood."

"Oh my God." Tears start forming in my eyes again.

"It might not be human, it could be from an animal." He hurries. I nod, not trusting my voice to speak.

23

CALLUM

I get Reese back to my townhouse. Constantly checking our surroundings for anyone watching or following, I'm certain we were clear. Reese decided she wanted to go to sleep, crashing from the adrenaline rush from earlier, so I sent her up to my room to lie down. I, on the other hand, have to call Saint and update him on what's happened today.

After retelling the events of the day, Saint sighs. "Shit man, I thought this was gonna die out. I thought the attack on the guy at the bar was a coincidence and he just took credit for it."

I lean over my phone on the counter, looking out of the window above the sink in front of me. "This guy pissed on causal obsession and fucked his way into psycho territory. We can't keep waiting for him to attack; I have a bad feeling he's gonna hurt her."

There's tapping on Saint's line before he speaks, I assume he's typing out a message. "Are you sure it was blood on the walls?"

I stare at the phone deadpanned, like he can see me questioning that dumbass question. "I've never used it to write messages on walls, but I've spilled enough blood to know what the fuck it looks like."

Saint hums his agreement. "Are you going to go after this guy?"

"I can't let anything happen to her." I watch the storm that's rolling in through the window, rethinking everything he's left us and searching for clues.

I can hear shuffling and keys jingling together on his end of the call. "I called for emergency church. It'll have to go through a vote, but you know we're gonna stand behind you on this." The rain starts to come down hard, and the only sound in the house is our conversation and the hum of the storm. "Stay home with the princess, I'll make sure everyone knows how much she means to you."

I just agree and hang up, I'm not going to correct him and sputter more bullshit about Reese and me just being friends. I know damn well everyone can see what's really been going on. We've just been trying to fool ourselves, but I know she feels the same way I do. I can see how she relaxes when I'm around and how she's letting me in. Trying to be just friends and ignoring how we feel is only going to make us second guess shit and drive a wedge between us, it could get us in trouble; it's exactly why I left her alone today, and look what fucking happened. I'm not doing that again. I'm gonna tell her what she means to me and if she wants nothing to do with me then I'll go back to the clubhouse and a prospect can move into my guest room. Aw fuck, I don't know what's making my stomach churn more, the thought of letting a girl in or Reese wanting nothing to do with me.

Shaking off the fear, because I'm a fucking man, I head upstairs to my room. Reese is laying on her stomach in the middle of my big bed messing with her phone, wearing nothing but little spandex shorts and a sports bra. I sit down beside her, but before I can say anything she puts her phone down and looks up at me. "I think I know how he got the security code." Fuck I didn't want to talk about that fuck, but it was a question I was trying to figure out; I nod for her to continue. She looks down at my dark comforter and focuses on her fingers. "I texted it to Emma to have her move a package into my apartment when we went to Seattle. I also told her where my spare key was."

I rub my eyebrow, well that answers that. "I didn't know you had a spare key laying out. I would have told you to get rid of it."

She interjects before I can continue. "I did after getting home. Telling her where it was reminded me I had it hidden."

I rub a finger over my chin, thinking. "So he had his own key made."

Reese drops her head into the bed. "And he was coming in whenever he wanted." Her voice is muffled in the blanket.

I rub my hand down her bare back, her skin so smooth and warm. "I don't think so, the video feed hadn't been messed with until today. I think he was content with having the key and being able to stay updated through your phone, then when we cut him off he got pissed and left you a message."

She sits up and climbs into my lap. "I don't want to talk about this anymore." Her mouth lands on my neck, placing wet, warm kisses down my neck until she reaches the collar of my shirt. Her hands slide under my shirt and lift it over my head, she continues her kisses down my chest. I grab her under her arms and lay her back on the bed. I want to taste her so bad, and I know if I let her hot mouth anywhere near my dick I'm not gonna be able to hold off. I slide her sports bra over her perfect tits and take one pink nipple into my mouth, nipping and swirling my tongue around it. She gasps and arches her back, pushing into my mouth. I do the same thing to her other nipple and push her shorts down her legs.

Sliding two fingers into her dripping pussy, I slowly fuck her with my fingers. "Always so wet for me, babe." I growl into her nipple.

"More." She grabs my face and pulls me towards her mouth.

I place my mouth on hers, sliding my tongue inside. I keep using my fingers to tease her, but I add my thumb to rub circles on her clit. She moans, breaking our kiss and I take the opportunity to move down her body and bring my mouth to her nub, replacing my thumb. I could eat this girl out for the rest of my life, it's one of my favorite things to do. Reese's hands weave into my hair and hold my head exactly where she needs me. I flick her clit with my tongue and stroke the inside of her pussy, I remove one of my fingers and use her soaking pussy to lube her ass. I'm able to easily slide one finger in and her body immediately tenses and her pussy clenches on the one remaining finger. She screams my name and intelligible curses, her legs shaking. I pause, letting her come down from the orgasm and grabbing some lube, but once she's back to me I take her right back to the edge, I stick two fingers back in her pussy and one in her ass and suck on her clit like I'm trying to suck it through a fucking straw. Her noises are mixtures of yeses, grunts, and moans, and it's fucking heaven to my ears. This time I don't give her any time to recover, I bury my dick so deep into her I'm sure I hit her fucking intestines, her moan is long and low. I fuck her as fast and hard as I can, her moaning and meeting me thrust for thrust. I can't hold off anymore, but I'm a glutton for punishment and call me sappy but I think it's sweet if we cum at the same time, so I pinch her clit between two fingers and suck one nipple into my mouth. "Cum for me, babe." Like I flipped a switch with my words, her back arches off of the bed and her pussy squeezes my cock, barely leaving me able to thrust, I push deep inside of her and come so hard my vision blurs. I collapse next to her on the bed. Both of us sweaty and panting. "If I haven't already made it clear, you mean a lot to me, Red." She rolls over and curls into my side, looking into my eyes. I see my entire future in her green eyes, all of the good and the bad, her on the back of my bike for the rest of our lives. I'd be running for the fucking hills if the love in her eyes didn't settle every nerve in my body. She kisses my chest in answer and buries herself into the crook of my arm, stunned I pull her in closer, surprised that she's consciously cuddling into me and shocked at how right this feels.

24

CALLUM

The transition to living with Reese has been surprisingly easy, and we've both been working from my townhouse. She hasn't left the house since she moved in a week ago, also no more crazy shit has happened, but I know it's only a matter of time and I'm waiting for the psycho to show his face again. As much as I didn't want to leave Reese, I have to go out to the warehouse and help oversee this shipment; we're making our first delivery to the O'Connell's.

Reese watches me slide a gun into the back waistband of my jeans and then another into the inside pocket of my cut. "Do you really need those?" She curls into my pillow pulling the blanket up over her, still naked from when I laid her out and made her cum on my dick after dinner.

"They're just a precaution. I promise" I lean down and kiss her forehead.

She grabs me by the back of my neck, her favorite place to hang on to me, stopping me from leaving. Her voice loses the lusty tones she once had and becomes serious. "Come home to me, Callum."

I kiss her hand before letting it go. "I will, beautiful. Now put on some clothes, Wyatt and Mason are coming to hang out until I get back." She crawls out of the bed and walks her sexy ass over to the dresser, pulling on a pair of sweatpants and one of my shirts; it's huge on her and hangs down around her knees. Smiling at that image, I walk downstairs and wait for the prospects to get here.

Once the prospects are at the townhouse and sitting on the couch finding a movie to watch, Reese walks down the stairs staring at her phone. I take the opportunity to make sure everyone's on the same page.

"No one leaves this house and no one comes in. If anything happens to Red I will cut off your hands and make you eat your own eyeballs." I know these two are smart because they both came with guns and knives strapped to them and they have the smarts to look scared when I threaten them; they both nod and I turn to the door.

Reese makes it to the bottom of the stairs and grabs my hand as I'm about to turn the handle. "It's Sophie's birthday this weekend and everyone is meeting at Mickey's to celebrate. I want to go."

I stare at her because she's got to be fucking joking. "Absolutely not." I turn to leave, considering this conversation over.

"I wasn't asking, Callum. I've been hiding in this house all week and I want to see my friends." She crosses her arms under her tits and stares into my eyes, unflinching.

I rub my eyebrow. She's not a prisoner, but that doesn't mean I won't fucking handcuff her to my bed to keep her from leaving. "I can't go with you tonight, Red, and you're sure as shit not going alone."

She looks over at the prospects. "Mason and Wyatt can go with me, right guys?"

I glare at them, warning them to shut the fuck up and stayed seated. "No."

Reese grabs my hands and brings them both to her cheeks, resting her face in them. "Please, I need to see my friends."

I stare into her green eyes knowing she's not going to give this up. Reese doesn't fight me on much, but when she gets an idea in her head she sticks to it. Sighing, I turn to focus on my prospects. "She doesn't leave your sight for a fucking second. Not even the bathroom, you'll stand outside of her stall while she pisses." I toss the keys to the Raptor at them. "Take my truck and don't fucking drink too much."

Reese kisses the one hand still on her cheek and Wyatt stands up and walks over to me. "We won't let nothing happen to your Old Lady, Callum." Old Lady. Holy shit, I haven't even told her how I feel and my brothers are already considering her my Old Lady. Reese and I need to figure this shit out between us or call it quits because every day I'm falling deeper and deeper.

I lean into his face and look him dead in the eyes, hoping he can see my sincerity through mine. "Brothers or not, I will make it as painful as possible for as many days as I can, and right before you die, I'll heal you, and then do it all over again until I decide it's time; then I'll slit your throats."

Mason clears his throat and stands from the chair beside the couch. "We know, brother."

I lean down and kiss Reese one last time before leaving. "At least wear something that covers your ass and tits!" I toss over my shoulder jokingly as I leave the house to head out into the warm night air to my bike.

The CM Roofing warehouse is far outside of town, deep in the mountains in a valley; it's where I store the supplies for my roofing business and where I run the company. The warehouse is also where the club makes illegal ammo. When I started the business, the club paid half of the cost to build the shop in exchange to run club business out of it. In the hidden basement of the warehouse, the club has hired people to make ammo for high powered rifles, including many that are military grade and not legally sold in many countries. The roofing employees have no idea there's a basement. There's not a lot of activity out here at night, which is why this is when we come to pick up the shipments. I pull up to the warehouse and see that I'm the last one to arrive. I walk inside through the giant rolling door and past the other two prospects standing watch outside. The warehouse is just as you'd expect it to look, a wide open space with all of the supplies lined up on the right, the offices, and a small lunch room on the left. Ronan and Tobi are standing by the black vans while Saint loads a case into the back and Finn is carrying another through my office doors. I incline my head to greet Prez and Tobi and make my way to help load the cases. The hidden entrance to the basement is in my office through a vintage Coke vending machine. It looks like a collectible, but it's really a door to the stairs to the basement; a cool fucking hidden door, but we can barely fit through it, especially Finn's giant ass. The basement is just rows of tables with bullet presses with chairs in front of them, a small bathroom, and a small break room. Normally we only have to make one shipment per order to the O'Connell's, but being as this is going to be a giant fight and we don't know when it could end tonight's only the first in multiple shipments over the next few weeks.

Once the vans are loaded and the prospects are behind the wheel ready to go, Ronan checks in with the guy that manages our "night crew", and then we follow the vans to the rendezvous point. Our meeting place is at the back of a logging yard behind tall stacks of wood, the owner is a club friend and turns his head whenever we have get-togethers here. We're the first to arrive, as we like, and we all stand at the back of the vans waiting. The yard is dark, the only lights coming from the moon above and the headlamps from our bikes. After talking and passing around a couple of joints, headlights shine over the piles of lumber. Killian and Conor get out of a sweet dark green '67 Maserati Sebring Series 2 Coupe, while his other lackeys hop out of vans similar to ours. The prospects open the back doors to the vans, the lights inside illuminating the cases of ammo, and the O'Connells start to transfer the cases. Killian and Conor bring over duffle bags and place them in our vans where the cases were. Killian shakes hands with Ronan and Saint, Ronan sharing the joint with him now. Tobi starts to count the cash with the prospects, and Conor walks over to Finn and me and shakes our hands.

"Pleasure doing business with ya, lads." He crosses his arms, watching his men loading their vans. We nod.

"When's Killian gonna sell me the Masi?" Finn smiles, looking at the classic Maserati he cum over every time we see it.

Conor laughs easily. "Ya'd have a better chance at gettin' his firstborn boy." We all laugh at that.

"What's this war over anyways?" I lean against the open back door of the van and shove my hands into my hoodie pocket, the air biting a bit.

Conor pulls a flask out of his back pocket. "What's any great war started over?" He holds out the flask.

I accept it and take a sip, whiskey warms my stomach immediately. "Can't be territory, the Segretos operate in Sicily." I hand the flask back.

He takes a swig from his flask. "Yeah, but in a less literal sense. A woman." I nod, feeling a sense of familiarity with that statement. I'm ready to wage war to protect my girl.

"Conor, let's crack on. We need to get back." Killian speaks over the small chatter happening between everyone. Conor shakes our hands and walks back over to the classic beauty. We watch them leave, and then we head back to the warehouse to drop off the vans and put the money in the safe. If we ever get raided, the clubhouse is the first place they're going to check, our places of business as well, but since the hidden basement isn't on any floor plans, it's the safest place to stash cash until it can be paid out to members.

25

REESE

After Callum left I ran back upstairs to get ready, in Allie's last minute text she said that the theme for Sophie's birthday tonight was Little Black Dress. I asked Mason if he would go back to my apartment and bring me the only LBD in my closet. I don't own a lot of black and since he's close to my age I trust him to know what clubbing attire is. I style my long copper hair into big loose waves and apply my makeup dark and dramatic with thick false lashes and a red lip.

When I'm halfway through with my hair Mason knocks at the bedroom door. "Princess, I got your dress!" He yells through the door.

I walk to the door and open it, he walks through and lays the dress on the bed, and places my black heels with the thin straps on the floor beside it. "Thank you. Good call on the shoes, I completely forgot I didn't bring any heels here."

He shrugs. "I wasn't sure and they look like the shoes girls normally wear to clubs."

I walk back into the ensuite and put the finishing touches on my makeup. "They're the ones I would have chosen." I meet his eyes in the mirror. "How's my apartment?"

Mason leans against the bathroom door frame and crosses his arms in front of his chest, his expression neutral. "Normal seems untouched and was locked up tight when I got there." I nod, letting out a sigh. "I brought pizza back, do you want me to bring you up a few slices?"

I smile at him, Mason and I had become the closest between the four prospects. We just have more in common since we're the same age, and although I know he takes Callum's threats seriously he isn't too scared to be friends with me. "Sure. Who can say no to pizza?"

He pushes off of the doorframe. "You got it, Princess." He puts his hand on my shoulder, making eye contact through the mirror. "Callum's gonna get you home as soon as he can. The whole club is working to find this prick."

I nod. "I know. Thank you for always babysitting me."

He walks out of the door, laughing on his way. "Anything for the Princess of the Devil's Outlaws!"

I inhale my pizza and then slip on the short black dress. It's really simple, just a plain black dress with thin straps and a deep v-neckline. I walk down the stairs, carrying my heels to put them on downstairs. Wyatt and Mason are both wearing neutral colored tee shirts with jeans, boots, and their cuts. Their cuts are a lot like Callum's, only instead of the devil's skull with the snake and the name of the club and state, theirs are plain with only a small prospect patch on the front and a larger one on the back. We drive to The District in mostly silence, and when we get to Mickey's the guys stick close behind me, watching me like my own personal secret service; I get a lot of scared looks from the other clubgoers, but at least they stay away from me. Everyone is already here when we arrive, it's pretty easy to make out our group since it's several girls wearing different variations of short black dresses and some guys dressed in black dress shirts or black tee shirts; Sophie is the only one not wearing black, she's in a painfully short, strapless, silver sequin dress that hugs her curves beautifully. She's laughing and dancing on the dance floor with her ex Logan. I use the word 'ex' loosely though because everyone, including them, is hoping they get back together; they just have to figure out their issues first. I walk to the table that Allie and Emma are standing in front of and give them both hugs and introduce them to Wyatt and Mason. I notice Allie's light blue and green eyes sparkle with interest when Mason shakes her hand, and Wyatt's eyes linger on Emma's exposed flawless dark skin, not in a creepy way, just interested. What a bitch, she's always had perfect skin, but poor Wyatt, there's no way Emma could forget The Devil's Outlaws long enough to even get to know him. Mason looks at Allie with wide eyes and I file that away to ask him about later. "ROX-ANNE" by Arizona Zervas starts playing through the loud-speakers and Allie drags Emma and me out onto the dance floor, the guys watching us from a table next to the one we had been standing at. Sophie screams when she sees me and pulls me into a bone crushing hug, releasing me to let me hug Logan after. Sophie's naturally tan skin beams against her sequined dress, with her dark hair freshly highlighted and pulled into a high pony. Allie starts rapping the song perfectly and Emma laughs next to her, her kinky curly bun bobbing on top of her head. I missed this so much, just having fun with my friends and forget-ting my guy drama and the stalker. I needed this. When the song ends we go back to our table and Logan brings us drinks.

When I catch Allie staring at Mason again I finally say some-thing. "Stop undressing him with your eyes and go talk to him, Al."

She flicks her mid-length platinum hair over her shoulder. "He's very cute but I've got my sights set a little higher."

I stare at her in confusion with my head cocked trying to

figure out who she's talking about. She smirks and winks, not letting anything slip about this mystery man.

"Invite him! You look too hot tonight to miss!" Sophie leans across the table.

Allie shakes her head. "He's working tonight." She yells back over the music.

"Go see him after then." Sophie counters. "A little black dress is like a weapon. Wield it."

Emma laughs. "That was a good one, Soph." We all laugh and Sophie shrugs.

I watch Mason get up from the table with his phone to his ear and walk towards the front doors of the bar. Wanting to make sure nothing is wrong with Callum I pull my phone out and see one new message.

CALLUM:

I like that dress. I can't want to see what you're wearing under it.

I scroll above his message to see the mirror selfie I sent him of me in the dress. I decide to mess with him a little bit, hoping he won't call my bluff here in the bar.

REESE:

What if I said nothing?

His reply is instant.

CALLUM:

Fuck.

CALLUM:

Shits about to get real awkward over here if I'm walking around with a hard on.

REESE:

smiling purple devil emoji

CALLUM:

I want you in my bed with nothing on but those heels when I get home.

My insides start to heat and I smile at my phone.

REESE:

Yes sir. *red heart*

Feeling a little parched after picturing the scene Callum just painted inside of my head, I walk over to the giant bar to get another drink. Although recently I've been doing a lot of social drinking, that really is the only time I drink, and every time my goal isn't to get drunk. I have a few drinks, literally just a few, and then I'm done for the night. I usually nurse my drinks so two or three last me all night. Finding Logan at the bar, I walk over to wait next to him. Ever since Logan and Sophie first started dating he has always been good friends with all of the rest of us. Luckily Sophie and Logan stayed really good friends after they broke up, so he still hangs around us and we all act like nothing has changed because, in a friendship way, nothing has. It's kind of sad watching them together though, seeing how much they both want to be together, but not being in the right space to do so. They both agreed that when they were both ready they would try again, Sophie just hasn't completely forgiven him yet. When they started dating he didn't know what he wanted and he hurt her; I know he regrets it, it's written all over his face when he's with her.

Logan slings his arm over my shoulder, with his eyes slightly closed as he sways and leans into me. "I missed you guys, Reesey." *What did he just call me?*

My spine stiffens and my heartbeat picks up. Reesey was

what my stalker called me in the notes he left. My breathing comes in short spurts and I turn my head to look up at him. "What did you call me?"

He chuckles. "Uh. Reeses. Like Reese's Pieces the candy duh," he slurs and I have to admit, with the slurring in his speech it did sound like he said *Reesey Piecey*. I'm losing my damn mind over this stalker.

I laugh, though it's mostly at my freakout and less at his new nickname for me, and Logan laughs too like it's the funniest thing he's ever said. I flag down the bartender and order another drink for me and water for Logan. Rolling his eyes he takes the water and we both walk back to the table.

When we reach the table, Wyatt walks over and leans down to talk into my ear. "Mase has been gone awhile, I'm going out front to check on him. Don't leave this table for anything, please." I nod in agreement and I watch him walk towards the front door.

A commotion breaks out a few tables over, causing all of us to look over, and then some guy brushes past us, pushing me into Allie and almost knocking us over. Allie yells at his retreating back and I roll my eyes. During the collision, I spilled half of my drink onto my leg and the floor. I grab a couple of napkins from the center of the table and wipe my leg.

Allie looks at my now half-empty cup. "Might as well finish it."

"Yeah, why not? It's my last one anyways." I raise my drink to her in a salute.

Allie shakes her head. "Are you even drunk?"

"No, but you know I don't like to get like that." I wave her off

"Yeah, yeah I know, Miss Responsible." Allie raises hers and we finish our drinks in a gulp. I cough when I swallow mine, almost choking. The cranberry juice must be bad because it was bitter, almost salty. I listen to the conversations around me for a bit and then I see Mason and Wyatt walk back into the bar. They stay by the front doors talking to the bouncer, Wyatt catching my eye and waving to me. I start to sway on my feet and sweat. I grab an ice cube out of my empty cup and suck on it, hoping to cool down, but it only makes me feel nauseous. I lean into Allie so I can talk to her without yelling. "I don't feel good, I'm going to the bathroom." She starts to nod, but I'm already walking away and towards the back of the bar to the bathrooms. I push past everybody, the spinning of the room making it so much harder. Thank the heavens there isn't a line to the bathroom for once. I run in and throw up into the toilet. I sit back against the wall of the stall and rest my head in my hands, my eyelids are so heavy and I just want to fall asleep on this dirty bathroom floor. I hear an unfamiliar voice.

"Reese, are you okay?" It's a guy's voice, why is a guy in the girl's bathroom? Please tell me I'm not in the guy's restroom.

"I'm really sleepy and I don't feel good." I keep my eyes closed, fighting unconsciousness.

"I'll take you home." I hear the stall door open and he lifts me from under my arms and slings my arm over his shoulder, wrapping his arm around my waist. I don't open my eyes, they're too heavy. I should try to fight this, but I don't think I'd be able to, I'm sure I'm safe, they knew my name.

My legs feel heavy too, making it hard to walk, good thinking that this guy is helping me. "I want to see Callum."

"Okay, I'll take you to him," he says.

"Who the fuck are you?" Another male voice booms, this one I think I recognize. Someone else is grabbing me and pulling me away from the guy from the bathroom.

"I know Reese. She said she wasn't feeling well so I was going to take her home." That voice was my bathroom friend.

I'm shuffled around again, making my stomach roll more.

"You were going to take advantage of a sick drunk girl?" The familiar voice hisses.

"What? No. I was going to drop her off at her house." That's the guy from the bathroom, I think. "I saw her stumble past my table and wanted to help her home. You know the frat guys are always drugging girls' drinks and taking them home."

I feel someone touching my arm, shaking me a little. "Princess, do you know this guy?" Oh I know that voice, that's Mason.

I smile, glad that he's back. "I don't know." I keep my eyes closed because that just makes sense right now.

I feel his breath closer to my face this time. "Please open your eyes and tell me if you know this guy." I can feel his presence back away. "Or I'm going to kill him for trying to leave with you."

That gets my attention and I snap my eyes open, well I try to but they still feel really heavy. I lean my head back against the hard chest behind me to find Wyatt with his arm around my waist holding me up and Mason standing in front of me with a puffy eye and his hands wrapped around my upper arms, his knuckles bleeding. I look around him to see who the other voice was, the one who saved me from taking a nap on the bathroom floor, my eyes go wide, my blurred through only registering two things: one, I don't know who this man is, and two, this could have been really bad if Mason and Wyatt hadn't found me.

I shake my head. "No, I don't know him." I look at Mason and he looks murderous. The stranger's eyes are so wide I can see the whites around his irises, his face pales under the dim lights in the hallway.

Mason glares at the stranger. "You chose the wrong girl, you piece of shit." He turns back to me and looks above me at Wyatt. "I got this, you take her home. Cales gonna murder us for letting this happen to her."

26

CALLUM

"So let me get this straight." Reese is asleep on the couch with her head in my lap and my fingers running through her long red hair. "You," I point to Mason, who is slouched over on one of my leather barstools that he pulled into the living room. He's icing what is starting to turn into a pretty decent black eye with his knuckles wrapped. "Went outside to get into a fight, and you," I shift my finger to Wyatt sitting next to him on another barstool. "Went to find him and left Reese alone to get roofied. Did I get that right?" My whole body is shaking but I'm not sure if it's more from anger or fear of what could have happened. "What the fuck did I say about leaving her alone?"

Mason slumps over more, burying his head in his hands. "I—"

"I called him to discuss another vendor for black powder," Ronan interjects from the tan leather armchair beside me. "He went outside to talk to me and that's when he was jumped. He dropped his phone without hanging up and I heard the whole thing." I look to Finn and Saint because what the fuck does Mason know about our gunpowder vendor?

"Elaborate please," Saint says from the armchair opposite Ronan.

Ronan looks around at all of us and then down at Reese asleep on my lap. "Mason came to me a few weeks ago with a cheaper vendor for the powder. I told him if he could pull it off he would earn his top rocker." We all sit in silence, me glaring at the two prospects and Ronan, Saint, and Finn looking at me, ready to hold me back from ripping them apart. If Red wasn't in my lap I would have done it already.

"I don't give a fuck. Give me one good reason I shouldn't kill you both for disobeying me and putting Red's life in danger," I snarl. I've decided my anger is stronger than my fear right now.

"Cale." Finn calmly shifts from his seat on the bay window behind Ronan, pulling my attention away from the two idiots who left my girl alone to get drugged. "Mason couldn't have known some drunk guy was gonna try to boost his ego by jumping an Outlaw, and Wyatt did what he needed to do. He left Reese at the table surrounded by her friends. It would have been worse for her to go outside into the fight."

I shake my head, why the fuck doesn't anyone else see how fucked this was? "What if it was Huntley?" Low blow, I know, but I never claimed to be above it.

Finn flinches, looking down before bringing his eyes back to mine. "Then I'd be just as pissed as you, but I'd need you there to keep my head straight."

I look back at Mason and Wyatt. They both look remorseful and they did find her before that fuck was even able to get her out of the bathroom. "Fuck." I sigh. "You're spared this time." I point between them.

"Thank you, Callum." Mason sighs, his shoulders relaxing.

"We won't let you down." Wyatt still looks tense, but I think that's 'cause he's too smart to know they're not off of the hook that easily.

I smile, baring my teeth. "I know because no one will be able to stop me from killing you both next time."

"Was Miles able to get the CCTV for the bar?" Ronan's voice is calm, steering the conversation away from my murdering threats to our prospective new brothers.

I pick up my whiskey tumbler from the arm of the couch and take a drink, it burns its way down my throat and pulls me down from my rage high I was stewing in. "Yeah. Her drink doesn't look messed with from the bar to the table, but her table isn't in the view of the camera so we lose her until she's walking to the bathroom." I sigh. "She was stumbling to the bathroom and then a few minutes later the guy walks in and then the guys show up when they're walking out of the bathroom."

"So she was drugged at her table." Saint surmises, his foot propped on his knee.

I nod my head, taking another drink. "Yeah."

He continues, "Do you think this was her stalker?"

I sigh. "I don't know. It could have been, that would be the best scenario, but it could also be some low life who likes drugging girls to get laid."

"You two can go talk to the bouncers tonight." Ronan gestures to Mason and Wyatt, and they both nod. "Get the name of the fuck wad that tried to take the Princess tonight."

I follow up Ronan's orders with something else because I have a better idea of how these two shitheads can get back into my good graces. "Wyatt can. I have another job for Mason." Everyone's eyes fall back on me and Mason perks back up in his chair. "I don't want to slow Miles down with another job, so would you be able to keep tabs on Reese's ex?" When Mason came into the club and found out we outsource a lot of our tech shit he saw an opening and decided to try to fill it. He has a degree in computer science, but he hasn't quite mastered the criminal shit we need, he's still a little straight laced. That's where Miles is teaching him to be a criminal mastermind.

Mason pulls the ice pack from his eye and nods. "Yeah, brother. I'll set up some barriers for them so I get alerts and then I'll go help Miles comb through footage from the bar."

I nod, pleased with his efforts. "Alright, just make sure to tell him before you head over to the cave; he's a panicky mother fucker."

Mason's eyebrows draw together. "He lives in a cave?"

I close my eyes and rub my finger between my brows. "No, you fucking idiot. He just has blackout curtains and never turns on any lights so it's always dark."

Finn doubles over laughing, his arms crossing over his stomach. "How would he have any electricity in a cave to run his computers?"

Mason huffs, looking up to the ceiling. "I don't know, maybe he has a high-tech, modern cave with glass walls, and generators and shit." Wyatt and Finn laugh at Mason while Saint looks genuinely confused with his answer, and Ronan shakes his head. Even though Ronan is only about seven years older than us, sometimes I think he feels like he's babysitting a bunch of rambunctious kids. We may fight like brothers, but we also love like brothers.

I rest my head on the back of the couch, closing my eyes. "Get the fuck out of my house before I lose brain cells because of you. The suns gonna be up in a few hours and I want to go to sleep." I hear chairs sliding into my kitchen and feet shuffling. Saint and Ronan pat my shoulder as they pass and Finn ruffles my hair.

I hear the door open and two more sets of footsteps walk behind me before pausing at the door. "I'll talk to the bouncer and get back to you by this evening," Wyatt says from behind me.

Without opening my eyes I answered him, feeling less murderous now and a little more rational. "I can't lose her." Admitting that out loud for the first time feels wrong and like I'm telling the world's biggest secret. Reese and I haven't talked about how we feel, I think she feels the same way, her eyes speak for her, but what if she doesn't? What if this is all one-sided?

I hear Finn laugh from what sounds like outside and I turn my head and open my eyes to see his big as fuck tattooed head peeking back into the house from the porch. "At least you're finally admitting it!"

I hold up my free hand and flip him off. "Fuck off, Finn." I hear his loud laughter before the door closes and it's just Red and me.

Fucking hell what a fucking night. I move out from under her body and kneel to carry her upstairs to my bedroom. The effects of the drugs had worn off about the time they got back and she was able to wash her face and change into a pair of sweatpants and one of my tee shirts, but she said she waited until I got home to fall asleep, which she promptly did on my lap on the couch.

Her eyes peek open while I'm carrying her up the stairs. "If I was drugged shouldn't we go to the police?"

I look down at her, sleepy and beautiful in my arms. "No more police, we're taking care of this on our own from now on."

She buries herself more into my chest. "What happened to the guy who drugged me?"

Sighing, I think of the best way to answer this. Deflecting should do. "Not tonight, Red."

Reese yawns, her delicate hand moving to cover her sinful mouth. "Did you hurt him?"

"Yeah." I'd say a bullet to the forehead probably hurt. Close enough.

We make it to my room and I lay her down and cover her up, then strip down to join her in bed.

"Sorry I wasn't waiting for you naked with my heels on," Reese whispers as she moves closer to my side.

I laugh, staring up at the dark ceiling. "Next time, babe." I open my arm and loop it around her back.

She cuddles into my side and rests her head on my chest. "I heard what you said." I pause, hoping she'll elaborate on what exactly she heard. She does. "That you can't lose me."

I weigh my options in my head, but having this talk right now with her coming down from being roofied doesn't really seem like a great time to ask if she likes me or just likes fucking me. "You're hearing things, Red."

She chuckles softly. "Okay, sure." Her arm squeezes my side tighter and she turns her face so she's almost laying face down on my chest, and soon she's asleep again. And for the second time since knowing Reese, and the first time since my last relationship, I fall asleep cuddling, and this time there wasn't any sex beforehand.

27

REESE

The evening after Callum's "club run", as he called it, and my drugging, I'm sitting at the kitchen island, running a credit check on a potential resident. Callum wraps his arms around my stomach and leans down to place kisses along my neck; I hum in appreciation.

Between kisses, he speaks into my neck. "Go get dressed, I have a surprise for you." I turn around on the bar stool, my brows knitting together. "Other than last night you haven't left the house in a week, and that shit was a fail, so I'm taking you out and showing you a *real* good time. Stalker or not, it's unhealthy to be inside so much and you can't survive just off of my vitamin D forever." He smirks and I roll my eyes, laughing. After waking up this morning I filled Callum in on everything that I could remember of the night before, which wasn't really much. Miles and Mason are trying to figure out who the guy was, but so far, he just looks like some college kid. We don't have any connections so they think it was random. I head upstairs to get changed all the same and he smacks my butt as I walk away, taking a seat on the stool I just left. "Wear a ball cap and something of mine if you want to draw less attention to yourself." He yells after me up the stairs.

A few minutes later I return dressed in ripped jean shorts and one of Callum's big black hoodies with the devil skull and snakes on the back. I braid my hair and pull on a black ball cap as he suggested. On our way out of the door, Callum pulls on his cut and I slide my feet into my nude sandals.

I have no idea where we're going, but we head out of town and start up a mountain. The view is getting more beautiful the higher we climb, and the roar of the bike is bouncing off of the mountain beside us and echoing around us, sounding like fifty bikes instead of just us. It's so freeing not to be confined inside of a car, you have a completely unobstructed 360-degree view of your surroundings and it's absolutely breathtaking. We reach the top of the mountain and Callum pulls onto a small outlook. We get off of the bike and walk over to the bench sitting at the edge of the cliff. Callum hands me a water bottle. "Have you ever been to Lookout Ridge?"

I look all around us, you can see all of Merrill Hill, Mt. Rainier, and the long line of mountains beside it. I've been to mountain attractions and lookouts before, but none had this view. "No." I finally answer. "This is perfect, thank you for bringing me." I bring my legs onto the bench and cross them in front of me.

"I've noticed that anytime you're staring at mountains you always seem to relax." He rests his hand on my bare thigh.

I lean back into the bench, letting out a sigh. The sun is close to setting, basking the world in a light orange color. "They remind me that the world is bigger than I think it is. Sometimes we can get so wrapped up in our lives, the good days and the bad, and we forget that it's not just us in the world. There's so much more to live for." I laugh, realizing how weird my reasoning sounds. "I guess they just put me back in my place." Callum nods, looking like he's really thinking about what I said.

He turns his head to look at me. "Tell me about your last relationship."

I really don't want to talk about this, but I care about Callum and he deserves to know; he shared his story with me. "He broke me," I say, trying to stay detached from the memory.

"I figured, tell me about it." He takes my hand and turns my chin so I'm looking into his beautiful blue eyes. "I want to know every part of you, even the darkest, most painful parts of your being."

I take a deep breath and turn off my mind, just letting the memory of Noah spill from my lips. "I just wanted to have fun, you know? It was my sophomore year of college and I just wanted to meet people and have fun. I was living on my own in a new city and at a new school." I roll my eyes. "I met Noah through a dating app and we hit it off. He was a senior and funny and new. We went out a few times and he told me he wanted to get serious. He was lying though, he just wanted me to stop seeing other people while he went and slept his way through every sorority on campus. Of course, I didn't know this at the time." I pause, taking a deep breath and looking out over the mountains. The breeze barely whispers by, the world is so still up here. "Even though he was supposed to be leaving after graduation, I agreed to start taking us more seriously and I gave him every part of me. I loved him so intensely that I went insane with jealousy when I finally did figure out what he was doing behind my back. I still don't know how many times he cheated on me or with how many girls, and to be honest I lost count of the ones that I did know about. I guess what hurt the most and still stays with me was reading the messages between him and his ex where he compared our sex to theirs, and how poorly he spoke about me to other girls." Callum starts rubbing circles over my hand with his thumb, leaving a flaming trail behind. I shake my head and laugh sadly, "there was one message where he was begging a girl to give him a chance, he said that if she gave him a chance he would leave me for her."

"Why did you stay with him if he was cheating on you?" I look into his eyes, but there's no judgment there.

I look down at the water bottle on my lap. "It was a mixture of a few things. I really did care about him, and I thought he cared about me, I mean why would he waste my time if he wanted to mess around? I had made it clear that we could continue to see each other without committing to one another. But more so I felt bad for leaving him, regardless of what he was doing to me. I've always prided myself on never giving up on people; I thought that made me a good person, or supportive, or strong I guess. Finally, I had enough. I had hit rock bottom and my absolute worst. I couldn't stop wondering why I wasn't enough for him and what was wrong with me. I asked him one night and he just apologized and told me he wasn't ready for a relationship; he never really gave me a real answer for why he did what he did. I decided that I couldn't keep living with how miserable the relationship was making me and I realized that I couldn't forgive him, so we broke up. At the end of that school year, he graduated and took a job at the college instead of moving home and I dropped out to go full time at Westbrooke. I haven't spoken to him since; I can't, he took everything from me. Before I met him I was the happiest I had ever been, I was confident and easy-going, and I loved my life. He made me cynical and hard. He made me look at myself with such disgust. For not only how I had acted in jealousy, but also because I started to see myself as someone who wasn't worth even the smallest bit of respect or love." I scoff. "I never really recovered." I pull my hand away and take a long drink of my water. I've never shared this much of that story, not even with my best friends. I've never felt this vulnerable with a guy, I've never bared this much of my heart, even when I thought I was in love with someone.

Callum grabs my chin and moves my face so I'm looking at him again. "You are the most beautiful woman that I have ever met, and it's not just because of how you look. You are smart, kind, and resilient. You radiate happiness and warmth and everyone around you loves you. You are worth every amount of love and respect, and your ex didn't realize what was really in front of him." He places his hands on my cheeks, not letting me look away from his heavy gaze. "I will happily spend the rest of my life making up for that asshole's mistakes and making sure you love your life again. I will never betray your trust, Red." Before he can promise anything else I lean in and kiss him, trying to portray how much his words mean to me. Callum has made me feel safe since the day I met him, and he hasn't failed me once. I don't want to fight my feelings for him anymore; I know he can make me the happiest I've ever been. He already has. He's put my pieces back together without either of us even knowing. "I love you, Red." He whispers it so softly between kisses that I'm not sure he really said it. As much as I want to say it back and take that step with him, I need a little more time. I want this time to be the last time I say it to someone. Luckily his phone starts ringing in his pocket, breaking the thick cloud of emotion surrounding us and giving us a moment to both collect our thoughts. He sighs and pulls his phone out of his jeans pocket. "What's going on, Miles?" Callum's body goes rigid, his eyes focus on the landscape in front of us. "Send me the address."

I grab his hand, still sitting sideways facing him. "Cale, what happened?"

He taps out a message on his phone and pulls me to stand with him. "Miles was able to find the ISP address of your stalker and find his house." He pulls me into his arms. "I'm ending this tonight."

My eyes widen. "So the guy last night?"

"Just a random piece of shit," he answers.

I fall into his embrace, too stunned to do anything else. "I'm going with you." His body grows tense again. "I need this, Callum. I need to know who he is."

He kisses the top of my head. "I know, babe, we'll meet Finn at my house and switch out the bike for the truck."

We walk to the bike and get on. I take in the view one last time before I finally get my life back and I can stop living in fear of my stalker and my feelings for Callum. I'm going to tell him I love him after tonight. I have to.

28

REESE

When we pull up to Callum's townhouse Finn is already waiting, standing next to his bike. Finn and I follow Callum inside of his house and the guys continue into a downstairs bedroom where Callum keeps his gun case. They step back into the living room shoving guns in the backs of their jeans and inside of their cuts. Finn nods to Callum before going back outside. "I'll follow you both on my bike." He squeezes my shoulder before opening the door.

Callum pulls me into a tight hug and captures my mouth with his, slipping his tongue inside and tangling with mine. "Let's go end this, Red." I nod and we walk into the garage to get in Callum's Raptor, he holds the door open for me, the windows are tinted so that the cabin is completely black except for the monitor lights. When he gets behind the wheel he gives me another kiss, my hands linking behind his head to hold him there. We take a deep breath together and then pull apart. He hands me a gun from the inside of his cut, looking somber.

I stare down at the small black gun, the once black trigger now shines a dark red. "My gun." I chuckle, never having imagined having to own my own gun.

He places his big hands over mine, calming my nerves immediately. Looking down at the gun he smirks. "I added your own personal touch to it." His eyes come to mine and his face turns serious. "You won't need it, but just in case; shoot anyone who isn't me or Finn." I nod and he opens the garage door and the loud rumble of the pickup starts; I pop open the glove compartment in front of me and gently close my gun inside.

Callum holds my hand during the drive, looking over at me every few minutes. The drive is silent, the only sound is the radio playing "Train Wreck" by James Arthur, and when we stop at a red light he leans over and kisses me, ending the kiss way too quickly for my liking. "I can't wait to kill this motherfucker for what he's put you through, babe."

As the light turns green and we start to move forward, I decide that I have to tell him how I feel just in case something terrible happens tonight. We have the element of surprise and two huge scary bikers against one deranged psycho, but you can't bet against the devil you don't know. So I say it. "Callum, I —" Before I can finish my confession I see a car barreling through the intersection we just entered, they're going so much faster than the posted speed limit and they're not showing any signs of stopping.

I yell Callum's name but it's too late, there's no avoiding it. He whips his head to the side and the car crashes into his side of the Raptor. The impact throws my head against the window and then my stomach flips several times, there's loud crunching and smashing, and stinging on my arms and face; and then the airbag slams into my face, the dust choking me and making me cough. "Callum!" I think I'm yelling, but I can't hear myself over the ringing in my ears. I can't hear any response so I keep yelling his name, trying to reach over to him; I can't see him through the smoke and dust. I start to hear my name being yelled through the ringing and I try to yell Callum's name louder so he can find me.

Through the slowly fading dust, I see my door being ripped open and big hands grabbing my arms to place on the roof of the car, which I'm now realizing is upside down. "Brace yourself, I'm going to cut your seatbelt!" The voice doesn't sound like Callum and that makes my stomach roll again.

I press my hands against the roof and feel the seatbelt being pulled away from me, the seatbelt gives way, and big hands catch me before I fall out of my seat and drag me out of the smashed door. I close my eyes and quickly pray when I open them I'm looking into the most beautiful, deep, steel blue eyes I've ever seen. I open my eyes to see Finn's panicked dark blue eyes, he's carrying me over to the curb and yelling more things, but I can't hear him over the panic now setting in. I look all around us, there are cars stopped and people standing around. Callum's white Raptor is upside down in the middle of the street with broken glass making a scattered trail leading from the intersection. The worst part of it all is that I don't see Callum anywhere. He's not waiting on the curb and he wasn't the one who rescued me from the crash. Finn runs back over to the crumbled Raptor and tries to rip the driver's side door open over and over, yelling to people on the sidewalk to call for help. With shaking legs I run to the car, realizing Callum is still in it. I drop to the ground making sure to stay out of Finn's way; he's grunting, cursing, and sweating trying to get the door open. A pain bites into my hands and knees, but I ignore it. I look up to see panic written all over his face, both of us know he's not going to be able to open it on his own, but we both know he won't stop trying until help comes. I look into the window and see Callum, he's so still. I can't see his chest moving, blood is dripping onto the roof from a giant gash on the side of his head and his neck from where the seat belt must have cut into him; there is so much blood I start to panic even more.

Without thought, I start yelling at him, trying to get him to stay awake if he's got any sense about him right now. "Callum, you have to stay awake dammit! I need you here with me." Tears start to run down my face, but I ignore them and say what I should have said so long ago. "When I first saw you at Mickey's I couldn't think of anything except for how the room seemed to stand still and you turned my world upside down. You made me trust, and believe, and hope for the first time in months, and you can't just leave me before we've even got to begin." I hear sirens in the distance. Finn starts banging his fists on the door. "Your eyes hold the universe in them and you have no idea of the spell you put me under every time you look at me. I hope you forgive me for not telling you how I felt when you told me you loved me today, maybe you didn't even mean to say it, but I heard you and I'm sorry I didn't stop you and make you repeat it. I don't know when I fell for you because I've been trying to deny it for so long, but I knew I loved you when you could turn around any day with your teasing and kisses. I knew when I started living to see your smile and heal your shattered heart. I knew when I wished that I wasn't broken so I could love you fully and give you everything you deserve. I knew when everything was easier when you were around, sleeping, breathing, eating. I love you, Callum, wholly, fully, and completely without end. Please don't leave me."

29

REESE

My whole body is shaking and the sirens drown out my sobs. Hands wind around my stomach and lift me from the ground. I watch two paramedics try to pull Finn away from the car, but he grabs one guy by the throat and leans into him, yelling something into his face, the look on his face would normally make me run in fear, but I'm too numb right now to be worried about anything other than Callum. The sirens mask his words, and the paramedic nods and holds up his hands. The guy who grabbed me puts me on a gurney and starts to check my vitals and dress the cuts on my arms and face from the windshield shattering. Finn sits next to me and we watch firefighters pry the door open and pull Callum's lifeless body out of the car, a scream rips out of me and Finn holds me down as I try to lunge out of the back of the ambulance. Callum is limp and not responding to anyone, they hurry and put him on a gurney and rush him into a second ambulance. "Is he dead?" I ask the paramedic who gets into the driver's seat.

He starts the vehicle and we speed behind the one that has Callum. "I don't know, ma'am."

I cry the rest of the way to the hospital, holding Finn's hand. He's silent and still, his eyes focused on our hands, but I see the tears rolling down his cheeks.

The nurses put me in my own room in the ER and Finn leaves to try to find some information about Callum. After assessing me they find nothing broken, only some scrapes and cuts and a minor concussion. They said I got really lucky that I wasn't on the side of impact, but I would trade places in a heartbeat so that Callum could be the one with such minor injuries instead.

I find Finn leaning over the receptionist's desk in the ER waiting room and speaking in a low tone, leaving him to his threatening, I take a seat in the waiting area and wait for him to update me. "If I Would Have Known" by Kyle Hume plays on the speakers and I swear I'm either going to cry some more or strangle whoever chose this radio station. Finn falls into the seat next to me and sighs. "They're sending a doctor to update us, all she knows is that he was taken into surgery after getting here." I nod, being thankful that Callum was at least alive enough to make it into surgery. "Did you mean what you said?" He's staring out of the window in front of us.

I rub the giant knot on the side of my head wincing. "Every word. I just hope he heard me."

He grabs my hand from my head and holds it on the armrest. "You guys are good for each other." I nod, trying to keep my tears from falling; I can't think about the possibility of Callum not surviving this.

A nurse comes out of the ER doors, looking around the waiting room. Finn and I rush towards her, needing her to be the nurse sent with information on Callum. "How's he doing? Is Callum out of surgery?" It's rushed and almost yelled, I need her to have good news, he has to be okay.

She looks at the floor and then meets my eyes, regret shining brightly. "I'm sorry, miss, the man you came in with passed before we could begin surgery."

30

REESE

My heart feels like it's in a chokehold inside of my chest. It's bound to burst with how tightly the nurse's words are squeezing it. "Fuck!" Finn roars right before his fist smashes into the wall beside him, I on the other hand stand still and watch as the nurse flinches away from us. His outburst didn't phase me in the slightest because of my state of shock.

"I'm really sorry. I'll send the doctor out to talk to you both." The nurse says as she clutches her badge in her hands.

Finn leans his forehead against the wall, his hands fisted beside his head. I softly place my hand in the middle of his expansive back, his size making my hand look smaller and the devil skull staring back at me. "No, he can't." His voice shakes. I try to say something but my voice is cut off by a sob. I place my hand over my mouth to stifle it and slide down the wall next to him, pulling my legs to my chest and resting my forehead on my knees. Finn turns around and sits down next to me, his legs stretching out in front of him.

I'm not sure how long we sit here together. Quietly mourning Callum on the floor of the ER waiting room. I hear shuffling and muttering beside Finn and me and without looking up I know it's Mason that has slid down to sit beside me. The bright presence that he brings with himself everywhere he goes is so powerful it pulls you in without any consent, well that and I can feel the softness of his hoodie rub against my bent leg. After what feels like hours I hear shoes squeak in front of us and I look up to see another nurse, this one older than the last.

"Are you here for Mr. Moran?" She asks sweetly, her smile not quite reaching her eyes.

Finn clears his throat. "Yeah." He looks down at me and the remorse in his eyes brings another sob to the surface.

"Would you like to see him? We just got him moved out of Radiology."

Finn and I nod and we all stand. He grabs my hand in his and looks down at me. "We're in this together now, Little Red." I look down at our conjoined hands as silent tears roll down my cheeks.

Saint clears his throat and it's then that I look around me and notice the entire club is standing against the wall with us. He looks between the two of us and the nurse. "You two go ahead, we'll wait right here." Finn nods and I look over to Mason, he smiles his beautiful smile but this is the first time I've ever seen it tinged with sadness. I nod and walk hand in hand with Finn through the doors of the ER.

The nurse takes us to an observation room outside of the ER and opens the door. "Take your time." She smiles and then pushes open the door.

Finn walks in first and immediately spins around and glares at the nurse's back. "Is this a fucking joke?" He yells. Confused, I look around him and my body feels like someone has slammed into it. All of the groggy and distant feelings I had earlier have been replaced with hypersensitivity. The lights are too bright, the monitors too loud. My eyes go wide as I see Callum laying in bed with IVs attached to one arm and hooked to a machine that's reading a heartbeat. Relief washes over me, he didn't leave me, he's not dead.

"Excuse me?" The nurse says, her sweet blue eyes wrinkling with the confused look.

I place my hand on Finn's giant bicep to hopefully restrain him some. He's shaking and breathing heavily through his nose, his jaw clenching while he glares at the nurse. I'm scared he's going to strangle the poor woman. "We were told Callum was dead."

The nurse frantically shakes her head. "What? No. He only had a small blood transfusion and had his shoulder reset." Her features transform from confused to remorseful. "Who told you he had died?"

As if on cue the young nurse who had talked to us first walked up to the desk behind the older nurse. Leaning against it and talking to the male nurse behind the desk she was completely oblivious to us and the sheer rage that Finn now transferred onto her. I point to her. "She did."

The nurse follows my finger and nods her head. "I'll go talk to her. Please go in and see Mr. Moran, he's just resting and should be waking up soon."

Pulling Finn with me, we walk into Callum's room and sit on both sides of him. He's laying in the bed just as still as he was in the car, but at least this time I can see his chest move with his breaths. He has a small line of stitches on the side of his head, one arm in a sling and the other covered in small cuts. They did the best they could, but Callum's neck and what I can see of his chest are still covered in dried blood, and strands of his blond hair are crusted as well.

"He's alive," I whisper. Wiping the tears from my cheeks with one hand while the other rests over the thin hospital blanket on his thigh, since his left arm is the one in the sling.

Finn chuckles, shaking his head. "He has too much to live for now." He slouches into his chair across from me, never taking his eyes off Callum; like if he looks away Callum will disappear.

There's a soft knock on the door before the older nurse walks in carrying a bowl with soapy water and a small washcloth. "I found out where the confusion was," she says as she sits the bowl of water next to Callum's thigh in front of me. She lays two washcloths next to it and I instinctually pick the washcloth up and soak it in the lukewarm water. She continues talking as I gently wipe the dried blood off of Cale's neck and the small amount on his chest. "Another man came in at the same time as you and Mr. Moran." She looks at me. "We were working so quickly that identities got mixed up." She looks between Finn and me and then down at Callum. "It is absolutely no excuse and we cannot apologize enough for what you went through because of our mistake." I submerge the washcloth again to rinse it before going back to clean off what small amount of blood remained on Callum's face and head. "As I mentioned before, Mr. Moran had a transfusion to help with the blood loss from the head wound, he had some stitches, his shoulder reset due to dislocation, and he has a few broken ribs." She smiles politely. "He'll be in a sling for a few weeks while his shoulder heals and his ribs should heal on their own. Once Miranda is done with her paperwork, she wants to come in here and apologize."

Finn shakes his head. "There's no need. Everything is fine now." He finally looks away from Cale and rests his eyes on the nurse; his murder stare finally gone.

Kelli, as her badge says, nods with a tight smile. "Stay as long as you like and press the button if you need anything." She turns and quickly makes her way out of the room again.

I finish cleaning the crusted blood off of Cale's skin and as much as I could get out of his hair. I pick up the second washcloth and dry all of the spots I washed. Laying the bowl and washcloths on the table by his bed I lay my head next to Callum's body, taking deep breaths. I finally let myself feel the relief that he is alive. I'd never felt such fear before when I wasn't sure if he was alive in the car, and then such agony when I thought he was dead.

"Look at me, Red. Let me see those beautiful green eyes." Callum's rough voice shocks me and my head snaps up to meet his drowsy eyes. His smile is weak, and it takes the breath right out of my lungs. I seriously thought I'd never see his smile again, never hear his voice. God, I don't know what I would have done without him. "There she is."

"You almost died," I whisper, tears sliding down my face again.

He reaches across himself and holds his hand out for mine. "Outlaws never die, babe." I grab his hand, shaking my head. His hold on my hand is weak but it's there, he's here with me. "Are you okay?" His brows crease together and when I nod he lets out a sigh of relief. Callum brings my hand to his lips and kisses my knuckles, turning to face Finn he smiles again. "You want a kiss too, Finny?"

Finn laughs. "Yeah, big boy, come here." He leans into Callum with his lips puckered. Cale lets go of my hand to push him back and then he reaches for my hand again.

Keeping his eyes on Finn, "How's the Raptor?"

Finn slouches back into his chair, resting his feet on the bed next to Callum's. He scoffs. "Fucked." Callum sighs, his eyes closing briefly. "I'll get the prospects to find you a new one and have it at your house."

"Who hit us?" With every sentence, it seems that Callum is gaining more strength.

Finn crosses his feet at the ankles. "We can talk about it when you get home."

Callum glares at Finn. "Fuck off. I want to talk about it now."

Finn rolls his eyes. "Fine, grumpy. It was a hit-and-run. I got off of my bike and ran towards you guys and the van sped off."

"Did you tell the club to look for the van?" Callum stares at Finn.

Finn's eyes go wide. "No, fucker. I was too busy thinking you were fucking dead!"

I interject before Finn strangles Callum. "Yeah, you might have a damages bill for that wall in the hallway." Finn waves off my comment, clearly not concerned about paying for the hole in the wall.

31

REESE

After a while of the three of us sitting together, the doctor came in to tell us that Callum would be staying the night for observation and be released in the morning. Much to Callum's disagreement we were finally able to convince him to stay in bed and rest.

"That was a close call," Mason says as he drives me to Callum's townhouse to get a change of clothes.

I lean back into the seat, staring out of my window. "I know. I really thought I lost him. It put a lot of things into perspective."

Mason nods, staring out at the road. "Near-death experiences usually do." The accident and the emotional whirlwind are starting to kick in and the adrenaline is wearing off. "When Finn called us on the way to the hospital everyone lost their shit. Ronan and Saint are good at hiding their feelings, but you could tell they were about to break too."

I close my eyes. "I'm glad they stayed at the hospital with him."

Mason chuckles his happy personality back again. "I don't think you could pry Finn away from that room right now."

I laugh too, remembering Finn convincing the nurse to bring

in a cot for him and Huntley to bring his Xbox for him and Callum to play. "I know, I didn't want to leave either but I figured Cale and I needed clean clothes."

"You mean you didn't want Cale to go home in that sexy hospital gown with the open back?" Mason asks, barely hiding his amusement.

I grin imagining Callum's naked tattooed back walking away from the bed after we slept together the first time. "He does have a nice butt."

Mason makes a disgusted sound. "Okay, now I've heard enough!"

I laugh, the most honest laugh I've had all day. "What did you expect when you brought up the hospital gown?"

Mason chuckles next to me. "Yeah, I guess I did walk into that one."

With that, we pull into the driveway and quietly walk into the house, me using the key Callum had given me when I kind of moved in with him. Mason drops onto the couch while I go upstairs to take a shower, change, and pack clothes and toiletries for Callum. I'm walking down the stairs with a small overnight bag when there's a knock at the front door. I pause on the steps and Mason looks back at me confused.

"Are you expecting anyone?" He stands from the couch and peeks through the blinds on the bay window. I shake my head. "Stay there, let me get it." I sit on the steps, hidden behind the door and Mason.

Mason opens the door a small amount and I can hear a guy talking on the other side. "Hi! I have a delivery for Reese Thomas."

"From who?" Mason stands tall, his back straight and shoulders rigid.

The guy on the other side pauses. "Uh. Says a Mr. Thomas.

Called right as the shop was closing, but said these were important so I brought them by tonight." *My father?*

Mason's shoulders relax and he reaches out for something. "Okay thanks, man." He shuts the door and turns around with a bouquet of flowers in his hand. I walk down the rest of the steps and drop my bag at the bottom, meeting Mason by the door. He hands me the bouquet and I carry them into the kitchen while admiring them. A bouquet of white roses with one deep red dahlia in the middle.

"They're from your dad?" Mason asks while walking around the other side of the long kitchen island.

I stare at them quizzically, because why is he sending me flowers and how did he know where I was? I haven't told my parents about my stalker or temporarily moving in with Callum, I haven't even told them *about Callum.* "Yeah, I'm not sure why though."

He plucks something out of the arrangement and hands it to me. "Well here's a card."

Opening the card my heart stops in my chest and I immediately wish I could take back the last 48 hours.

> "YOU WEREN'T SUPPOSED TO BE IN THE CAR, REESEY.
> GET RID OF HIM OR THE NEXT ARRANGEMENT WILL BE
> FOR HIS FUNERAL."

Two sentences are all it takes to make my world crash in on itself. My stalker was the one who crashed into us today, and he did it intentionally. He did it to hurt Callum. Now he's sent this bouquet, pretending to be from my father, to force me to break up with Callum. The last few weeks flash before me and the pieces start to click together, this is the second time my stalker has hurt a man because of me

"Everything okay?" Mason snaps me out of my inner spiral.

My eyes flick up to his, clutching the card in my hands I shake my head to think of an excuse.

"Uh, yeah. Um…" Shit, I can't think when I'm being watched. "Why don't you take Callum the bag while I call my dad and then you can come back and take me to the hospital?"

Mason chuckles. "You're funny, Princess. I like my balls and my hands, and my eyes, and my life, which has all been threatened if I leave you alone again." He shrugs. "I'll just step outside and you can come out when you're ready to go."

I nod. "Okay, I'll just be a second."

Mason walks around the island smiling and towards the door. He picks up the overnight bag from beside the door and steps outside. What am I supposed to do? I have to tell them right? But if I do that then Callum and the club will one hundred percent go after my stalker harder than they already are. *But isn't that what I want?* Not if the cost is someone's life. Callum's face flashes through my mind. The crash, the nurse telling us he was dead, him laying in a hospital bed. Then his slate eyes when he stares into mine after sex, his ruffled blonde hair in the mornings, his long dark lashes fanning over his cheeks, his sweet smile with perfect white teeth. *No.* Then I see Finn. Him joking with Callum, the silent tear rolling down his perfect face in the ambulance, the pictures of him and his dad hanging in his dad's bar, the way he looks at Huntley like she hung the stars in the sky. *No.* Mason is next. His infectious smile and laugh, his witty banter, his ambitions of becoming a techie and a fully patched member of the club, us having dinner at my kitchen table, and him choking down my burnt food and still smiling like it was the best meal he's ever had. *I can't risk them.* I have to leave and I have to make it look like my idea. I have to make sure Callum won't fight for me.

I find a small notepad and a pen after searching through the drawers on the island. I scribble a short note, knowing that I won't be able to do this to his face. I tear up the card and throw it in the trash with the flowers, and then force myself up the stairs not knowing any other way to do this. I come back downstairs a few minutes later with all of my stuff packed and I carry them outside. Mason is sitting on the porch steps, scrolling through a girl's Instagram, but he quickly closes it before I can see the girl. He stands and slips his phone into his back pocket with a smirk on his face, when he sees my bags in my hands his head cocks and his brows scrunch together.

I look to the ground, not able to say this to his face. "I need you to take me home."

He pauses, confused I'm sure. "Uh, is all of that for the hospital?" He chuckles, typical sweet Mase. "I didn't think Cale needed his makeup and curling iron in the hospital."

I close my eyes, trying to hold back more tears. "I'm not going to the hospital and I'm not coming back."

The noise is sucked out of the atmosphere, I swear the light breeze completely stops, and you could hear a pin drop. "Oh shit." I see him move his weight around. "You're not gonna make me tell him right? He's gonna kick my ass, sling and all."

I exhale a heavy sigh. "No Mase, I left a note. It explains it all."

Mason gently takes the bags from my hands and sets them on the ground next to us. "Can he convince you to stay? Can I convince you? Reese, he's never let anyone in like he does with you."

Shaking my head violently so he'll stop talking, I whisper, "No. I have to go."

After a beat, Mason sighs and picks up the bags from the ground. "Okay. I'll have Leo come get the bag to take to the hospital and I'll tell him you're staying at your house tonight."

I finally look up at him and shake my head slightly. "You don't have to lie to the club for me."

Mason flings one bag over his shoulder and we walk towards his Chevy pickup. "If I don't, nothing is gonna be able to keep Cale in the hospital. Not even a 6'5" tattooed giant with resting bitch face." I want to laugh, but I know that will only make my tears spill over my eyes so I just nod and walk to the pickup. Not letting myself turn to look back at the townhouse and everything I'm leaving behind with it.

32

CALLUM

Finn shuffles into the room and kicks the door closed behind him with his boot. He sets a cup of water on the table beside my bed and slumps back onto the chair next to me. "Mase called and said Little Red is staying at her apartment tonight. Leo is bringing you some clothes."

I set the Xbox controller down and turn to face him. "Why is she staying there and not at my house?"

He shakes his head and shrugs. "I don't know man, she asked Mason to take her home." This is weird, she was fine when she left and said she would be coming right back. I have a bad feeling about this, we get into an accident and now she's skipping out and staying at her apartment, the same place that was broken into a few weeks ago. Something's not right. I sit up and swing my legs over the bed, slowly, very slowly because my body feels like it was hit by a truck… 'Cause you know, it fucking was. Finn's voice rings through the pain.

"What the fuck are you doing?" He looks at me like I'm dense.

I shake my head, still slowly trying to move my legs. "What's it look like, shithead? I'm going to see Reese."

He scoffs behind me. "The fuck you are. Sit your ass in bed and I'll call her."

Angry at my body and how much pain I'm in but also at the bossy asshole behind me I growl. "Fuck off."

Finn stomps to my side of the bed and stands beside me. "Motherfucker, I will goddamn sedate you. Sit your ass back and I will call her." I give up and sit back in bed because fucking ouch and I know he really will sedate me; I'm choosing my battles. He walks back over to the chair he has claimed as his and he pulls his phone out, dialing Reese on speaker phone.

The call rings for what feels like forever and then goes to voicemail. Feeling my heartbeat quickly fucking rising. "Call her again." Panic evident in my voice. He calls her again but the call rings through with no answer.

Before I can try getting up again he halts me. "Before your fucking heart explodes and the nurses rush in, let me call Mason." Mason picks up instantly.

"What's up, boss?" I can hear faint typing on his end of the line.

Finn sets the phone on the bed next to my legs and leans forward resting his elbows on his knees. "Where's Reese, she's not answering her phone."

The typing stops and I can hear my heart in my goddamn ears during the small pause he gives. "I'm outside in my truck and she went in a little bit ago. All of the lights are off, so I assumed she went to sleep. I can go knock though." I hear a car door open through the phone.

"No. It's fine. She had a crazy day, let her sleep." I rush before he gets to her door. He's right, she's sleeping. Her body always crashes after some crazy shit like today. "Why did she want to go home instead of stay at my house?" I ask the question that keeps nagging at the back of my mind. Call me insecure, but it feels like she's pushing me away.

Mason closes the car door on his side and then is quiet for another moment, a long moment. "She didn't say." *What the fuck?*

Before I can think about it any more Finn pipes in. "Miles finished replacing everything right?"

My head turns to face him again and I nod. "Yeah, locks have been replaced, code has been changed and the system has been upgraded, and the cameras are even more sensitive and alert when there is any type of movement now."

More typing on Mase's end. The guy is always messing with his tablet or his laptop, but he really is learning a lot from Miles. "I'm almost done with the block for Reese's phone so it can't be copied again, and so far it hasn't been."

I sigh, deciding that she's safe at her apartment tonight with Mason since I can't really do anything else from where I am. "Fine, I'll be over in the morning."

"Got it, brother. See you then." Mason hangs up and Finn takes his phone back, and the gaming controller with it.

"Chill the fuck out, she's fine. Now, what do you want to watch since you can't game with one arm, gimpy?" We both laugh and I flip him off with my good arm.

33

CALLUM

I'M CAREFULLY PULLING MY BLACK T-SHIRT OVER MY HEAD WHEN Nurse Kelli pushes a wheelchair into my room. Finn trailing behind her with his shit-eating grin. "Kelli, you better turn that shit around. I'm walking out of here." I grab my bag of belongings off of the table next to my bed, luckily the paramedics were able to preserve my patches but not so much my cut. The scrapes of it are in the giant ziplock along with my wallet, beat-to-hell phone, and useless Raptor keys.

Nurse Kelli rolls her eyes, completely used to Finn and I's attitudes. Finn and I convinced her to join us in my room last night for pizza and a round of COD. She kicked Finn's ass and I will never let him live that down. She said she has three boys at home and she sometimes plays with them. "You're no fun, grumpy gills." She parks the wheelchair outside of the door and steps aside to let Finn through.

"Look what I got!" Finn sings while dangling car keys from his finger.

"Already?" I ask while slipping on my tennis shoes.

Finn hands me the keys to my new Raptor since the previous one will definitely be totaled. "Saint and Wyatt went to pick it up last night in Seattle. Brand new, white just like the last one, but with red stitching inside."

"Why did Saint go?" I ask while slipping the keys into the pockets of my gray sweats.

Finn shrugs and grabs my bag of stuff. "He said he couldn't just sit in the waiting room all night, he needed to do something." He stares at the cut up leather with a sad expression. "The new one's already on its way, brother. We're glad you're in one piece though." He looks at me with a sad smile.

Nurse Kelli hugs us both as we exit the hallway and round into the waiting room. Cheers and whoops ring out loudly, all of my brothers, plus Wyatt, Leo, and Jack all stand in the waiting room, Ronan's old ass holding a small teddy bear and an "It's A Girl!" balloon. He makes his way to us first. "I'm glad you're okay, kid. I don't know what we would have done without our three muskerfucks." We both laugh at his name for me, Finn, and Saint.

"Thanks for the balloon." I point up to the pink balloon floating above us.

"Anytime." He smirks at me. Old motherfucker, not really all that old but we like to tease him, is always joking around; even though most people see him as the hardass president. He says we deal with too much shit on the daily and he likes to bring light into serious situations, needless to say, he and Finn get along fucking great!

Saint steps around Ronan and claps me on the back. "Good to have you back, brother." Aw that was nice. "But next time you scare us like that I'll put you in the hospital myself." And there's our grumpy VP. The complete opposite of Ronan, yet they make the perfect pair. Grumpy or not, Saint is a goddamn great friend and with me and Finn, we make the perfect threesome. I love every single one of the men in this club, including the prospects, this is my family and they've treated me better than anyone ever has, even my own blood.

I look around, the only people missing are Reese and Mason. As if reading my mind, Finn nudges me. "Go get your girl."

Hell yeah, that's what I needed to hear. "Gotta shower first, brother. I can't go over there looking like this." Finn shakes his head as we all walk outside and Finn and I get into his Hellcat so he can take me home to my girl.

———————

I'VE ALWAYS LOVED my townhouse, it's the only place I've ever lived on my own. Going straight from my parent's house into the clubhouse when they kicked me out. My Raptor was the first thing I bought with the money I was making from the club, and then I started renting the townhouse after I started CM Roofing. Even though I love being alone in my own space, this place has been so much better with Reese around.

I walk through the front door and immediately smell Reese's perfume in the air. I'm sure no one else can smell it, but it just lingers in the air all of the time since she moved in. Moving through the living room and into the kitchen I toss my giant ziplock bag onto the counter and go to reach for the refrigerator door when I notice a piece of paper on the island with Red's perfect script. Pulling out a bottle of water I open it and take a long sip while reaching for the note.

"TODAY PUT EVERYTHING INTO PERSPECTIVE FOR ME. I CAN'T DO THIS ANYMORE, I'M SORRY."

What the fuck? I set the bottle of water on the counter and rush up the stairs, taking three at a time, and to my bedroom. Pulling open the drawers I cleared out for Reese, I find them empty. Same with the spot in the closet that held her clothes and the organizer with her shoes. I hurry into the attached bathroom in complete shock to, of course, find all of her makeup and toiletries gone as well. I run back down the stairs and jump into my Raptor, like literally leap, ignoring Finn waiting for me in his car.

"Your dick can wait, you're not supposed to be driving!" He yells out of his driver's window laughing. I wish I was hurrying to Red's house to get my dick wet, but he didn't see the note, he has no idea. He backs out of my driveway and goes in the opposite direction of me. I don't care, I break every speed limit on the way to her apartment. There is no way in hell she is leaving me with just a fucking Post-It note on my goddamn counter. She said she thought I was dead and this is what she wants to do? What the fuck got put into perspective that she needed to pack all of her shit and leave when I wasn't around? When I pull in front of her building, not even worrying about parking in an actual spot, I bypass Mason's truck and stomp straight for the door. I'm panicking by the time I make it to her apartment, but I take a deep breath before I knock on her door. After what feels like an eternity she finally opens the door, but only enough to talk to me, not let me inside. She looks sad and tired, her green eyes red and dim, not vibrant like they normally are. Her long red hair is pulled into a bun on top of her head and she's wearing an oversized sweater and shorts.

I try to stay calm, not show her how much I'm freaking out inside. "What's going on, babe? What the fuck is up with that note?"

She stares down at her feet, only looking up at me every few breaths, and never into my eyes. "The accident put everything into perspective for me, Callum—"

I interrupt her before she can say anything else. "Put what into perspective for you?"

"I don't want whatever it is that you want." She takes a long breath and my heart stops beating. The only thing I can focus on is what she's saying. "We were moving too fast and I don't want to do it anymore."

I can feel my heart shattering in my chest, my stomach clenches and makes me want to puke right here on her welcome mat. Caught completely off guard with this entire morning I still ask questions, not completely sure what's going on. "You moved in with me." I trail off.

"For my safety," she whispers. "I'm sorry you developed feelings for me, Callum, but I told you from the beginning that this was just sex."

She softly closes the door and everything seems to hit me at once. I turn to leave, but I can't go. I slide to the ground with my back against her door. "Please don't do this, Red," I beg, I fucking beg! My ass on the ground, knees bent, with one elbow resting on them and the other clutched to my stomach in my sling. Being hunched over like this kills my ribs but I don't have the strength to sit up any better. I rest my head in my hand; I'm begging the woman I swore not to fall in love with to please open the door and tell me she loves me. Minutes pass with just silence, the only sound is my ragged breathing. She never opens the door. I finally realize that I can't make her love me, no matter how badly I want it or how much I beg her to talk to me. So I pick myself and what is left of my fucking dignity up and I leave.

Before I start my truck and drive home I walk over to Mason. He rolls down the window as I approach, his iPad in his lap. "You knew?" It came out as a question, but we both know I already knew the answer. He sheepishly looks into his lap, avoiding my eyes.

"I couldn't tell you while you were stuck in the hospital without a way to fight for her, brother. I'm sorry." I can tell in his voice that he means it. Mason isn't like the rest of us, he has a romantic side to him that wanted Reese and me to make it. Not only that but I know he loves both of us individually as well as together.

I sigh, not actually angry with him. Just curious because I was honestly blindsided by Reese's note and now this. "I'll send Jack to get some food for you. Keep watch here and if anything feels off or you see something, get her to my house immediately." He nods, biting the inside of his cheek. "Let her know that she can take my townhouse, I'll move into the clubhouse so she can have it to herself."

I shake my head and turn to walk away, still not mentally accepting what the fuck has happened today, I can't even call it a breakup because we weren't *actually* in a relationship; not officially at least.

Mason's voice cuts through my thoughts. "What if she doesn't want us here anymore?" He calls from his seat.

I turn around a few steps away from the truck. "Then sit further away. I'm not risking her life just because she doesn't want to be with me." He nods and rolls up his window as I walk back to my Raptor. I sit in the seat with the engine rumbling underneath me. I take one last look at Reese's apartment; I'm leaving my entire fucking heart in that apartment. To hell with it anyways, it never did me any good.

34

REESE

I sit on the floor of my apartment with my ear pressed to the door and listen to Callum's pleas and his breathing for forty-five minutes. When I hear the rumble of his Raptor I drop my head to my bent knees and break out into sobs. I wanted to take back the hurtful things I said to him, none of it was true.

35

CALLUM

When I roll up to my house I see Saint's bike and Finn's Hellcat parked in my driveway. I pull up beside them and get out. Walking to my house I find my brothers making themselves comfortable like they normally do. "NUMB" by Chri\$tian Gate\$ plays on my sound system while Finn is slouching on the couch with his hat on backward, and Saint and Leo are in both armchairs, with Saint's feet kicked up on the ottoman. They all get quiet and turn to look at me when I walk through the door.

Finn is the first one to speak up. "Mason called, we thought you could use these." He holds up handles of Wild Turkey and Jack Daniels.

"And this." Leo raises a handle of Titos.

I shake my head, a small smile appearing on my face. Leave it to my brothers to be able to help me when I most need it. I look over at Saint. "What did you bring, asshole? Or did you think you could just sit here with your dirty boots on my furniture?"

Saint laughs and holds up a normal-sized bottle of Grey Goose. "I didn't bring enough to share if I'm going to have to watch you cry into Finn's lap."

I deftly drop onto the tan leather couch next to Finn and take the Wild Turkey from him with my good arm. "Oh that's right, I forgot you like the prissy shit." I take a giant gulp, feeling the whiskey burn in my stomach.

Saint shakes his head and pours his vodka into a short tumbler. "I just have taste buds."

"You know it's only ten AM, right?" I gesture with the bottle to Finn.

He turns his head toward me, his eyes see right through my banter, they all do. They know I'm putting on a front, trying to pretend that I'm not completely destroyed inside. "You wanna be sober today?" *You got me there, brother.*

I slowly nod, agreeing with his reasoning. I hold the bottle up to his and we clink the giant handles of liquor together. "Fair enough." We both take long pulls from our bottles and Finn clears his throat after his.

He pulls a gun from the inside pocket of his cut. "Jack and Leo were able to save this from the Raptor." He hands me Red— Reese's gun.

I sigh and bite the inside of my cheek. "Thanks." I take the gun from him and toss it onto the ottoman.

"This doesn't go down as well as that shit Sebastian Segreto gave us." He rubs his chest with his left hand. I notice a fresh "H" tattooed on his ring finger. Good for him, but fuck him right now. I choose to ignore the new tattoo for now and ask when I'm a little less testy about women.

"I haven't even tried it," I admit, looking over to the bar cart by the sliding backdoor, where the bottle is sitting displayed.

Finn chuckles. "Let's keep with the cheap shit today, brother. That stuff doesn't deserve to be used for drowning your sorrows."

After some more pulls from our bottles with Saint using a glass because he's too good to drink straight from the bottle. Our conversations range from bikes to cars, to what bars we need to go to tonight, then to food because we're all getting hungry. The hurt is still definitely there but stings a little less with my buzz and my brothers' company. Saint pulls out his phone and answers a call, our conversations continuing in the background. Finn laughing loudly at Leo's dumbass ideas to earn his top rocker. The kid is barely twenty-one, which in truth is only four years younger than us, but he still seems like such a naive kid sometimes.

"Yeah, Ro, you're on speaker." That sentence gets all of our attention, and we quickly stop talking and turn toward the phone that Saint is placing in the middle of all of us on the black tufted ottoman.

"Are you sober enough? I just need a minute." Ronan's gruff voice comes through the phone speaker.

Finn leans forward, placing the bottle on the floor beside his feet and resting his elbows on his knees. "Yeah, Prez, we're good. What's going on?"

"Richards just called, said that the murder of Michelle Davis is being ruled as gang related. The FBI is looking into all of the organizations in the state. It shouldn't affect us, but we need to lay low just the same," Ronan says.

"Who's Michelle Davis?" Leo's dumbass cuts in and Finn and I laugh at him.

Saint rolls his eyes. "Senator Buxley Daivs' wife, you idiot." He rubs his eyes and then holds out his hands and squints at Leo. "Do you even watch the news?"

I interrupt the argument before Saint can lecture Leo on his knowledge of current events, or I guess the lack of. "So going back to Miles' call the day of the accident. You guys didn't find anything at the address he sent me?" I got very vague details at the hospital but I wanted to know everything now that I wasn't on pain meds, well not as much, and everyone was here.

"So," Saint answers for Ronan. "We went but it was an abandoned house. Been empty for years, kids go there to drink and get high. We called Miles and he said that the signal was probably bouncing around to make it look like it was coming from there."

"What the fuck?" I drop my head onto the back of the couch. "We're running in fucking circles."

"He just has to slip up once and we got him, brother," Leo says gently.

I shake my head. "Yeah but that requires him to keep doing shit," I snap.

"You know he's going to though, he's not just going to grow bored of her." Ronan, ever the voice of reason. A lighter sparks on his end of the phone. "What were the results of the blood on her wall."

"Uh." I blink a few times, trying to clear my head. "Human, just like we thought."

"Are you gonna tell the Princess?" Ronan asks, everyone else quiet as a mouse.

I bite my lip, thinking of the decision I've already made. "No. I found out the day of the accident and I was going to but then everything happened. I think it's best not to freak her out with that now."

Trying to lighten the mood Finn asks. "We having a party tonight, Prez?"

Ronan lets out a sound like he's exhaling smoke. "Yup. Already got the bartenders and strippers booked from Second."

"Perfect." Leo smirks from the armchair.

Saint and I shake our heads, but Finn bellows, loving Leo's promiscuity. "Brother, you're gonna catch something fucking with all of them strippers." Ronan chuckles through the phone.

36

REESE

"You can't tell anyone, Al," I say after I finish telling Allie everything that's happened.

She blows out a breath and runs her fingers through her blonde hair. "I don't understand why you won't just tell him what's going on, Reese."

I shake my head, tears threatening to spill over at the reminder of what's happened. "Because he'll try to fix it and get hurt again. This way he stays away from me and when the club figures out who's behind it then I can come clean with him."

"But what if he doesn't want to hear you out after this is over? And what if something else happens and he's not here?" She counters, turning on the couch to look at me.

"It's not worth his life, Al, and nothing else is going to happen as long as I stay away from him. My stalker is threatened by other guys."

She scoffs. "Yeah, 'cause he's a fucking perv."

I interrupt her rant because everything that she's asking and saying is things that I've already gone over a million times in my head. I hate being without Callum. He was the only thing keeping me sane and being without him now feels like a part of me is missing, but I cannot have anything happen to him. My stalker isn't messing around, he's not playing pranks on us. He's messing with people's lives and he's not afraid to hurt people. I would rather Callum hate me and be alive than love me from a grave. "Can we just watch movies and eat a ton of ice cream? You were supposed to come over and help me, not make me feel worse."

Allie frowns and sighs. "Shit you're right, I'm sorry, Reese. Which flavor do you want?" She stands and walks into my kitchen and to the freezer.

"Cherry Garcia, no bowl. Just bring the whole thing," I say, sliding down so I'm laying on the fluffy white couch, picking up the remote and turning on 365 Days. Allie grins devilishly and brings two tubs of ice cream into the living room, handing me mine and getting comfortable next to me with hers.

I really hope Callum will listen to me when this is all over. I hope he will believe me. First, I have to figure out who my stalker is.

"Okay." Allie starts. "Let's start from the first note and go from there."

37

CALLUM

"Slide" by Chase Atlantic booms through the speakers in Purgatory. The red LEDs are the only lighting in the room as the stripper spins around on the main pole, flipping upside down and pulling her legs into the splits. It's a true club party tonight with the clubhouse completely filled. Girls are walking around with their tits out and people are fucking wherever they can get their pants down. Okay not everywhere, mostly outside and in the rooms upstairs if they have the key to a room. Hell, there's even a stripper riding someone's cock in a chair across the room from us. I'm sitting with Jack, Leo, and Saint. Jack's barely paying attention to any of the girls like he normally does, his blonde hair is hanging in his eyes as he stares down at his phone and his sharp jaw is set. Leo is sitting with Jessica on his lap, periodically kissing her neck and staring at her fake tits. And Saint is slouched in his chair next to me constantly checking his phone like some heartbroken bitch, or like me. The only reason I'm not doing the same fucking thing is that I left my phone at home so I *couldn't* do it. After the millionth time, I've finally had it. "Just go fucking call her." I lean over the arm of my chair and yell over the music.

My voice startles him and he looks up at me. "What?" He asks like he didn't just hear me.

"Go call her, whoever she is," I repeat. Finn and I have noticed him being a little fidgety recently, checking his phone a lot more than usual.

Saint shakes his head and yells back. "She's busy tonight."

I scoff. It's not often we're turned down, which is probably why our egos are so damn huge. "Who the fuck says no to Saint fucking Viotto?"

He chuckles, taking a sip of his vodka. "She had other obligations."

"Fuck her then!" Alcohol makes me a little more careless than normal. I left buzzed a long time ago and am heading straight for blacking out.

Saint smirks. Purely fucking evil. "That's what I'm trying to do."

I side-eye him, suddenly not in the mood to talk about pussy anymore. "Fuck you."

Saint laughs and sets his glass down on the table in front of us. "Stop sulking and just take Sasha home."

Just as he says that Sasha steps onto the small stage and "Grind On Me" by Pretty Ricky starts to play. She sways as she walks, her long legs swinging her slim hips. The red lights reflect off of her beautiful skin and her shiny bra and matching thong. Every guy in the room turns to watch as she takes the stage and completely ignores the pole choosing to do floor work instead. Sasha is a phenomenal dancer, having trained since she was younger. She's not like the other girls at The Second Circle, she's just trying to make a living to open up her own dance studio. She drops to her hands and knees, pressing her chest to the floor. Then she rolls so she's laying down, arching her back with one hand laying over her pussy and the other moving from her mouth and sliding down her torso. Never once does she break eye contact with me. I guess she still has that crush on me. I watch a little longer and when she turns and stands, bending over completely, balancing with one hand on the floor and the other covering her pussy again, I stand and toss five hundred dollar bills at her and flick her a kiss. The beat drops and she stands, watching me as I walk out of Purgatory. Well, walking is more of a stretch, I definitely stumbled out, almost bumping into the wall as I got out of the door.

You know how you don't really realize how drunk you are until you stare into the bathroom mirror? That's how I feel right now while I awkwardly try to wash my hands. Being drunk and in a sling are not two things that mix well. The room starts to sway and I lean my forehead against the cool mirror which helps in cooling myself down. I don't even realize someone else is in here until I'm being turned around and pushed into the wall. Lips crash into mine and a hand sneaks under my shirt. *Why aren't her hands around my neck? Whatever.* My eyes are still closed but I know this is Reese. My girl came back to me. "I missed you, Red." I sigh when her mouth moves to my neck. I run my hand up her body from her under her butt, along her side, and end on the side of her face. Her body doesn't feel the same, her hips are more narrow, her torso longer, her jaw sharper.

Reese chuckles, but it sounds too throaty to be from her. "I'm not that little redhead you brought around last time, Cale." Ah hell, it's Sasha. My eyes snap open and the chubby I was starting to sport immediately goes down; well I guess that takes care of that.

I take her hands off of my chest and gently push her a step back. "I can't, Sash."

Sasha looks at me, I mean genuinely looks at me. "She really did a number on you, huh?"

I push my hair out of my eyes and look at my boots. "Yeah,

she fucking did."

Sasha nods, we've always been friends. Hooked up a few times and I know she started feeling something for me, but always friends before anything else. "Okay. Call me if you need a distraction."

I lean down and kiss her cheek. "You know I will, babe." I step around her and walk out of the bathroom and into my old room; crossing through the room to the door.

I step out and hear Finn and Huntley talking in the hall a few doors down from me. Finn's back is turned towards me and neither of them sees me walk up, so I catch a part of their conversation.

"Finn, this is not what he needs right now." Huntley snaps at Finn. "Hooking up with random strippers isn't going to fix anything."

Finn sighs and drags his hand down his face. His voice is different when he's with Huntley, softer, kinder. "I know it's not, Angel, but it will at least make him feel better for tonight."

By that time I'm right behind Finn and I can see his big hand on her thin waist and her with her arms crossed and shaking her head while she glares up at Finn. I rest my hand on Finn's shoulder, more for balance than for friendship but that's beside the point. "Take me home."

He turns, shocked to see me I assume. "What about Sasha?"

I shake my head. "I can't."

Huntley steps forward. "I'll take you home, Callum." I nod and we start for the stairs. When I start to sway Huntley and Finn put their arms around me and help me out to Huntley's car.

The last thing I remember before waking up in my bed alone is sliding into her front seat and Finn buckling my seatbelt. I close my eyes and lay my head back against the headrest, "Please Don't Go" by Joel Adams plays through the car speakers. "You'll get through this, brother," Finn says next to my ear before pulling away and shutting the door.

38

REESE

It's weird how much can change in one month. I started April being friends with Callum, and now in May we don't even speak. I haven't seen him in over a week. Since I moved home I started going back into the office. It's been nice to have my old routines back and to see my residents and the maintenance guys. No matter how busy the day gets though, my mind always drifts back to Callum. His broken pleas through the door, his easy smile. It breaks my heart every time. I miss him so much. I feel like a part of me is gone, like I'm walking around looking for something that isn't there anymore. I still take meals out to the guys surveilling outside, but they don't really talk to me anymore. I think they're scared I'll send them away. Honestly some days I think I should, they're a reminder of Callum too. Mason still comes in to eat dinner with me, though not as often as he used to. He says he's working on tracking down my stalker who has been radio silent; I guess because he got what he wanted: me alone. The first week drug on, and once I got into a routine the days went by almost like I'm reliving the same day over and over, just going through the motions. Allie, Sophie, and Emma come by in the evenings when they aren't busy, and they usually stay until I fall asleep, making sure to turn on the alarm when they sneak out. The only thing that's getting me through is the nights that Allie and I try to put clues together to figure out who's behind the letters and threats. So far we haven't gotten very far. We thought it might be my ex for a while, but he seems pretty happy with his new girlfriend. Tonight Mason invited me out to go get dinner and eat it in his pickup. I think he was tired of my cooking and wanted to get a change of scenery. It's silent while we wait for our food at the little drive-in diner.

"What's the name of this song?" I ask when I've had enough of the silence.

"Uh." He looks at his phone. "'After Hours' by Charlieonafriday. It's good right?"

I take in the soft melody. "Yeah, I really like the beat."

Mason taps the back button on his phone and the song plays again. "Yeah, I heard it at Cal—." My breathing halts at the mention of Callum's name and he immediately stops talking and looks at me out of the corner of his eye.

We haven't spoken about Callum since the day Mason helped move me home. I shouldn't, but I really want some sort of information about him. "Go ahead."

Mason shifts in his seat, looking down at his hands in his lap. "I heard it at Callum's. He's been listening to it a lot."

When the waitress brought our food out I went to Spotify and downloaded the song.

We eat mostly in silence and when I'm done I pull my legs into the chair and wrap my arms around them, Mason sighs into his phone and I look over at him. "What's up?"

"Nothing," he sighs again. "Just Jessica."

I raise my eyebrows. "You're still seeing her?"

"Sometimes." Mase puts his phone in the cupholder between us and slides down in the driver's seat a little.

"Is it getting serious?" I ask, turning in my seat to face him.

He scoffs, shaking his head. "No."

"Then why are you still seeing her?" I lean my back against the window behind me.

Mason turns his head to look at me, resting it on the head-rest. "Because she's easy."

"Mason Underwood!" I scold.

He chuckles. "Not like that." He pauses. "Well, yeah like that too, but I mean she understands when I have to cancel or dip early for club shit. She doesn't try to change me or control me. She's there when I want her and gone when I don't."

I nod because his reasoning does make sense. He's always busy doing something for the club and I could see someone thinking he could do better. He has a computer science degree from a great university and could do anything but he chose the club instead.

"Honestly I wish I could find something like what you and Cale had." His confession jolts me from my thoughts.

I shake my head, my thoughts then drifting back to Callum and fresh tears threatening to fall. "We didn't have anything that special, Mason," I lie.

His unique green eyes lock onto mine and I can tell he's thought about this a lot. "Yes, you did. You two were it for each other. You still could be if circumstances were different, I guess."

Too choked up to say anything else I say, "You'll find who you're supposed to be with too, Mase."

He bites the inside of his lip, still deep in thought. "Maybe."

39

———

CALLUM

I wish I could still live without my heart. I don't need it anyway, it doesn't do anything good for me. After Kaity cheated on me it hurt for months. Day in and day out it felt like fucking heartburn until slowly the burn eased into nothing and eventually that's all I felt: nothing. I went a long time with it not feeling anything; just pumping blood. Fucking nothing, just sitting there. Reese came along and my heart finally started fucking doing something again; it started beating for her. Then she left and she took it with her, and now all I'm left with is a constant tightening feeling in my chest. It's hard to breathe, every fucking day it's a struggle to breathe.

My pounding headache wakes me and I know it's one of those headaches that won't go away until I get up and do something about it. I roll over and sit on the edge of the bed, dragging my hands down my face to clear some of the fog from my brain. I flick on the bedside lamp because the blackout shades have made it completely dark in here and I can't see a damn thing. Honestly, I don't even know if it's day or night. After sitting with my head in my hands for way too long, I finally get up and take a shower. I can smell the alcohol bleeding from my pores and it's making me nauseous. I grab my new cut off of the chair beside the door and slide it on over my gray tee shirt. I was able to stop wearing the sling a few days ago and it feels great to be able to dress easily and move like normal, even if my ribs are still a little sore sometimes. I walk down the stairs of the clubhouse hoping I can convince someone to make me some food and find me the Tylenol.

I'm at the bar eating my breakfast and sipping on some whiskey to hopefully clear up this hangover when Saint takes the barstool next to mine.

"Mason told me you're staying here." Well hello to you too, asshat.

I roll my eyes and take another sip. "I can't go home." I actively avoid looking at his cocky face.

"Why?" He sets his keys and phone on the bartop in front of himself.

"Every room I walk into smells like her; she's just fucking everywhere." I had to leave, I wallowed in my self pity for a few days and then my sadness turned into rage and I almost destroyed everything in my townhouse. I've been staying at the clubhouse since, drinking all night and sleeping most of the day. I know I need to clean my act up, my company can't stay in the hands of my office manager for much longer.

Saint sighs. "You're Callum fucking Moran, Sergeant at Arms for the Devil's Outlaws. Clean the fuck up and remember who the fuck you are. You don't cry over some bitch."

That gets my attention. I turn to look at him and glare at his stupid fucking face. "Call her a bitch again and I'll cut your tongue out."

Saint's face breaks into the biggest shit eating grin. "Good to know you're still in there somewhere." We laugh, breaking the tension that has been hanging over me for weeks. I might be in the shittiest mood, but I love this man. He looks down at my first meal of the day. "Why are you eating a grilled cheese?" He scrunches his nose in disgust. Of course, the prince doesn't eat grilled cheese sandwiches.

I take a bite of my sandwich. "It's all Tracey knows how to make."

He cocks his head, still staring at my sandwich. "Is it good?"

I finish off my small glass of whiskey. "Not at all." We break into laughs again.

Saint grabs his keys and phone off of the bar. "Come on, let's go to Big Dawgs. Randy will make you something edible."

I take another look at the pitiful sandwich, it really was terrible and Randy is a great cook. I push the plate away and stand from the bar. " Tracey, your grilled cheese was shit!" I half-heartedly yell into the kitchen.

"Fuck off, Cale!" Tracey screams from the kitchen as Saint and I are about to walk out of the front door.

40

REESE

A FEW MORE DAYS HAVE PASSED WITHOUT ANY PROGRESS IN finding my stalker. We've had the notes and my apartment examined for fingerprints, but that led to dead ends. Now Mason and Miles are scanning through my cameras to see if there was any activity we may have missed. Maybe the cameras caught him lurking around the building or maybe he didn't completely cut everything from when he broke in. We're hoping for some sort of mistake, but combing the cameras from my house, the stop lights surrounding my complex is a very slow process. Since Mason and Miles have been working together, Jack, Leo, and Wyatt have split his shifts to watch over me. Tonight is Leo's turn, but Mason is coming over for dinner so I invited Leo to come along as well. I made a really great kielbasa pasta dish that I found online. It's really great but honestly, I'd rather be eating ice cream.

"Holy shit, Princess. This is actually good." Leo says through a mouthful of pasta and sausage.

I glare across the table at him. "Wow thanks, Leo." Mase and Leo laugh at my expense, bringing me out of my head and back into the moment. It's been great seeing my friends more often since I ended things with Callum, but these boys just have a way of making their way into your heart and making everything feel like it'll be okay for a few hours. I think it's the bond they share with one another. They devote their lives to the club and would do anything for each other; sometimes it feels like they feel that way about me too. Trying to keep the mood light, I try to think of something I can talk to Leo about; we've never really talked that much before. "How's the blonde?" It was the first thing that came to mind and I immediately feel like an idiot for bringing up the girl they are both sleeping with.

"Which one?" Leo smirks as he lifts the beer bottle to his lips.

Well, I guess I'm stuck riding this conversation out. "The short one with big boobs?" I try.

Leo shakes his head. "Nope. Still doesn't narrow that down."

Oh God, what have I gotten myself into? My cheeks flush. "Um. You and Mase were both with her at the clubhouse party that I went to." Why am I still trying?

"Jessica is fine. Stop making Reese uncomfortable, Leo." Mase finally interjects, laughing.

Leo chuckles and I can see why he apparently has a horde of short blondes, he has a boyish charm that reminds you of that bad boy in high school that your parents didn't want you to date. His confidence and smirk are going to get him in too deep one of these days. "I guess your type is blondes too?" I raise one eyebrow, refusing to let Leo's charm shake me.

A roguish smile spread across his face and I know he's about to say something perverted. "Nah." He shakes his head. "Daddy issues."

Mason barks a laugh and almost chokes on the drink he just took, while I internally facepalm myself. I know he's only a few years younger than Mason and I, but he makes me feel so old in the sense that I would not be able to keep up with this kid. His wit and confidence make him a perfect fit for The Devil's Outlaws, especially with Finn... and even Callum.

After dinner Mase and Leo load the dishwasher. Mason always insists on cleaning up when I cook for him, and I guess Leo has some manners under all of his cocky smiles because he started to help without any thought. I'm sitting on the couch, watching them over the counter when my phone vibrates on the arm of the couch.

UNKNOWN:

Attachment: 1 Video

What is this? I look up at the boys. They're laughing, Leo trying to whip Mason with a hand towel while Mason is rinsing dishes at the sink. Mason picks up his long leg to keep Leo at a distance. I look back down to my phone, swiping it unlocked to see what the video is. The message is from a number I don't recognize, I check to make sure the guys aren't watching me while I turn down my sound and click on the video.

The video is dark and I have to make sure my brightness is turned up. It looks like dark boots walking through grass, and then the camera pans up and a building and some light come into view. It looks like a window, the light shining over the top of the curtains and through a small gap in the middle like they weren't closed all the way. The phone gets closer to the window and that's when my heart drops into my stomach. Allie is standing in front of a bed, in a sports bra and thong, pulling sweat pants up her short legs. She grabs a shirt off of the bed and that's when I notice my comforter. Before I can recover my breath, a long hunting knife with a wicked looking point waves in front of the window and camera, then the video abruptly cuts off. Panicked and angry, I text the number back.

REESE:

What do you want? I already did what you
wanted and broke up with Callum.

I place my phone down. My stalker recorded Allie changing in my room one of the nights she stayed with me. I'm trying to remember what she wore on which nights she stayed here so I can place him here on a certain night. My phone vibrates in my hands and I drop it to my lap like it's on fire when I see another message from the unknown number. In truth I didn't think I would get a response, all of our communication has been physical messages from him without a way for me to reply.

UNKNOWN:

There's a package waiting for you by the
dumpsters. Better hurry.

I drop my phone on the couch and walk into the kitchen and grab the bag of trash from the trash can in the small pantry. I've seen too many scary movies with body parts in boxes and the video of Allie has me thinking it has to do with her. Ignoring the guy's conversation, I walk straight to the back door and once I'm outside I sprint to the giant trash bins behind my building. I toss the bag in, half full and not even tied shut. I look around the dumpsters, not seeing anything in the dark. I shouldn't have left my phone, I could have used the flashlight.

"Reese, run!" Mason screams. My spine snaps straight at the sound and I see Mason running towards me while a black van that was parked next to the dumpsters speeds away; the tires squealing. Before I can move, Mason reaches me and pulls my hand to drag me back with him. We run back around the building and into my apartment. Mason pushes me into the hallway and to the floor while he barks at Leo to check the locks and set the alarm. I stand back up and slowly step out from behind the wall of the hallway and into the living room. Mason is scrolling on his phone, looking for a number I can only assume is Callum's.

I'm not sure if there was really a package or if it was just a ruse, but I need to know for sure, nothing else matters right now. "Mason. He left a package." My voice is weak, distant.

"What?" He looks up from his phone, his eyes are wild, his chest quickly rising and falling with his heavy breathing.

I step more into the living room and to the couch, picking up my phone. "My stalker sent me a video and said he left me a package by the dumpster." I offer my phone to him. He looks to Leo, who is leaning against the wall in the dining room, peeking out of the curtains of the big window, and angles his head toward the back door that I ran out of earlier. Leo nods and walks towards the door, he disables my alarm and unlocks the door, but before he opens it he pulls a gun from the inside of his cut and pulls back the slide, cocking it. He opens the door and quietly walks out, closing the door behind him. While I'm staring at the spot Leo just left, stunned by what just almost happened and the sight of Leo pulling a gun from his vest, Mason takes my phone and walks to stand at the back door. He stares at my phone with a hard expression on his face and then taps a few things on the screen, he tosses it onto the couch next to me before he opens the door for Leo and then locks it again behind him, turning on the alarm once more.

"There wasn't a package anywhere," Leo says, slipping the gun into his waistband behind his back.

I shake my head, grabbing my phone to look at the message again. "There has to be."

Mason walks over to me and rests his hands against my arms, leaning down to look into my eyes. "He said that to get you outside and take you, Reese. He knew we were both in here and wanted to get you outside and alone." Mason's eyes probe mine, probably wondering why I'm not crying in the corner from this near miss.

Just as I'm about to suggest Leo go look again, my phone vibrates in my hand. Mason and I both look down at my phone, and his hands tighten against my forearms at the name.

UNKNOWN:

1 New Message

With a sigh, I slide my thumb across the message to open it, keeping the phone low so Mason can see it too.

UNKNOWN:

I won't stop until you are mine and mine alone, and your time is running out, Reesey.

Holding back tears I look into Mason's sincere blue-green eyes. "Take me to Callum."

41

REESE

I step off of the back of Mason's bike, pulling down my short jean shorts that had ridden up my thighs and smoothing out my brick red v-neck shirt. A deep bass thumps out of the clubhouse and I look around the gated compound. There aren't as many cars and bikes as there were at the last club party, but definitely quite a few. I turn to look at Mase as he walks up beside me, pulling his hood back up over his head. "Is there a party tonight?"

He looks down at me and shakes his head. "Not that I was aware of."

We walk into the clubhouse side by side and I look around to take in the sight. Immediately, the scent of cleaning products hit my nose, a much welcome improvement from the last time I was here. The lights are bright and a few girls are walking around in their push-up bras and little leather shorts. Saint's gaze flicks up to us as we walk in. He leans over to the pretty brunette sitting next to him and whispers into her ear, smirking. A few tables and chairs are pushed aside to make room for a tattoo bed with Saint sitting in a rolling chair next to it, my eyes stop on who is laying on the bed. Callum, shirtless and face down, his arms crossed under his cheek as he faces Saint on the other side of him. My heart stops at the sight of him. I haven't seen him since the day he came to my apartment and I told him I didn't want anything to do with him. He looks good from what I can see of his muscled back and the back of his head, his hair is messy like he hasn't styled it, only showered and run his fingers through it a few times. It takes everything in me to not run over to him and hang onto his back like a koala, swearing to never let go again. The girl next to Saint picks up a phone on the rolling cart next to him and the song playing loudly through the large speakers abruptly changes to "F*CK YOU, GOODBYE" by The Kid LAROI and Machine Gun Kelly. Mason and I walk over to Saint and Callum in the middle of the clubhouse, but I stop when a girl perches her barely covered ass on the bed next to Callum and starts slowly rubbing his lower back right above his jeans. I stand there stunned, not able to look away. I feel like I deserve to watch him with someone else since I broke his heart, even though I feel the nausea roll up my throat at the sight. To my immense pleasure, Callum reaches his hand behind his back and lifts the girl's hand off of him, and pushes it away from him. She gets the hint quickly, probably something he said because Saint throws his head back and laughs before the girl stands and rolls her eyes as she walks towards the bar. Mason pushes me forward, and I walk straight to the table, never taking my eyes off of the beautiful mural covering Callum's back. The walk is too short and I never thought of what I was going to say to him. The entire ride over I was still thinking of the kidnapping attempt, but now that we're here and I see Callum in person, all logical thought has left.

When I get to the head of the bed, Saint looks up at me with an evil grin on his face. "Hey, Princess. Look who it is, Cale." His smooth voice drips with acid and I know he takes my break up with Callum personally, I mean the song change when I walked into the clubhouse was pretty telling.

Callum's voice is gruff, angrier than normal. "Shut the fuck up, Saint. Just start the tattoo."

"Callum," I squeak, then clear my throat. Callum's entire body goes rigid before he slowly raises his head to look up at me. His eyes are bloodshot and his normal light dusting of facial hair has grown into a short beard. My heart breaks even further than I thought it could, I knew he would take the break up hard but seeing the evidence of it makes me hate myself.

His gaze goes from shocked to straight hate, his normal steel blue eyes are a dark gray like storm clouds, and I can feel the venom before his words even leave his mouth. "What the fuck do you want?" He spits the words as he moves to sit on the edge of the bed, Saint pulling off the black latex gloves he had on.

I inhale sharply, he's never spoken to me like that. I let out a shaky breath, pushing forward. "To apologize and explain."

Callum shakes his head and bites the inside of his lip. "Nah. Fuck your apology and your explanation."

"Callum, please." I plead quietly, not enjoying the small group that has a front row seat to this conversation.

He glares at me with his lips in a snarl. "I will never give you the power to hurt me again." He shoots his dark gaze to Mason who stood at the foot of the bed, opposite me. "Take her the fuck home."

"I don't think she should go home, brother. She was almost kidnapped tonight." Mason says, not at all deterred from Callum's angry gaze.

In a flash, Callum is standing in front of me, his slate eyes locking on mine, the hatred morphing into concern. It broke me all over again, his hatred of me, his sorrow, his concern, the kidnapping, all of it was too much and I started to cry, tears falling down my face as I stared up into his beautiful eyes. "Are you okay?" He asked quietly, his big hands wrapping around the tops of my arms.

"He made me." I gasp through the tears.

His brows furrow and he squints. "He made you what?"

"Break up with you." The tears come faster and I almost choke on the next sentence. "He was the one behind the accident."

"Fuck," Callum breathes out as he turns his head.

He bends down and picks me up by the back of my thighs. I wrap my legs around his slim waist instinctually, my arms going around the back of his neck. He walks us through the clubhouse and kicks a door closed. It's only when he sets me down on the edge of a table do I take my eyes off of his and look around the room. The room is rather bare, with only a long table with the club insignia carved into the center with several leather chairs around it. A few club mementos hang on the walls. Callum takes a seat in the chair in front of my spread legs, still shirtless he leans back and opens his legs wide, his arms resting on the chair arms. He's a work of art, all muscles and tattoos. I've never once stopped thinking about how absolutely perfect his body was, he's like a wild animal, beautiful to look at but deadly to contain. His gaze lingers on the apex of my thighs before he slowly travels up my body to my eyes. "Tell me everything. Now"

42

REESE

I TELL HIM EVERYTHING: THE FLOWERS, MY STALKER CAUSING THE accident, the threat to his life, the video and texts from tonight, and the kidnapping attempt.

"Fucking Christ, Reese." Callum drags his big hand down his face and over the scruff that shows he hasn't shaved in a week. "I wish you would have said something instead of taking everything into your own hands."

I tuck my legs underneath me on the table. "I couldn't let anything happen to you. Or to Mason or Finn. I couldn't live with it if something happened to anyone."

Callum sighs and slides further down in the chair, laying his head back to rest against the back of the chair. "I'm tired of waiting for him to fuck up and leave a trail. I want to go after this fuck and end this."

I look down at my bare legs on the table, trying to avoid his eyes for my next question. "Do you still love me?" I whisper. At the top of my vision, I can see his legs stiffen. The pause feels like it extends for several minutes and the air thickens with tension.

"You heard that," he finally says.

I look up and am immediately pulled into his intense gaze as he stares at me. "Yeah." I manage to push out while looking into his eyes.

Callum stands and takes one step towards me, everything seeming to be in slow motion. He places his hands on either side of my body and leans over me, forcing me to lean back with my hands behind me. He's inches from my face when he finally speaks. "Depends. Did you mean what you said at your apartment?"

My gaze drifts to his lips, closer than they've been in weeks. "No. Not a single word," I truthfully say. I expect a smile or a kiss, instead, he straightens and takes a step back.

"I guess you can come see if I still mean it." His voice is flat, not giving anything away as to how he feels. Then he turns, walks to the door, and walks out.

I quickly slide off of the table and follow him back into the main room of the clubhouse. He's striding back to the tattoo table in the middle of the room, and Saint sets his short tumbler down on the bar top at the sight of us. Callum lays on the bed on his stomach and Saint and I both get to his side at the same time.

"Ready?" Saint says as he pulls the rolling stool up to the head of the bed.

"Yup." Callum reaches out and grabs my hand, pulling me towards the bed to sit next to him. After I'm seated he tucks his hand under his forehead and lays his head down on the table..

"Do you do this often?" I ask Saint as he starts pulling things out of a metal case on the floor.

Saint pauses his movements with his head still down and moves his eyes between me and Callum. "Tattooing?" He asks when I continue staring at him. I nod my head and he lets out a laugh and continues his setup. "Yeah, quite a lot actually."

"Saint owns SINdicate with a really talented guy named Rich," Cale says.

I try to place the name for a moment and then remember the tattoo shop in The District. "Oh. Cool!" I nod. I've passed the place several times when going to restaurants or bars, and the place has always looked cool with the exposed black brick and neon lights inside. I never knew it was affiliated with the club though, or that Saint was a tattoo artist. The shop is always busy though, and I've heard people talking about how long the wait time is to get an appointment.

Cale and Saint both laugh at me. "In fact, I've done all of your man's ink."

"You're really talented," I say honestly because he is. I love every single one of Cale's tattoos, they're beautiful and creative. The lines are perfect and clean, they flow and just overall look like an art piece.

"I know." Saint winks and I laugh at his confidence. Or arrogance, Saint has both in spades.

I watch in silence as Saint readies everything for the tattoo on a little rolling table next to him. He dips the tattoo gun into a little tub full of red ink and then he starts drawing a line on the back of Callum's neck, above the mural I love so much on his back.

The tattoo is quick, only about five minutes, and when it's done Saint wipes it with a paper towel to get rid of the excess ink and leans back. "What do you think, Princess?" I look down at the mountain range outline that Saint freehanded in red ink.

I reach out and hover my hand above the fresh tattoo, confused. "It's beautiful," I say to Saint, then I look down at Callum. "But why?"

He stays laying down while Saint cleans the tattoo and starts on the aftercare. His head turned to look at me. "It's you. Simple, to the point." He breathes a laugh. "Red."

Tears prick my eyes and I blink to clear them. "Me?"

"I'd never seen such peace or beauty in a person until I saw you look out over those mountains. You changed me. I never thought I would open myself up to anyone again except for my brothers, but you came along and you changed everything for me. So for better or worse. With or without you. I wanted to remember the way you looked out over the mountains and a reminder that there's real beauty and peace in this world." Callum's eyes have always portrayed his feelings, whether his face was schooled or not, I can always read him through his eyes, and right now they are giant pools of every emotion. Grief, relief, love, lust, even a little anger, but mostly sincerity. I know he means everything he's said, I can read it clear as day in his eyes.

Before my mind can catch up with my mouth and I almost blurt out that I love him, Saint claps a hand on Callum's shoulder. "All done, Cale." I break eye contact with Callum and stand up.

Callum sits on the side of the table, giving Saint a quick hug and quietly slipping a few folded up bills under a clean paper towel on the cart next to him. Instead of putting his shirt back on, Callum slings his heathered gray tee shirt over his shoulder. "Come on," He says and holds his hand out to me. I walk to his side of the bed and put my hand in his. His big hand envelopes mine and he pulls me towards the stairs leading to the rooms upstairs.

Right before we make it to the stairs, Saint yells behind us. "Motherfucker, you know I don't take money for small pieces, especially from brothers!"

Callum turns and shrugs his shoulders. "I don't know what you're talking about, that's not mine." He smirks slightly as he keeps ahold of my hand.

"Come get your fucking money, Callum." Saint glares at him.

Cale turns around and pulls me up the stairs, yelling behind us. "Not mine."

43

REESE

"Slow Down" by Chase Atlantic starts playing downstairs, louder than the music that was playing when I walked in so I guess they decided to start partying. Callum pulls me down the hallway and into a door at the end of the hall. He closes the door and pushes me against it, the only light is the streetlamp peeking through a gap in the curtains and the light from the hallway slipping in under the door. He falls into me before my eyes have had time to adjust. His mouth devours me like I was his source of oxygen and he hasn't taken a breath since we last kissed.

I press my hands to his bare chest and push him away. "Wait." I breathe.

"What?" He asks, pushing his hands under my shirt and slowly sliding them up my stomach.

"I'm sorry for hurting you." I grab his face and force him to see the truth in my eyes. "I'm so sorry, Callum." I can see the wall starting to build behind his eyes, he's trying to shut me out again. So I push on, hoping I can save this. Us. Because nothing feels better than being in his arms. "I was trying to save your life, he was coming after you because of me and I can't be selfish. Not with you."

He sneers. "Be selfish, Reese. I am. I'm choosing to love you over anything else because you are the most important thing in my life. I love you no matter what it does to me, Red. I love you whether you hate me or it gets me killed. I would bleed out on the floor for you and it still wouldn't be enough, so stop fighting it and tell me you love me too."

"I love you." I breathe, tears welling in my eyes.

Callum throws his head back. "Fucking finally!" He pushes my mouth open for him and his hands come up to palm my breasts under my shirt, sliding his thumb over one nipple.

He pulls away, pulling my bottom lip between his teeth. "Where are you?" Callum breathes, his eyes searching mine.

"Right here. With you," I whisper, looking down at his full lips.

His gaze follows mine and his tongue darts out to wet his lips. "If you come back to me you're never leaving again. I let you go once, I won't let that happen again."

My eyes snap to his, his blue eyes burning with lust. "I'm not going anywhere."

"Good," he says right before he rips my shirt over my head and unbuttons my shorts in the next breath, pushing them and my panties down my legs. I kick them aside while he undoes his belt buckle and unbuttons his jeans, pushing them down as well. He stands inches from me, throwing his tee shirt to the floor and stroking his long length, his stomach muscles clenching with the motion. "Take off your bra." His voice rough with arousal.

I slowly slide the straps of my bra down my arms and unhook it before letting it fall to the floor beside us. I watch him continue to slide his hand up and down his shaft, sliding his thumb over the tip. He steps forward and lifts me straight onto his hard length, burying himself completely inside of me with the one thrust, with his palms on the backs of my thighs. I yelp at the sudden intrusion but moan as he starts fucking me hard against the door. I lay my head back against it and he takes the opportunity to suck and kiss along my neck. "Fuck, I missed you, babe." I nod my agreement because his thrusts are taking my breath away. His movements slow as his hand shifts under my thigh and he slips two fingers into my pussy with his cock, fucking me with both. I raise my head to look at Cale, my eyes going wide with the new sensation and I moan his name. He picks his head up from my neck and looks at me, smirking at the pure satisfaction written all over my face and I feel myself get even wetter at the look of his dirty smirk. He growls in approval before removing his fingers and slowly pushing them into my ass. I moan loud and throw my head back against the door again. "You're so tight, baby," Callum says before he picks up his speed again, fucking me hard against the door with his cock and fingers buried inside of both holes. I bring my lips to his and I come apart, screaming his name into his mouth as he swallows my moans. He stills, his dick thickening as he comes deep inside of me. He pulls himself out of me and drops my legs to the floor. "Once wasn't enough." He growls and quickly spins me around and pushes my front against the door before I can even make sense of what he's said. He dips his finger inside of my pussy again playing in both of our releases, leaning down into my ear. "Are you on birth control?" He asks.

I lean my head back against his chest and nod. "Mhmm."

"Good. I'm not using a condom anymore." He grabs my hair and moves my head so he can capture my mouth again. He uses his fingers to spread our combined cum onto my clit before sinking three fingers back inside of me and fucking me with his fingers and his palm pressing against my clit. Every press against my sensitive clit sends a jolt through my body, but Callum laughs darkly and continues his ministrations. He keeps a tight grip on my hair and the sting in my scalp and the pleasure in my pussy is enough to have me coming again within minutes, but before I can he slams his cock back inside of me, moving his soaked fingers to my clit. I cum around his dick, pulling away from his mouth to moan through my release. "God, you feel so good cumming on my dick." Callum envelops me with his arms, wrapping around me with one hand cupping my cunt, and the other grabbing my boob and rolling my nipple between his fingers. He fucks me with short and deep thrusts, hitting that spot deep inside of me. He presses the heel of his hand into my clit and moves it in slow circles. I feel myself climbing the cliff again, our juices running down my leg and soaking Callum behind me. "That's right, baby, cum again for me." His words set me over the edge and his palm presses against me harder, pinching my nipple with his other hand. He comes with me again and although we've done this many times before it feels different this time. "Please don't leave me again," he whispers into my neck, so quiet I almost thought I made it up. "You have my fucking heart, Red, always have, and if you leave with it again you're gonna kill me."

We both know our feelings are real and we're tired of lying about it. This feels like making love, even though it was against a door and nothing about it was romantic. I feel a new strength build inside of me, like putting on another layer of armor against my stalker. I can do anything with Callum by my side, especially take my stalker down.

44

CALLUM

"We can leave," I say into Reese's ear when we take the last step and walk into a full on club party.

She turns around, pulling me down to her. "No, let's stay." I pull back to look into her green eyes and make sure there isn't any double meaning like she actually wants to go but thinks she needs to please me by staying here. After a moment I finally give in and grab her by the hand and lead her to Saint, Mason, and Finn at the bar.

Finn pulls Red into a big hug before I pull a stool out for her and stand behind her. She's sitting between Finn and Mason and he leans over and bumps her shoulder with a big smile that they share. I couldn't be happier that she's made genuine friendships with my brothers and that they care for her like they do, and fuck it feels so damn good to be here with her. I feel like the air has cleared and I can breathe again. With everything out in the open with us, I feel like we can take on anything, and we will. We're gonna end this fucked up game her stalker has been playing with us and finally figure out if we can make it work in a normal fucking world.

I rest one hand on Finn's shoulder to get his attention.

"Where's Huntley?" He turns his head to look at me and then tilts it in the direction he was staring at a moment ago. Huntley is behind the bar at the opposite end doing blow job shots with a few strippers and Leo and Jack.

"You're cool with her wearing that?" Saint asks, for once not glued to his damn phone. Huntley's wearing a black lacy tank top thing, that honestly looks like lingerie, and high-waisted black shorts with rips all in them. Her long hair is pulled back into a ponytail and she's pouring shots and dancing and singing "Party Girl" by StaySolidRocky behind the bar with Peyton. She looks like the life of the party.

Finn doesn't take his eyes off of her, a small smile creeping onto his face. "I don't mind, I know how to fight."

"Not like anyone would try anything here," Mason adds. He's right, the only guys here are our brothers and they know Huntley is Finn's.

"And she looks fucking good and happy. That's all I want for her," Finn says. I pat him on the back. I know he's in deep with Huntley, I think he was from the first moment he saw her. He bangs on the bar a few times to get Huntley's attention over the music. She snaps her head over at the sound and he motions for her, she grabs a bottle of JD before walking over.

"Want a shot, Pretty Boy?" She asks, biting her bottom lip with a brow raised.

Reese swivels in her seat, pulling my attention back to her. "What's going on, Red? You good?" I ask, thinking she's had enough and is ready to go home.

She nods her head. "I just wanted to tell you how sorry I am again, and that I'm really glad to be here with you right now."

I lean into her, not wanting anything separating us. "Oh yeah, and why's that?" I ask, smiling like a fucking loon.

She chuckles and smiles her beautiful smile. "Because I love you."

I let my head fall back and sigh. "I'll never get tired of hearing that."

"Can I get you guys anything?" Huntley interrupts back behind the bar again. Red and I order and Huntley brings another beer back for Mason with our drinks. "I'm glad you two came to your senses. We were getting worried there for a while." She smiles and steps away to lean over the bar and talk with Saint and Finn.

I watch Reese bob her head to the music and laugh at what Mason is saying. She fits in here so well, with me and my brothers. She's everything that I could have ever asked for. Loyal, strong, resilient. She makes me the happiest that I've ever been, and being loved by her makes me feel like I'm on top of the world. I set my beer bottle onto the bar and lean in to talk into Red's ear. "Hurry up and finish that, we're leaving."

She turns to look at me, concern in her eyes. "Why?"

"Because I need to be inside of you right now. I need to feel your love." Her eyes widen, still acting like a blushing virgin even though my finger was in her ass not even an hour ago, and she gulps down her drink, almost jumping off of the barstool.

"Hey, Reese!" Huntley yells, catching us before we can make our quick escape. "Meet me at the University gym tomorrow for some self-defense training?"

I'm not fucking stopping, so Reese nods her head vigorously while I drag her out of the clubhouse.

45

REESE

I walk out of Callum's bathroom to him pulling a navy tank top over his head and letting the loose fabric fall over his abs to rest above his black athletic shorts. His eyes meet mine and roam my body in a white sports bra that pushes my breasts together and up and black high-waisted ⅞ leggings. "Ready, Red?" He asks, pulling a pair of short black socks from the drawer and dropping onto his bed to put them on. I nod and pull my long hair into a high pony. I sit next to him and we both pull on our tennis shoes.

"Thank you for coming with me." I bump his shoulder with mine.

He chuckles. "Are you kidding? I wouldn't miss a girl fight, especially with you in such a tight bra."

I push his shoulder more forcefully than the bump earlier. "Shut up!" I laugh and he leans in, his mouth inches from mine.

"I wouldn't want to be anywhere else. I want to be wherever you are." He braces himself against the bed on my other side, his arm burning against my back and casing me in.

I place my hand on the back of his neck where he has my

tattoo, my favorite place to hold him when we kiss. "I love you, Cale."

He closes his eyes and groans. "Fuck, say it again."

I lean into him, using my grip on his neck to pull him into me. "I. Love. You." I punctuate each word with a kiss.

"Fuck. Okay, we have to go before I end up laying you down and giving you a different kind of workout." He pulls me up by hand and leads me downstairs to his new Raptor.

———

WE PARK in the parking lot of the university gym and walk towards the front doors. The gym is new and the university put a lot of money into it. It's a giant modern two-story building with the entire front wall made up of windows. Through the windows, you can see the check-in desk, a rock climbing wall, a weight room, and a few private yoga studios.

When we get close to the doors Huntley strides through with a giant grin on her face. "Hey, love birds! Ready to learn how to beat a bitch's ass?"

I giggle, Huntley's optimism is always infectious, she's a lot like Mason in that sense. Will make you laugh, but could also knock you out. "Finn's waiting for us in a yoga studio."

We follow Huntley through the entrance and pass the reception desk without a look at it.

"Hey, you guys need to check in!" A guy yells from behind the desk, jumping to stand as we walk by.

"They're with me," Huntley calls over her shoulder, not even bothering to turn around or stop walking.

"You can't do that. You already brought that big tattooed guy in without checking in and the rules only allow one guest per student!" He leans over the desk on his skinny arms.

Huntley whirls around, anger making her angelic beauty

twisted. "Remember what happened when I caught you lurking outside of the girls' Pilates class, Craig?"

"Uh." Craig's face turns bright red and he sputters.

"That's what I thought. So sit down and swipe cards."

Callum bellows a loud laugh while we turn and walk down a long hallway with several workout studios. "What the hell did you do to him?"

"Almost broke his arm and told him if I caught him again I'd gouge his eyeballs out so he'd never be able to look at another girl again." Huntley shrugs and I'm slightly worried she might accidentally kill me while trying to teach me how to defend myself.

We reach one of the last doors in the hallways and she pushes it open to find Finn laying on his back on a giant black mat scrolling through his phone. The room is beautiful, with light hardwood floors, and two connecting walls of floor-to-ceiling windows that look out to the football stadium with the mountains in the background. One of the walls opposite the windows is covered in mirrors and the other is filled with lockers.

"Alright, Finny, I need the mat so you'll have to move your big ass now," Huntley says as she stands at his feet looking over him. He extends his hand and she grabs it, helping him up although it's clear she didn't pull more so just guided him to tower over her. He leans down, placing his big hand around her slim neck, and kisses her. His hand placement looks firm but the way their lips meet is gentle and loving. The kiss represents them perfectly as a couple, rough and loving, able to withstand anything.

After Huntley shows me how to hold my body to protect myself but also provide maximum damage during a fight, she shows me how to throw a proper punch so I don't break my thumb while doing so. Now she has us in front of the guys while she demonstrates moves that I'm supposed to use to get away from Callum. She stands tall in front of Finn, and even with her height he almost dwarfs her. Regardless she still looks fearless as she raises her chin and stares into his eyes.

"Let me know if it gets too real." Finn's rough voice makes Huntley falter as her eyes cast down before refocusing on his, a small crack in her strong exterior but it's enough to remind me of the reason she learned to defend herself. She quickly nods her head and he raises his head and relaxes his arms at his side, ready for her demonstration.

Huntley focuses her attention back on me. "Okay, so fighting aside, your best defense is going to be your intuition. If you feel scared or you think that something is off, it probably is. Your body is great at letting you know when things are wrong, trust it. Furthermore, never get in a car with someone, I don't care what they threaten you with, staying where you are will call their bluff, but going with them will one hundred percent end up making the situation worse for you. You have a much better chance at getting away in your original location than if you go with them." She lets out a breath and motions Finn to stand next to her. "So with that being said, if they don't give you a chance to make a decision and they decide to just take you, we want to work on how to get out of holds." Huntley looks at Finn. "Grab me by my ponytail." Finn licks his bottom lip before complying, sinking a hand deep into her hair and tugging her head back. Huntley looks at me before placing both of her hands over his on the back of her hand and turning and twisting under his outstretched arm. His hold on her hair breaks and as she's facing him and holding his arm, with him slightly bent she practices shoving her foot into his groin. Instead of nailing him right there and definitely sending him to his knees, she places her foot on his stomach and pushes back, making him land on the mat on his butt. She turns to look at us while Finn smirks at her from the floor. "Your turn!"

I turn my back on Callum so he can grab my tied-up hair from behind and take a deep breath, trying to put myself in the headspace I would be in if this wasn't Cale behind me. I feel his hand grab ahold of my ponytail, I do the move exactly as Huntley did. I twist under Cale's arm until we're facing each other and I show myself kicking him in the balls. We both straighten and Callum gives me a giant grin like I've accomplished something astronomical and he's proud of me. I can't argue, it does feel good to be able to take some control into my own hands and learn to fight back. After practicing the move a few more times we start on a new one.

"This one is for if they are grabbing you from behind and it's really easy." Finn steps in behind her and wraps his giant tattooed arms around her slim body. She wedges her hands under his arms and arches her body away from him then slowly pulls her lower body back into his and pushes against his hands at the same time, making him let go of her. "With this one, you'll want to use a lot of force when you're bringing your butt back into whoever is behind you. Depending on their height you'll either line up with their groin or their stomach and either way that's going to hurt. You want to make sure to push on their arms at the same time so they release you as they're bending over; after, run like hell. Ready?" She asks. "Come on over, Cale!" She calls, turning to face Callum who's sitting on the floor by the wall of mirrors and taking a drink from a water bottle.

He saunters over and wraps his arms around me from behind, leaning into my neck and placing a kiss there. "Reminds me of our first time." My face flushes remembering our first time together just a few months before. It feels like so much longer with everything that we've been through already.

Just as I'm getting ready to practice the new move, Callum's phone rings from where we laid our things on the floor by his water bottle. "Hang on." He taps his hand against my hip before walking to where we left our things and bending over to pick up his phone. "What's up, Mason?" He says into the phone. I watch him and his posture straightens and his eyes fly to me. My brows pull together, trying to question what Mason is saying without words. "Alright, I'll head over now."

"What's going on?" I ask before he's even pulled his phone from his ear. He bends to pick up his keys and wallet from the floor and I close the distance between us. Finn and Huntley are standing next to each other, watching us.

Callum grabs my hands in his and looks into my eyes. I can already tell he's going to say something I don't like by the apologetic look in his eyes, but there's something under it too, fear. "I need you to go home with Finn until I can send a prospect to stay with you."

"Why?" I shake my head. "What did Mason say?"

I can hear two sets of footsteps behind me but I keep staring at Callum, trying to pry his brain open and see what's going on.

He squeezes my hands quickly. "Mason said they got your stalker's face on camera."

I think my heart stops, I'm scared and hopeful all at once. "He found him?" I breathe.

"He thinks so. We're getting the club together to go now," he says, never taking his eyes off of me but I know he's speaking to all of us.

"I want to go." My voice rising and my eyes boring into his, hopefully portraying that this isn't a request.

Callum shakes his head. "Absolutely not. Remember what happened last time we had a lead on this guy?" There it is, there's the fear. "We're walking in blind and I'm not taking you into that." I can tell in his voice he won't budge on this, but I want to push him. This guy has been tormenting me for months, he's tried to kill Callum, broke into my house twice, and tried to kidnap me. I need to be there.

"He's my stalker, Callum." I rip my hands from his and cross them under my sports bra.

"I'm aware." He snaps. He drags a hand down his face and takes a deep breath. "I promise I will have you brought in when we get inside and get a handle on things."

"But—" I start to protest again.

"I can't worry about you and keep a clear head. We know what this guy is capable of." He closes his eyes and sighs. "Please don't fight me on this, Reese." His slate blue eyes open onto mine again and I lose every argument I might have had. His eyes pool with emotion and I'm rendered speechless. He's right.

"Okay," I whisper and I see the tension marginally leave his shoulders; one fight down, one more to go.

Callum grabs my hand and pulls me towards the door. When we're about to walk out of the door we turn to see Finn and Huntley standing facing each other. His deep blue eyes are locked on hers. "Lock up here and then go to my house. Don't open the door for anyone except for the club or me." He rumbles.

"I'm going. You could use me." Huntley has a defiant tone to her.

Finn buries his big hand in her pulled-up hair and yanks her head back. "No." He growls with her throat bared and her head immobilized.

I'm about to step in, because who puts their hands on someone like that, but then she smiles. Callum pulls on my hand again and leans into my ear. "She's fine," he whispers.

"What?" I ask. Kind of mesmerized by watching their wills battle in their eyes. Huntley's head still pulled back and Finn standing over her staring into her eyes.

"They like their love rough." He chuckles behind me.

Huntley rises on her toes and gently bites Finn's bottom lip before placing a kiss on his lips. His grip loosens in her hair. "Good girl." He quietly growls before placing another kiss on her forehead and turning to follow us.

As the three of us are about to walk out of the door, Huntley speaks. "You better be home tonight, Finn, or I'll come find you."

Finn turns around, his smile so big it almost splits his face in half. "I know you will, baby."

The walk back through the gym and out to the parking lot is a blur, I just stare at Callum's back as he leads me, hoping this tip isn't like the last one we got. When we get to Callum's Raptor he opens the passenger side door and pops open the glove compartment. He pulls my gun out and hands it to me. "Just in case," he says when my eyes widen. "Shoot anyone who's not us. Ask questions later." I nod my head, my throat closing and not allowing for any words to leave. The last time he said that a van drove into the side of us and I thought I lost him. He leans down and captures my cheeks in his hands, pulling me into a kiss. His tongue slips inside of my mouth and caresses mine.

"Cale," Finn interrupts, and Callum and I pull away. "We need to get going, brother."

Callum nods and kisses me one more time. "We're ending this today, babe." He promises before nodding to Finn and walking around to the driver's side of his pickup.

Finn guides me to his gunmetal gray Hellcat with his hand on my back. Climbing inside, I watch as Callum tears out of the parking lot, his truck roaring just as loud as a bike. His tail lights disappear around a corner as Finn starts his car and I pray this won't be the last time I see Callum.

46

REESE

Finn unlocks Callum's front door and pushes it open, switching on the lights for the living room and kitchen on his way to the refrigerator. I follow him and sit on the barstool across from him while he leans against the counter, I place my gun down before he tosses me a bottle of water.

"He's gonna be okay, Princess. I got his back." Finn rumbles his blue gaze hard.

"I know, I just can't relax until this is over, we've been here before." I turn the bottle cap over and over in my fingers. "I think I'm gonna go shower and change," I say, standing from the island, and Finn nods.

Being back in Callum's house is so comforting, we've had nothing but great times here. It's comforting to be around his things. I close his bedroom door before walking into the master bath, I lean into the mirror over the sink and swipe at the smeared mascara under my eyes. I turn around to switch the shower on when I hear a loud crash downstairs. I pause, listening intently, and then hear another. I run through the bathroom and bedroom and rush down the stairs. I round the corner and stop. My brain takes several seconds to take in the scene and catch up to what's happening. The bar cart by the back sliding door is in pieces with several of the bottles smashed and liquids pooling around it, next to the cart is a giant hole in the wall. My eyes land on Finn panting on his knees, a line of blood trickling down his face from his eyebrow. He's glaring absolute murder at me. Finally, I look behind him to see the absolute last person I ever expected to see.

"What are you doing, Eli?" My eyebrows inch together on my forehead.

Eli stands behind Finn, sweating and breathing heavily, holding a hand to his side and a gun pointed to the back of Finn's head. I try to subtly look for my gun that I left on the counter, but it isn't there anymore. "Looking for this?" Eli asks cheerily, pulling my gun from behind his back and my heart sinks.

"Run, Reese," Finn says, his voice calm but there's a very slight waver of fear laced into it.

I turn my head towards the door, contemplating doing just that, but before I can make a decision Eli calmly says, "Run and I'll kill him." I turn back around to face Eli, ready to ask what he wants.

"Fucking run!" Finn bellows, the walls seem to shake with the volume, and this time I listen.

I turn and sprint for the front door, behind me I hear a loud smack and I can't help but turn my head back. Never look back. I see Finn laying in a heap on the floor right before Eli barrels into me and tackles me to the floor. His hands enclose my throat and squeeze tight, and mine fly up to dig into his wrists, hoping the pain will cause him to loosen his grip a bit. He doesn't let up even though I can feel my nails breaking skin and I kick my legs trying to crawl away from him but it's no use, his weight and tight grip keep me pinned where I am.

"I'm sorry, Reesey," Eli says before he lifts my head off of the floor and slams it back down against the hard floor. The first hit has me dazed, but the second hit had my eyes rolling back and me falling into blackness.

47

CALLUM

I walk through the clubhouse, Tobi, Wyatt, and Leo are sitting around a table and Tobi points me towards the stairs. I take them two at a time and stalk to Mason's room, which is the one next to my old room, at the end of the hall. I push the door the rest of the way open and stalk in. Mason and Miles are hunched over several monitors with Saint and Ronan standing behind them with their arms crossed whispering to each other.

"Okay, what's going on?" I snap, everyone turning to look at me.

"I called Miles over to help and stay behind in case we needed anything." Mason starts, his dark hood hanging around his neck.

"That doesn't answer my question," I reply, annoyed.

Mason looks at me like he's ready to throttle me for being rude, but he has the decency and brains to back down. "We caught another glitch in the camera feed. We don't know how it went undetected but when he wiped the cameras he cut out too soon and didn't erase him leaving Reese's apartment."

My eyebrows pull together. "So he broke it another time?"

Mason nods. "The morning after we hosted the O'Connell Family."

I shake my head, that can't be right. "But I was there that morning. Nothing happened. Pull the feed up, I want to see it," I demand. There's no fucking way this guy got into that apartment with me there.

"Give me a minute," Miles says from a few feet away from Mason, tapping at his keyboard. "Here ya go, Cale." He points to one of his screens and then leans back in his chair.

I watch the camera feed of Reese's front door, the sun barely coming up but the frame is empty, then the feed goes completely black, then it flicks back to Reese's door and a man locking the door. He keeps his head down, avoiding the camera, but something alerts him and he quickly looks over his shoulder exposing the side of his face to the camera. I still, recognizing him instantly.

"We've already started running facial recognition, but it takes a little while with only half of his face. Got any idea who he is so we can speed this along?" Miles rubs his thumb and finger along his dark bearded chin.

"Yeah," I answer, still stunned. "His name is Eli and he works at the University with Reese's ex."

"I'll check the University's website directory, got any idea what department?" Mason asks.

I chuckle darkly, a lot of shit starting to make sense, but the biggest question is still unanswered. "Fucking IT."

Mason nods his head while he pulls up the website. "Well, that answers some things." He searches the website and the room is silent. Saint and Ronan are still standing behind us in the small room, not saying a word. "Elijah Murphy." Mason finally announces.

"Running it," Miles calls next to him. "712 Cornice. Go!" He yells and all four of us rush from the room and down the stairs.

When I push through the door of the clubhouse and into the parking lot my phone buzzes in my pocket. I pull it out and see Jack's name on the screen. Panic rushed through my stomach and I quickly answer the call. "Don't tell me somethings wrong," I say as a greeting.

"The house is empty," Jack says down the line and I stop, Ronan, Saint, Mason, and Leo fanning around me.

"Maybe they stopped somewhere before going to my house." I turn around and face my brothers. Praying this is the reason they're not home.

"Finn's Hellcat is in the driveway—"

"Check the entire fucking house!" I interrupt him.

Jack huffs out a breath. "I did. There's a giant ass hole in the wall in the kitchen and all of your alcohol is broken on the floor."

I end the call without saying anything else to him. "Fuck!" I yell. I look around at everyone surrounding me. "Let's go. He took them." I stalk to my truck, Saint and Ronan following me while Mason and Leo walk to their bikes and climb on. Saint comes to the driver's door beside me and pushes me to the back door. "Excuse the fuck out of you, dickhead?" I push his shoulder hard.

"You're too fucking wound up right now, you'll lose focus and kill us before we get there." He pushes me back a few steps and opens the door for me. "Read me the directions and Ro will text Jack the address."

Reluctantly and with a glare I step into the backseat of my own fucking truck and sit down.

WE MAKE the trip in half the time it was supposed to take, screeching to a halt in front of a normal looking one story house with flower beds in the front yard and a wooden bench swing on the porch. My brothers and I storm up the lawn, clearing the three steps to get to the porch and I brace myself before kicking the front door in. It swings into the wall behind it, the handle busting the plaster and staying wide open for us. We all rush in and clear all of the rooms of the small house, before finding a door to a basement. I quickly check that everyone is behind me before turning the knob and quickly making my way down the stairs, luckily someone flipped the light at the top of the stairs because I was coming down blind. The basement is empty as well, but based on the scene down here I'd rather Reese and Finn still be missing than be here. In the corner is a large kennel, like that which a dog would be in with a padlock laying on the floor in front of it. In the middle of the room is a gambrel hanging from the ceiling and on the floor beneath are dark splatters with a perfect untouched circle in the middle, like a bucket was placed there. I walk towards the back wall and look at several pictures of Reese pinned to a board. Pictures of her on the back of my bike, us riding into the clubhouse, walking into my house, her in her office, and so many others, but the one that makes my blood boil is of her leaning with her head in her hands on what looks like a bathroom floor. I recognize the dress she's wearing as the dress from her friend's birthday when she was drugged. Eli had something to do with the guy that drugged her and he took a fucking picture of her before trying to kidnap her.

"Cale, you need to see this." I turn around to see Saint holding up the lid of a giant deep freezer.

I walk over and peer inside. A naked woman lay crumbled inside, her throat slashed but dried blood covers her throat and over her face, making sense of the gambrel. I can't make out any facial features because of the blood covering her entire face, but her red hair, the same shade as Reese's, tells me all I need to know. "We need to find them. Now." My voice shakes.

"We have one more thing we can try." Mason quietly speaks from the corner where he's kneeling next to the empty cage.

"Have Miles track her gun," I say, closing the freezer and walking towards the stairs.

48

REESE

THE THROBBING IN THE BACK OF MY HEAD MAKES ME KEEP MY EYES closed, but when I try to bring my hands to my head to cradle it I snap my eyes open when they won't give way. I frantically look around me. My hands are handcuffed behind me around a pole and I'm in a giant empty room with cement floors and walls with tall ceilings, safe to say I'm probably in some warehouse. I see Finn's arms also looped around a pole some ten feet away from me. He's still slumped over and I can't see if his chest is moving or not.

"Finn!" I hiss, trying not to be too loud just in case Eli is near. "Finn!" I whisper yell again when he doesn't answer the first time.

Whispering his name the second time must break through his unconsciousness because he groans and raises his head, his eyes screwed shut. "You should have run, Princess," He says without opening his eyes.

"He would have shot you!" I argue, my eyes wide.

He rests his head against the pole behind him. "Still." Finn opens his eyes and takes in our surroundings. "Why the fuck are we here?"

My eyes narrow at him. "You know where we are? Where are we?" I whisper yell again.

"The warehouse." His voice is laced with confusion, he blinks several times and he looks around the building. *The warehouse. Well, that's quite obvious, I had already figured out we were in a warehouse.*

Before I can question him further, Eli steps out of a room from behind me. Turning my head I can barely make it out but it looks like an office. "Where's Huntley?" Finn growls at our captor.

"Who?" Eli's face almost splits with his creepy smile. "Oh your girlfriend, she's fine. I only told you I had her so you would surrender."

Finn jerks against the cuffs and the pole creeks. "Why are we here?" He sneers.

Eli paces between Finn and me, his hands clasped behind his back looking calm and smiling. Seeing him so at ease and knowing he was the one watching me this entire time makes my stomach roll. "Well I knew your club of criminals would never let Reesey and I go easily, so I brought you both here to see what your club is doing in the basement. I know you make bullets. With that and trading you, the club would be wise to allow us to calmly leave town."

I shake my head, so confused with what's going on right now. "Why are you doing this?" I try to stay calm, Eli and I were friends.

Eli turns to face me, bending down and gently cupping my cheek with his hand. "Isn't it obvious?" I stare at him, blinking, hoping maybe that will wake me up from this weird nightmare. "I love you, Reesey, and we can finally be together." I shake my head, trying to pull my face away from his hand. "You were too good for my stupid best friend and way too good for a criminal." He sneers, pushing away from me to stand back up.

Finn scoffs. "You really think Callum is going to let you kidnap Reese?"

"He will if he doesn't want your little operation to be turned over to ATF and for you to make it out of this alive." Eli snaps, seeming to lose his cool a little.

Finn shakes his head laughing. "You chose the wrong club to fuck with and the wrong woman to stalk."

Eli's evil Cheshire cat smile creeps back onto his face. "We'll see." Eli walks toward me and I instinctively push back into the pole, trying to get as far away from him as I can. "Now if you'd be so kind as to pass my message along to your little club, Reesey and I will just be on our way."

He steps behind me and frees my hands, but before I can make a run for it or turn and punch him, he's snapping the cuffs back onto one of my wrists. I look down, confused, and see that he's handcuffed me to him. He yanks me up, using his hand that's cuffed next to mine.

I swing my fist back, intending to take the slack he gave me and punch him in the face when he presses the barrel of his gun into my forehead. I freeze, staring into his eyes and seeing no hesitation in them.

"I wouldn't." His voice is even. "In fact, just to make sure you comply." He moves the gun from my forehead and fires it right next to my ear. My ears ring and I drop to the ground to get away from the gun, but then I remember what was behind me. Finn slumps forward again, growling with a small hole in his shoulder and blood pouring out.

"Finn!" I yell, scrambling to go to him, but forgetting that I'm handcuffed to Eli. He yanks me back and I land on my butt at his feet.

"Let's go." He barks and tugs me up again. "Or else the next one is more serious."

"Don't move those fucking feet, Reese." Finn hisses between clenched teeth.

I shake my head while Eli drags me past him and out of what I think is the back entrance of the warehouse, hoping Finn can sense my apology.

49

CALLUM

"WHY THE FUCK ARE THEY AT MY WAREHOUSE?" I SNARL, STILL from the backseat, while Saint flies around the bends and down the dirt road leading to CM Roofing's warehouse.

"No clue, but that's where the tracker is leading us." Saint deadpans. *No shit.*

Saint slams on the brakes in front of the warehouse and we all fly out of the pickup, dirt that was kicked up by the truck washing over us. Ronan holds up a hand to halt us as Mason, Leo, and Jack pull up behind us on their bikes.

The night is completely silent, the only sound is the wind blowing the leaves on the trees. "There aren't any vehicles here," he says, puzzled.

"I'm not waiting to figure that out." I snap, already making my way to the front door of the warehouse.

Saint grabs my arm and yanks me back. "Use your fucking head." He slaps me in the back of the head. "We can't just storm in there, it could be a trap."

"I don't care!" I yank my arm out of his grasp.

Ronan grabs my chin in his strong hand and forces my face to his. I don't know when the ancient fucker got over to me, but apparently, he got a new hip recently and can move faster. "Go in smart and with backup." He growls, barely an inch from my face. "Jack, you're going around back with me. The rest of you with Callum," he says over his shoulder and then he lets go of my chin and quietly sneaks around the dark corner of the warehouse.

Without looking to see if anyone is following, I run as quietly as I can to the door and when we are all in position, Mason swings the door open and we storm in with our guns raised. Except the warehouse is quiet, dark, and empty. Save for my brother with his arms looped around a post behind him. Blood pours from his shoulder and pools on the ground next to him. We all rush over and Saint and I kneel to inspect him.

"Get me out of these fucking cuffs!" Finn growls, yanking said cuffs and banging them against the pole. Mason and Leo quickly wander off to find a bolt cutter.

"Where's Reese?" I ask while Saint shines his phone flashlight over Finn's injury which looks like a gunshot. *Where the fuck is she?*

"He went out the back with her. Some fucker named Eli," Finn says and then growls low in his throat when Saint presses his discarded shirt into Finn's shoulder.

I stand but before I can move, there's a shot and scream behind the warehouse. *Please be okay.*

50

REESE

Eli and I are running through the grass, him pulling me by my wrist that is still handcuffed to his. It's so dark out here that I can't see where we are going.

"We're almost there, Reesey," Eli says in front of me as he pulls a little harder on my wrist.

Oh my God, I need to do something. We're away from Finn so he can't shoot him again, and I cannot get into a vehicle with him. My mind is running, what can I do out here? I can't see anything to look for a weapon and he has a gun, but would he shoot me? I don't think he would. I have to take a chance, if I go with him I'll wish I was dead, so I might as well fight now. I dig my feet in hard and yank my hand back, halting Eli.

He turns around. "Come on, Reesey, we've got to go!" He pulls my wrist again, turning to run, but when he turns his head I cock my hand back and hit him as hard as I can in the side of his head.

He groans, staggering a little to the side, and I bring my hand back to hit him again. Before I can, a shot pierces the air, the pop echoing, and I scream as I'm pulled to the ground. I fall next to Eli and I use my hands to move over my body and check for the wound. When my hands reach my head I can feel warm liquid splattered on my face, but I don't have any pain. I turn my head, realizing if I'm on the ground then Eli has to be too. Eli lays on his stomach with his eyes closed. I watch him let out one big breath and then doesn't breathe again.

"Help!" I scream, realizing that someone shot Eli and it has to be the club. "Callum!" I yell again and then I hear soft foot-steps running on the grass towards me. I sit up, trying to make out who is coming for me.

"Reese." A rough voice answers me. "Reese, it's Ronan; you're okay." Ronan kneels in front of me and captures my face in his hands, looking deep into my eyes. "Are you hurt?" I shake my head. I can't force words past my lips, I'm so overcome with relief. It's over.

Ronan moves his hands from my face to my hands and notices the handcuff on my wrist. He lets go and starts to roll Eli's body. "He's dead right? You killed him?" I ask while Ronan searches Eli's pockets.

He pulls out a small key and slides it into my handcuff. "Yes he's dead, but Jack shot him. He's a better long-distance shot." When the cuff unlocks from my wrist Ronan tosses the key beside Eli's body and I rub at the raw skin. The cuffs really dug in when Eli was dragging me along behind him. Ronan pulls a dark bandana from his back pocket and lightly swipes at what I can only assume is blood splatter from the side of my face and then slides his arms under my bent legs and lifts me, carrying me back the way we came. "You're safe now Reese. He's dead. He can never come for you again." He talks to me as we walk and I start crying in his arms, laying my head on his shoulder. "You're safe, Reese. You're safe. Cale's coming for you right now. He's going fucking crazy with worry for you, Princess."

"Reese! Reese!" I hear a familiar voice yell. A beautiful voice, a voice that slides into my heart and wraps it into a blanket.

Warm, strong, full of love, and mine: Callum. "Do you have her? Is she okay?" He yells again, coming closer.

I pat Ronan on the shoulder, asking him to put me down, and he obliges. Setting my feet gently on the ground and then I take off running in the direction of the big body running towards us that I know is Callum.

When we're a few feet from each other, I launch myself at him and he catches me, pulling me into his strong body and almost crushing me. "Are you okay?" He asks in my ear, brushing stray hair that had fallen out of my ponytail away from my face. I nod my head and snuggle my face into his neck and take in a lungful of his scent. He's always smelled like comfort, like home; the leather from his cut mixed with his cologne. It's him and I love it. "Fuck, Red, I woulda died if anything happened to you. I wouldn't be able to handle it if I lost you again. Fuck!" He swears, holding me tighter and turning to keep walking back toward the warehouse.

"Wait. Finn!" I panic, pulling away from his neck to look into his eyes.

His face is grim and I brace myself for what he's about to say. "I know," he says. "Saint is with him and they're loading him into my truck now. We need to get him to the hospital." With my face not buried in his neck, I can see that he's almost running with me wrapped around him like a koala.

I see Ronan and Jack running behind us, Ronan reaches forward and squeezes one of my hands that's wrapped around Cale's neck, and Jack is carrying a big rifle with a scope on the top. I turn to see where we're running and see headlights up ahead and the sound of bikes and Callum's truck. "Put me down, we can get there faster," I say, turning back to look at him.

"Absolutely not. You're not leaving my side for the next, probably fifty years." He huffs, his eyes briefly switching to mine before back to the direction we're running in.

We reach the truck and Callum finally puts me down but he quickly grabs my hand and keeps a firm grasp on it. Mason and Leo are sitting on their bikes ready to go and the back door of Callum's Raptor is open. I can see Finn laying across the seats with his head in Saint's lap while Saint holds his bunched-up shirt to Finn's shoulder. Ronan steps up into the back and Callum and I take the front seats with him driving. Jack tosses Ronan his rifle before running to his bike and we all speed away from the warehouse.

I turn around in my seat and look at Finn laying on Saint, sweating, and kind of pale. He's already looking at me and the tears that I managed to stop, start again seeing him shot and in pain because of me. "Nice to see you, Princess," Finn says softly. His eyes locked on mine.

"He shot you," I squeak.

He scoffs, scrunching up his face. "You think this is the first time I've ever been shot?" He jokes, but his usual banter tone is weak. "You're hurting my street cred with that shit."

I laugh through the tears, and he laughs softly trying to reach me with his opposite, non-injured arm.

"Quit moving, dumbass!" Saint snaps, flicking Finn on the forehead.

Finn huffs and lays back. "Yes, Doctor Viotto." Saint rolls his eyes, but Finn keeps eye contact with me. "I'm sorry I didn't do more," he almost whispers. "I was just so—"

"Scared for her," I finish for him, knowing he means Huntley. I knew Eli must have threatened her in some way when Finn asked about her. "I know. I wouldn't have done anything differently had I been in your position."

"He said he had her, that he was going to do what those frat guys did to her." His eyes close shut in what looks like agony. "I couldn't let her go through that again."

"She's okay, brother," Saint says, his voice softer than I've ever heard it. "Leo called her, she's meeting us at the hospital."

I turn back around in my seat and look over at Callum, his knuckles are white around the steering wheel, and his eyes flit up to the rearview mirror and back to the road over and over.

When we pull into the hospital's emergency bay, nurses rush out and Saint and Ronan help load Finn onto the gurney, Saint runs alongside them through the sliding doors, speaking to the nurses and Ronan gets back into the backseat of the Raptor. After parking, Callum hands me a black Devil's Outlaws hoodie from under the backseat to pull over my blood-spattered sports bra. I cleaned up my face and chest the best I could with Ronan's bandana, but I won't be clean until I have a shower. Knowing this is a person's blood on me, a person I used to think of as a friend still makes my skin crawl. We walk into the waiting room with Callum holding onto my hand with a steel grip. *I guess he was serious about me not leaving his side.* When we walk through the sliding door, a blonde blur smashes into Callum and grabs him by the shoulders.

"Where is he?" Huntley growls.

Ronan steps around us and grabs a hold of Huntley's hands. "We just brought him in." He leads her to a chair and they sit down, still holding hands. "Saint went back with him and he'll be out with an update soon." She nods, seeming to calm down for the moment and then her gaze turns to me.

She stands and walks slowly towards me. I'm ready for her to hit me or tear into me; it's my fault Finn is hurt. She stops in front of me and bends slightly so we're more eye to eye. This is a really inappropriate time to notice this, but she's stunning close up. She looks like a walking filter. Her skin is pale and flawless, like literally no flaw in sight. She looks angelic with her deep blue eyes, long dark lashes, and high cheekbones. *Shit, wrong time to check her out, Reese.* She places her hands gently on my arms. "I'm so glad to see you, Reese. I was so worried when Leo called and said you were taken."

I open my mouth to say something, but Saint walks through the double doors leading back into the ER, wiping blood off of his hands with some sort of disinfectant wipe. The doors swinging closed snags Huntley's attention and she turns to face him.

"He's fine, the bullet didn't hit anything major, just lodged itself into his obnoxious amount of muscle. I guess being a giant fucker finally paid off for him. They're removing the bullet now and will transfer him to a room so they can continue to replenish some blood."

Huntley lets out a loud sigh. "He's okay?"

Saint smirks and shakes his head. "He's perfectly fine now that he's gained some strength back. When I left he was carrying on a conversation with the doctor about her '65 Stingray."

"Of course he was." Huntley laughs.

Saint takes Huntley's hand and leads her to a chair. "So let's just sit and wait for a nurse to come back and escort us to his room." She nods and follows him to sit.

Callum and I sit a few seats away, my hand encased in his strong one. Something Eli said keeps playing in my mind, and I can't make sense of it.

I lean into Callum's side so I don't have to speak so loudly. "Callum, what are you doing at CM that could get you in trouble with the ATF?"

His head snaps to the side to look at me, and his hold on my hand tightens. "What?" He asks.

"Eli said he was going to turn ATF onto CM to ensure that you let me go." I hold his eyes, I need these answers. I'm tired of being left in the dark when it comes to him and the club, not anymore.

Callum breaks eye contact briefly, looking down and

scratching his eyebrow before speaking. "It's nothing you need to worry about, Red."

"Stop." My voice drops dangerously. "Stop shutting me out. If I'm supposed to be your Old Lady then I want to know everything from here on out." His eyes widened in surprise. "So what is going on at your roofing company?"

"My Old Lady?" Cale asks with a grin. Of course, that's the only part of that he heard.

"Yeah." I smile.

Callum chuckles. "Damn, Red. You didn't even let me ask you." He sobers and nods slowly, seeming to think about what he wants to say. "Okay. The club makes ammo in a hidden basement under my warehouse."

"And that would get you in trouble because?" I hedge.

"Because we make them for illegal rifles and sell them to," he pauses, squinting at the ceiling. "Unsavory characters."

"Okay," I say slowly. "It could be a lot worse." Callum laughs and bites his bottom lip while nodding his head. Things start to click together, the club helping him buy the warehouse, the weird meeting with Sebastian, his immense knowledge of guns, and his seemingly endless amount of money. "Is that what the meeting with Sebastian was about in Seattle?" I ask to confirm.

He nods. "Sebastian is the head of the Segreto Mafia in Italy. Some shit is going down with him and the O'Connell Irish crime family."

Now it's my turn to be surprised. "The mafia? And you're involved in it?" *Never mind it's getting worse.*

Callum grabs my other hand and leans closer, looking deep into my eyes. "Only as far as the bullets go, we're not in any danger. You're not in any danger. I promise, Red. The club and I will always protect you, I think we proved that tonight."

After checking on Finn, Callum and I walk out of the hospital, his arm draped over my shoulders. "What are we supposed to do now?" I ask. I mean what do you do after you spent months being stalked by your ex's best friend, fell in love with a criminal, found a new family with said criminal's organization, and then killed your crazy stalker? I mean no one called the cops to report mine and Finn's kidnapping or Eli's dead body. The only phone call I overheard was Ronan calling some doctor and giving him the warehouse's address and the area where we left Eli's body. When I asked Callum about it at the hospital he told me that they know a debarred doctor that buys human bodies and harvests their organs to sell through the Red Market. Just knowing that the club has someone on speed dial to dispose of dead bodies for them, plural, was enough to make me start to spiral so I stopped asking questions after that. I know Callum is good and I know the club is too, I don't need to know all of their dark secrets.

"Live our normal lives, maybe finally have some fun." Callum laughs, pulling me in closer and placing a kiss on the top of my head.

I look up at him as he guides us to his truck. I don't think I'll ever get used to his beauty. His blonde hair is always messily tousled, his steel blue eyes that always draw me in, and his strong jaw. Damn, he's handsome. "How are we supposed to do that after all of the excitement over the last few months?"

We reach Cale's Raptor and he turns me around to face him. His hands fall to my hips and mine wrap around his neck to rest on the place my tattoo sits. "You could start by moving in with me," he says, looking into my eyes. My eyes widen with surprise, but I already know my answer. Wherever Callum is, that's where I want to be.

I lean up to press a kiss to his lips and when I pull away, his eyes bore into mine, searching out my soul and capturing it. "Yes," I finally answer him.

EPILOGUE
ONE MONTH LATER

Reese

I WALK INTO MINE AND CALLUM'S TOWNHOUSE AFTER GOING INTO the office for a few hours. Callum is where he usually is now in his free time, sitting in front of the bay window at the keyboard I got him, with his headphones plugged in and lost in his music. He's started playing almost daily. Recently he won't share what he's been working on but I know he's writing something special because when I'm sitting on the couch behind him I see him erasing and scribbling notes onto a sheet of music. He's composing something special, I can feel it. He seems a lot lighter these days, we both do. When he said we should have fun and live our lives that's exactly what we've been doing. Honestly, you could say it's been downright boring. We grocery shop together every Sunday, Cale goes to the gym, we go to the movies and spend way too much on their dine-in service, but seriously who could resist that chicken bacon mac and cheese? We go on a lot of bike rides and go to our favorite mountain spot a lot just to talk and enjoy being together.

I lean down and wrap my arms around Callum's shoulders and kiss his cheek. He startles, not having noticed me coming home. "Hi," I say after he's slid his headphones off and stopped playing. "What was so important I needed to hurry home for?"

"I'm not reason enough?" Callum scoffs, placing a dramatic hand to his heart.

"Always." I laugh and kiss his cheek again.

He turns on the bench, breaking my looped arms from his neck. He scans my outfit taking in my white button-up with the sleeves rolled up and half tucked into light jeans and my short strappy heels. His eyes pause on my thighs and hips and his hands come to rest on them, slowly rubbing up and down. "I have something to show you," he finally says, bringing his eyes back up to mine. "We gotta take a ride though."

We cruise through the curved roads, the trees thick and the air fresh, the late afternoon sun barely peeking through the ceiling of trees. Finally, we turn onto a small paved road, the trees creating a tall arch over the road, and at the end of the long drive I can make out a sort of clearing. When we get to the end I see that I was right, the massive trees clear away to show a perfect view of a strip of mountains in the distance. I don't know how Callum always finds these spots with the most perfect views but he does, and this one is by far the best one he's taken me to! I get off of the bike while Cale parks it and walk further into the clearing and take in the view. This spot is a little odd as it's flat clear ground with nothing around and a little out of the way.

"What do you think?" Callum says coming up behind me. He wraps his strong arms around me and rests his chin on my head.

"It's beautiful. I love it," I say, laying my arms over his and leaning back into him. I look out over the land, it stretches for a few acres before dropping off and leaving nothing but the amazing view. The mountains border Mt. Rainier, the sky is clear today, which gives us a front row seat to the volcano. The summer heat feels good, the slight breeze making the June sun comfortable. I take a deep breath and let everything absorb; everything that matters to me is right here. Callum's spicy cologne is swirling with the fresh air to make a heady combination, but that's probably mostly just the man holding me. I love my life right now, it has never been more perfect. I love my job, my home, my man, and my friends. Everyone is happy and safe.

"Well good because I bought it for us." Callum's voice breaks my train of thought.

I turn in his arms to face him. "You bought what?" I ask.

"This land. To build a house on," he says, his steel blue eyes locking onto mine. "So you can wake up every day and see this view. Wake up and sit in a big armchair in front of a giant window with a cup of orange juice, or walk out onto a porch or balcony and watch the sun rise and set. Whatever you want." I blink a few times, completely surprised that he had bought us land, and the perfect lot at that. "Hey, come back to me, Red." He laughs, rubbing my arms. "I just bought the land, we can start building whenever you're ready; whether that's in two months or ten years."

I look over my shoulder at the beautiful view one more time and then turn back to look at the beautiful man in front of me; the man of my dreams. "What about now?"

The grin that splits his face is probably the biggest I've ever seen on him, and it instantly makes me smile. "We can start looking into contractors tomorrow, but there is one thing I want to do here first." He lets me go and walks back to the bike. He looks around for something in the box attached to the side and then turns to walk back towards me. He stands in front of me, looking every bit the confident gorgeous man I met only three months ago. "Goddamn, you take my breath away." He shakes his head and looks down at his hands. He clears his throat and looks back at me. "I've never met anyone who fits me so well, it's like you were made for me and I was made for you. You are my best friend and coming home to you and your terrible cooking." He stops to laugh at my glare. "Is the best part of my day. You've taken to club life so easily, so I know you'll know just how big this is of me to ask you." He pulls something out of the breast pocket of his cut. "Will you be my Old Lady?" He asks and I see what he pulled out is a beautiful thin black band. I stare at the ring and before I can answer him he continues. "I know you already agreed in a roundabout way, but you're the type of woman who deserves to be asked." He sounds almost nervous like he actually believes I would say no.

"Yes!" I almost scream before he can ramble on anymore. I pull his face into mine and kiss him so he knows exactly how serious I am.

He pulls away and chuckles, his giant grin back on his face. "Good," he says, sliding the thin black band onto my left hand, the same place an engagement ring should be. I guess that makes sense since this is the biker version of a marriage. I look down at the ring and see it's encrusted with black stones on all sides of the ring and completely around. It glistens beautifully in the sunlight. "Because I have something else for you too." Callum breaks my attention from admiring my ring and I snap my eyes back up to meet his again.

"More?" I ask confused, what more could he possibly have?

Callum sinks to one knee, pulling a small black box from his back jeans pocket and I suck in a gasp. "I want to marry you, Reese Thomas. I want to marry you in front of our friends and family, I want you on the back of my bike, burning my meals, carrying my kids for the rest of my life. I want you forever, as my best friend, my Old Lady, my wife, and eventually the mother of my children." I don't know when the tears started, but I finally noticed them falling when he finished. "It feels like I've loved you for my entire life, and I'll love you long after it ends. Will you marry me, Red?" I nod my head, too emotional to speak because Callum has felt like the missing piece that I tried so hard to make Noah fit, but he just wasn't it. I know not only am I safe with Callum but so is my heart. He will never hurt me, and I will never stop loving him. Cale hangs his head and I can hear a breath I didn't know he was holding rush out. He focuses intently on the box in his hand and opens it, sliding the biggest oval diamond I've ever seen with a gold band onto my finger in front of the thin black band.

"They're so beautiful, everything you've given me today is so beautiful. Thank you," I say as Callum rises in front of me again. I raise my hands to cup his cheeks when I notice on the bottom of the black band, right in the middle of the myriad of black stones, is a bright red one. Callum notices my staring and grabs my hand to kiss.

"You're beautiful, nothing else compares to you." He pulls me into him and I wrap my hands around his neck. "The engagement ring is classic, like you. The Property Band is designed by the club, but I was able to customize it a little bit to something that reminded me of you, and the land was too perfect to pass up."

"'The Property Band'?" I ask.

"It symbolizes that you're my Old Lady, and 'Property of Callum Moran' is engraved on the inside of the ring." His hands rest on my hips, heat seeping in from his touch.

I roll my eyes lightheartedly. "How caveman of you."

Cale shrugs. "It's how we do it, baby." He leans down, capturing my chin in his fingers and guiding my lips to his. I melt into his lips and wrap my arms around his neck, resting them right above his tattoo for me. He pulls away too soon, and I groan in response. "I love when you do that," he whispers against my lips. "But I want you to see the sunset out here." He spins me around and I look out over our land. It really is beautiful out here, the sky is clear and turning a beautiful hue of pinks and oranges over the mountain range. "I have a blanket, we can sit and watch the sunset if you want?" He asks, his lips grazing my neck.

"Why do I get the feeling we won't be watching the sunset?" I ask, still taking in the view in front of me.

He squeezes my hips. "You'll still be watching the sunset, Red."

Callum walks back with a blanket and another small box in his hand. "What's that?" I ask while he lays the thick blanket over the soft green grass.

I follow him as he sits on the blanket, his legs straight out in front of him. "Get on your knees in front of me, facing the view." He licks his bottom lip and I watch the motion, entranced.

I obey, sinking to my knees between his legs, my back towards him. His big hand reaches around and flicks the button to my jeans, pulling the zipper down slowly. He tugs my tight jeans down over my hips but leaves them above my knees. His hand slides up my back until he rests it between my shoulder blades and he pushes me down onto my hands. I hear a buzzing behind me right before he slides my black lace thong to the side and starts to slowly rub a silicone vibrator against my clit. I moan at the contact and Callum increases the pressure he's holding the vibrator against me. I feel his finger swirling around in my wetness and then he pushes two fingers inside of me. Pumping slowly in tandem with the slow back-and-forth motions of the vibrator, pushing a little harder on the up motion of the silicone toy. Just as I'm reaching my peak, he removes the vibrator and his fingers. "Cale—" I start to whine, then I feel the bulb of the toy slowly enter my pussy.

"Is this okay?" He asks, pausing just halfway into me.

"Yes." I breathe out, and he pushes the toy the rest of the way inside. I sigh as he fucks me with the vibrator. After getting me used to the toy, he pulls backward on my hips. "Ride me, Red."

I pause. "But the vibrator," I protest.

He slides a finger in beside the toy. "We can both fit. I'll hold the sensor that's on the outside and it'll stay still." At that, I look down and notice a long pink almost string type of thing sticking out of me and Callum controlling the vibrations from his phone.

"Uh." I hesitate.

I hear Cale's zipper and his jeans sliding down his legs. "I'll help you, baby." Callum's hand guides my hips back until I feel the head of his dick at my entrance. He slowly pushes into me while pulling me down onto him. "Oh fuck, fuck baby." He moans. "Oh fuck. Relax, Red. Let me all the way in." I moan and whimper at the tight feeling of him alongside the toy. When he's fully in me, I rest on my heels over top of him with my hands resting on his thighs. We stay like that while I adjust to them both inside of me, Callum has the vibration low and I lay my head back.

I slowly start to rise and fall over him. Short movements while Cale increases the power on the toy. "Oh, Cale." I moan as I pick up the pace. Bouncing faster, trying to match the vibrator, and chasing a quickly coming orgasm.

"You're so fucking wet, baby. Ah," he moans. "Yeah, babe just like that." His finger starts circling my clit, encouraging me closer to my release, and right before it hits I slam down onto him and grind my ass against his pelvic bone.

Our cries ring out together around us as my pussy spasms. My body twitches while Cale wraps his arms around my stomach to hold onto me. He's turned down the toy slightly while I ride out the intense orgasm. When my body is done, he pushes us up, Him on his knees and me with my face pushed into the blanket. He quickly turns the vibrator all the way up before grabbing ahold of me and pounding into me. He's fucking me so fast and hard that if he weren't holding onto my shoulders I would fall over into a boneless heap. If I walk away from this without bruises on my shoulders and ass I would be surprised. Our moans entangle with one another, the sound of skin slapping against skin is the only sound out here.

"I love how you just take me, Red." Callum grits between his teeth, still plowing into me. "I'm gonna come, baby," he moans right before I feel his cock thicken inside of me and the warm spill of his seed triggers another orgasm for me. My pussy tightens around his coming dick and he moans again. "Yes, baby, just like that. Squeeze me dry, Red."

Man, I really love my life.

We lay on the blanket, my leg laying over Callum's and my head resting on his chest. He brings my left hand to his mouth and kisses it softly. "I can't wait to marry you, Red."

"I can't wait either." I sigh happily. "This ring is so beautiful, you did a great job."

Callum bites the side of his lip, holding in a smile. "I had a little help."

I raise up on my elbow so I can look into his eyes. "Finn?" I ask. Callum shakes his head, looking up at me. "Mason?" I try again.

"Someone closer to you." His smile grows more.

I laugh, shaking my head. Of course, I should have known. "Allie."

Cale nods. "I wanted to make sure you'd love it, so after the jeweler was done with it Allie came to approve of it."

My emotions are all over the place, and with tears threatening to spill over I lean down to kiss Callum. "Thank you so much for including my best friend. It means a lot," I say when I pull away.

"Yeah." Callum chuckles. "She cried when she saw it." He

pulls me into another kiss with his hand on my cheek. "Come on, babe, I gotta head in for church and Allie has something planned for you."

———

I STEP off Callum's bike and onto Allie's driveway. Before I can even finish kissing Cale goodbye, Allie is swinging the door open with two champagne flutes in her hands. "Did you say yes?" She yells from the porch.

I bite my bottom lip, trying to hold back my giant smile and failing. I extend my left hand into the air and the squeal that rips out of Allie's throat is almost inhuman. She tosses the champagne flutes into the air in her excitement, them falling to the wooden porch and spilling, luckily they were plastic. She runs from the porch, almost knocking me over in her excited hug. She lets go of me and hugs Callum, who's still sitting on the bike.

A few minutes later, we're relaxing on the patio sectional on the back porch with new plastic flutes filled with champagne and raspberries. It's just Allie and me while we wait for Sophie, Emma, and even Huntley. When Callum and Allie went to see my ring, Allie decided all of us needed to get together to celebrate and I decided to invite Huntley.

"I can't wait to see what you design, Reese. The house is going to be so beautiful," Allie says, her elbow bent on the back of the couch with her head resting against it.

"So much changed today." I chuckle, shaking my head. I'm slouched on the couch with my legs resting on the round fire pit in front of me. It looks like a giant tree trunk, but it's off right now due to the early summer weather.

Tears well in Allie's eyes and she swipes at them. "I'm so happy for you, babe. You got everything you always wanted."

She lets out a shaky breath. "God, I was so scared when Saint called me after your abduction. I don't know what I would do without you."

I wipe a stray tear. "I know, thank you so much for coming to check on us at the hospital and bringing everyone coffee."

She waves me away. "It was nothing, I just wanted to help."

I grab her hand. "I love you, Al." I look into her eyes.

"I love you too." She squeezes my hand. "I know I already said it, but I really am happy for you and Callum. He loves you so much, he didn't even laugh at me when I threatened to kill him if he hurt you." She laughs and another tear falls.

"Why are you crying, babe?" I chuckle when she takes back her hand to wipe at the tear.

"Nothing, I'm sorry. We're here to celebrate you and Callum." She shakes her head.

I grab her cheeks in my hands, her sea green and blue eyes sparkling with the moisture. "Not yet, the party hasn't started yet. What's going on?"

She rolls her eyes. "It's stupid." She huffs. "I just wish I could find something like what you Callum have."

My heart breaks. Allie has always been the toughest out of all of us, but really she just wants to be loved. She's dated of course, but she says she's never been in love. She's liked the guys she's dated and cared about them, but it's never been that deep to her. "You'll find a love like this someday. All consuming, endless, exciting, romance novel worthy love." I laugh at the last part.

Allie laughs along with me, her eyes moving to the patio lights strung around the covered porch. "That doesn't happen for everyone, Reese. You and Callum got lucky." I start to say something, but she keeps going. "And that's okay. I made peace with it a while ago, I just still hope sometimes."

I watch her, refusing to believe that. "But it can, Allie. Just don't settle."

Callum

I DROP Reese off at Allie's and head to the clubhouse for church. I'm pulling through the security gates still in a daze. She's my Old Lady and she's going to be my wife. I meant every word I said to her today, she's fucking it for me. Made for me. I park my bike next to all the others and walk into the clubhouse, everyone's already here and filing into the chapel, including the prospects since we have to discuss Red's stalker. I cross the clubhouse to join them.

When we're all seated Ronan is the first to speak. "Well don't keep us in suspense, brother. Did she wisen up and ditch your ass?" I look around to see everyone staring at me intently.

My tongue darts out to wet my lips as I shake my head smiling. "She said yes." My grin widens. "To it all."

Cheers erupt around the table and Finn claps his big hand on my shoulder. "I told you she was the one, didn't I?" He flashes his shit eating grin.

"Yeah, yeah." I roll my eyes. "Can we get on with it? I got shit to fill you all in on."

"Go on." Ronan waves his hand at me, not doing anything to hide his smile.

"Alright, so first things first, I talked to Red and found out that the morning of the break-in that we caught on camera, I was in the bathroom when Eli snuck into the apartment. He fucked with Red's hair, but she didn't think anything of it; she never saw him and he wasn't in the room when I walked back out." I feel the anger course through me again, I wish I had been the one to kill that fuck, but Jack and Ro were already there and knew saving Reese was more important than my want for vengeance.

Finn shakes his head. "Fuck, he was brave breaking in with you there."

"Why didn't he take her before he did then?" Saint asks from across the table. "I mean, he obviously wasn't afraid of us. Breaking in with you in the house and taking Reese while she's with Finn, our fucking giant ass club enforcer. He had plenty of other, better opportunities, so why did he wait so long?" His straight face looks so unaffected and if I didn't know him any better, I'd knock his fucking head in for not giving a shit about something like this, but that's just who he is. He's so analytical about literally fucking everything, he always puts his feelings aside to assess any problem, threat, or situation. I know he cares though, I've seen the way he looks at Red when she's around, there's a softness in his eyes that's not normal for him.

I shake my head, not really sure what was going through that psycho's head. "That redhead in his freezer probably kept him busy for a while."

Mason clears his throat from the end of the table. The prospects are never allowed in church, but since they were involved in the protection of Red and saving her and Finn from Eli, we allowed them in. "Well, he could have been alerted when we started looking into the video feed or his personal information. There isn't a way for me to see if we tripped something that notified him."

"So you think he was notified that we were onto him and went after the Princess before we could get to him?" Ronan asks.

Mason nods. "It's possible."

"I have another theory." I interject.

"Go on." Ronan looks at me.

I lean back in my chair and let out a long breath of air. I've gone over this a million times since Red told me what Eli said at my warehouse. "I think he was digging into the club for dirt, something solid to hold over us." I look around at my brothers, Finn hasn't shared this with the others yet, I asked him not to until I could make some sense of it first. "He told Finn and Red he knew about the bullets. I think the spy we found a few months ago had to do with him. I think he hired someone to watch us and get information and he found something out through that. When I sent Jack and Leo back to the warehouse they were able to tell that Eli had gone down to the basement. He knew what we were doing and had threatened to call in ATF so we would let him go with Reese." I turn to look at Mason. "Did you find anything about The Brothers Coalition?"

Mase nods. "Yeah. Not a lot, but they are an amateur spy agency on the dark web trying to make a name for themselves. They're not super expensive and since they are just starting they don't ask a lot of questions." Mason adds from next to Tobi. "I saw that Eli comes from a wealthy family, I can look into his financials and see if he's taken out any large sums of money recently."

Ronan nods. "Do that. I doubt we could track his business on the dark web." Mason shakes his head confirming Ronan's thought. "So we can at least track it this way. I think it's a pretty safe bet that this is what happened and I want to put this spy shit to bed." We all nod in agreement, glad all of this is finally behind us. "Good." Ro raises the gavel to indicate the end of church, but before he can slam it down on the table a loud bang echoes through the clubhouse. All ten of us are out of our seats and running through the chapel doors, pulling our guns from our waistbands or holsters within seconds, but when we round the corner into the main room, the people pouring in are the last I ever expected.

Finn

"FBI! PUT DOWN YOUR WEAPONS!" A woman with short brunette hair yells, all the other agents joining her to raise their handguns and rifles at us.

We all pause, looking back and forth between us, there's no way we're going to get into a shootout with fifteen fucking federal agents, even if we could successfully take them all out, there's no walking out of this. Ronan starts to slowly bend to place his gun on the floor and we all follow, kicking them away from us after we've placed them down.

"On your knees, hands behind your head!" The brunette yells again, and we all obey, except for Leo of course. One of the agents has to force him down to his knees and then kicks him square in the back so he falls to his stomach, while they handcuff all of us. Two other agents hold rifles pointed directly at mine and Ronan's heads while the others trash the clubhouse.

They start tossing all of the liquor off of the shelves and letting them shatter on the floor, they flip tables and cut open pillows on the couches. They're destroying everything.

"I hope you have a fucking warrant because I'm gonna wring you fucking dry for throwing my prospect to the floor and holding a gun to mine and my brother's head." Ronan growls to the brunette who seems to be in charge and is watching the mayhem taking place around her.

"Oh, I assure you we do, Mr. McKenna." The agent smiles.

"For fucking what?!" Saint yells and tries to stand before being kicked down onto the floor by the agent still standing over

Leo's prone body. "Fuck!" Saint yells, smacking his face on the wood floor.

"For the murder of Michelle Davis." The agent who kicked down Saint and Leo spits out, kicking Saint in the side.

Why does that name sound so familiar?

Oh fuck. The senator's wife.

To be continued...

ACKNOWLEDGMENTS

Writing this Acknowledgement is very surreal. I don't know if I ever truly believed I would finish this book. I started writing in 2017, partly because at the time there weren't a lot of MC romances on the market, and also because I was trying to hit on a guy that was apart of a local MC. It didn't work out, the guy or the book. I gave up several times, only writing a chapter every few months until I didn't touch it for years.

I had a baby and was staying home at the peak of the pandemic: I was bored. I picked up reading again after stumbling upon BookTok, and I found a new love in dark romance. I decided in February of 2021 to start completely over, a whole new story with new characters, a new plot, and a lot darker content. I took weeks off at a time, but here we finally are.

I just wanted to say thank you if you read even a page of this book. The characters are so close to my heart, and I can't wait to continue to tell the other's stories. I plan for The Devil's Outlaws to span over six books and two novellas, with every book following a different couple. So I hope that you will stick around because the story isn't over, and my favorites are yet to come.

Thank you so much. I'll never be able to express how much your reading this book meant to me.

Bethany

FOR EXTRA CONTENT

To discuss spoilers, ask questions, and read deleted scenes from Only The Strong, join our Facebook group, The DO Chapel.

You can also follow Bethany on TikTok @queeenb17 or on Instagram @bethanydawnauthor

ALSO BY BETHANY DAWN

The Devil's Outlaws:

Only The Strong

Will Survive

This Mess (May 2023)

Of Bikes and Men (September 2023)

Outlaws Never Die (January 2024)

The Devil Always Wins (May 2024)

The Devil Didn't Want Me (September 2024)

A Devil's Forever (December 2024)